Praise for the work of A

"De Alba's Puritans are as rich anc recent historical fiction."

—*Kirkus Review* *y of the Witch*

"De Alba has a firm grasp of her historical material and portrays the pirate life as convincingly as the witch trials."

—*Publishers Weekly* on *Calligraphy of the Witch*

"Gaspar de Alba proves again that she is a meticulous historical novelist who understands how to write a complex, suspenseful story that also remarks upon our present."

—Emma Pérez, author of *Gulf Dreams* and *Electra's Complex*

"Gaspar de Alba not only crafts a suspenseful plot but tackles prejudice in many of its ugly forms: against gays, against Hispanics, against the poor. An in-your-face, no-holds-barred story."

—*Booklist* on *Desert Blood: The Juárez Murders*

"Offering a powerful depiction of social injustice and serial murder on the US-Mexican border, this is an essential purchase for both mystery and Hispanic fiction collections."

—*Library Journal* on *Desert Blood: The Juárez Murders*

"In her first novel, poet and Chicano studies scholar Gaspar de Alba brings to life Sor Juana Ines de la Cruz, a prolific, brilliant, and complex author and nun of 17th-century Mexico. Gaspar de Alba has artfully combined excerpts from the writings with explicit, fictionalized journal entries to create a vibrant, if sometimes anachronistic, account of a complex life. Eminently readable."

—*Library Journal* on *Sor Juana's Second Dream*

"As Gaspar de Alba tells it, Sor Juana was not only a woman who questioned a patriarchal and superstitious society, but also a lesbian. She makes a convincing case by juxtaposing the nun's own poetry with actual events and fictional journal entries. Commendably, Sor Juana's flaws are not glossed over; she is portrayed as vain, prejudiced and difficult. This work of fine scholarship and vision should increase awareness of a compelling historical figure."

—*Publishers Weekly* on *Sor Juana's Second Dream*

ALICIA GASPAR DE ALBA

Arte Público Press
Houston, Texas

The Curse of the Gypsy is funded in part by grants from the City of Houston through the Houston Arts Alliance and the National Endowment for the Arts. We are grateful for their support.

Recovering the past, creating the future

Arte Público Press
University of Houston
4902 Gulf Fwy, Bldg 19, Rm 100
Houston, Texas 77204-2004

Cover design by Mora Des¡gn
Cover art by Alma Lopez

Names: Gaspar de Alba, Alicia, 1958- author.
Title: The curse of the gypsy : ten stories and a novella / by Alicia Gaspar de Alba.
Description: Houston : Arte Público Press, 2018. | Includes bibliographical references.
Identifiers: LCCN 2017061344 (print) | LCCN 2018011214 (ebook) | ISBN 9781518504938 (epub) | ISBN 9781518504945 (kindle) | ISBN 9781518504952 (pdf) | ISBN 9781558858626 (alk. paper)
Classification: LCC PS3557.A8449 (ebook) | LCC PS3557.A8449 A6 2018 (print) | DDC 813/.54—dc23
LC record available at https://lccn.loc.gov/2017061344

∞ The paper used in this publication meets the requirements of the American National Standard for Information Sciences—Permanence of Paper for Printed Library Materials, ANSI Z39.48-1984.

18 19 20 21 5 4 3 2 1

Dedication

Para Alma, el amor de mi vida,
and to our daughter, Azul Fernanda

Table of Contents

THE CURSE OF THE GYPSY: A Deconstructed Novel in Ten Stories

The True and Tragic Story of Liberata Wilgefortis, Who, Having Consecrated her Virginity to the Goddess Diana To Avoid Marriage, Grew a Beard and Was Crucified

THE Curse OF THE Gypsy

TEN STORIES
AND A NOVELLA

THE CURSE OF THE GYPSY:
A Deconstructed Novel in Ten Stories

Lorca's Widow

I didn't say I was his wife. I said I was his widow, in the Gypsy sense of the word, not the Spanish. I guess it won't hurt anybody now to tell you the story, to explain to you why I wept so much when you gave me that book of García Lorca's poetry for Mother's Day that year. But if you want to hear the story, promise that you will believe everything I say. Do you promise? Listen, then, and don't ask me anything until I finish.

Everyone knew Lorca liked men. Even though his best friends were always women, it was men he loved. Men he wrote about in his verses. Men he wept about when he came to the Tavern of Los Vargas in the Sacromonte and sang to the black dregs of his heart about a love that was killing him. Still, he drew women like bees to jasmine. Always he was surrounded by the *payo* girls who accompanied his flock of rich friends. The minute he started to sing, the women had eyes for no other. His voice was like the finest *jeréz*, and we were all intoxicated by it. My mother, my three brothers—Elías, Moisés and Nahum—and me, most of all. Margarita Petita, he called me. Everyone loved Lorca's voice. I loved those Moorish eyes of his that seemed always on the verge of spilling their sad liquid down his face.

I fell in love with Lorca the first night I saw him in our family's tavern. He was young and clumsy on his feet, but that didn't stop him from challenging Moisés to a duel of voices. Elías plucked madly at his guitar, knowing that Moisés had never been able to sustain that tempo, but Lorca did. Kept time with my elder brother's music as though he, too, were a Gypsy. Afterwards, Moisés and Elías hugged him and called him "cousin."

I was sixteen and married to a soldier who had gone off to fight the Prussians in the first big war of the world. Lorca was not much older than I, barely getting his whiskers and his voice, but already such a romantic. Two seasons went by and he did not return to the tavern. I didn't see him again until the Saturday before Easter. The Gran Vía was filled with smoke from the burning of the Judases. My brothers all stood around me as we watched first one effigy then another go up in flames. Suddenly, there stood Lorca, reciting something that sounded like a Gypsy verse, empty wineskin dangling off his belt.

"*¡Primos!*" he said to Elías and Moisés, who scowled at his familiarity. "Don't you recognize me?" he asked Moisés. "I'm the green man who beat you at our duel of voices." He turned to Elías. "Your guitar," he said, as if that explained everything. "You called me '*primo*.'"

"I recognize you, Cousin," said Nahum, the youngest. "You said you were a Vargas."

"My great, great grandmother was a Vargas," said Lorca, his words slurred into one, "and my great grandfather Antonio married a Gypsy from the Albaicín, and my middle name is Sagrado Corazón de Jesús"—he pretended to stab a dagger into his heart—"which is why I must know the name of this dark beauty before I die!"

"*Me llamo* Margarita," I said boldly, knowing that my brothers would never introduce me to the young man. Elías cut his eyes at me and Moisés pinched my arm.

"Margarita Petita," said Lorca, and proceeded to invent a drunken verse that sounded like he was using the letters of my name: "*Morena, la angustia me retuerce la garganta, arrepentido recelo del imán de tus tobillos, ampárame.*" I memorized it instantly, though it made no sense. "Dark Lady, agony twists my throat, a forlorn distrust of the magnet of your ankles, protect me." He bowed low and reached playfully for my ankles, but Moisés stopped him.

"She's married," he said gruffly.

Lorca straightened up, stared at my brother as though he'd lost his five senses, then howled with laughter, slapping his thighs like a jester. A group of his university friends appeared and whisked him away into the crowd. I watched the blaze of the last Judas, my face hot with a virgin's excitement.

"Just wait till I tell Mamá how you were flirting," said Moisés in my ear.

But all I could think of was seeing Lorca again. Margarita Petita, he'd called me, and made my name into a poem. Every morning before I opened my eyes to a fresh sky, and every night after the lamps were snuffed and the doors barred, snuggled up in the bed covers next to my mother, I whispered the poem to myself, like a prayer.

"Protect your heart," my mother told me one day as we ground the coffee for breakfast. "It's getting away from you, Margarita. What will you tell your husband when he returns from the war and finds out that you've given your heart to another man? It is *mala leche* to deceive your husband. Do you want to ruin us?"

"He isn't going to return," I told her, and my mother, knowing my predictions to be true, only shook her head and made a sign against bad luck. Later I learned from Nahum that she had gone to visit the King of the Gypsies, old Chorrojumo, who even at his age still gave counsel.

For an entire year, I took to following Lorca around the city. From his family's house on the street overlooking the river—66 Acera del Darro, I remember the exact address—he would walk up into the Alhambra wood, eyes down, hands deep in his pockets, pausing here and there in the dense shade of the poplars to take out his notebook and his pencil. Then he would amble down to the Alameda to meet his friends at the same café every afternoon. There they sat for hours playing dominoes and arguing about literature. He never saw me. Not even when I'd walk up to their table and brazenly offer to read their palms. He had eyes only for his friends and his verses. Sometimes after the Alameda he walked as far as the *cementerio*, and sat for a long time writing in his notebook, surrounded by graves.

Once, he caught me peering into the *zaguán* of his house and had me dragged into the courtyard to be questioned by his mother. I was nearly eighteen years old by then, much too old to be spying at doorways.

"What are your intentions?" the mother asked. "Are you looking for work? Are your children hungry? What do you want?"

I stared at my feet. "I tell fortunes," I said, my voice barely above a whisper.

"We don't need our fortunes told," said the mother. "You Gypsy thieving *ratera de mierda*. And if I ever see you lurking by our door again I'm calling the authorities."

I was pushed out to the street by one of the servants, humiliated not so much because the woman assumed I was either a beggar or a thief, but because Lorca didn't recognize me. I stopped following him after that.

As I had foretold, my husband came home in a box before the war was over. My mother warned me to observe the tradition, and I had to wear black and not be seen in public for an entire year. I was not permitted to talk to men, not even my brothers, for I was polluted with death, and this would bring bad luck to any man whose path I crossed. The year of my mourning passed slowly. My brother Elías' wife gave birth to another son and Moisés got married and had a big wedding that I was not allowed to attend. His young wife took my place serving the wine to our customers and telling their fortunes, if they asked. But she was no good at it. She couldn't really see anything, just pretended. And she did not have any grace for dancing.

We didn't see Lorca in the Albaicín or the Sacromonte for a long time. Some of his friends who frequented our tavern would talk about how he was traveling in the north, in the land of the witches called Galicia, and then we learned he had gone to Madrid to attend the university. Here and there we heard that he was becoming famous, not as a singer or a musician, but as a writer of poetry and plays. Then, suddenly, there he was again in his usual circle of young men and adoring women, looking much the same, except thinner and more haunted. I was much changed. I was a widow, now, with a plump belly good for dancing, and breasts and lips full of mystery and desire, eyes as sad as his own.

I could see right away that he was in love. Heard him telling my brothers one night after all the customers had gone that he wanted to leave Granada once he finished his degree, leave Spain altogether, escape the prison of his heart that produced such dark songs of deep unhappiness. It was Paris he wanted to see. Most of his friends from that café on the Alameda had gone to Paris, and he wanted to follow them there. But his parents would not allow it, forcing him to remain in the sterility of his broken heart. He confessed all of this to my brothers in between rounds of the wineskin and the guitar. I listened to his words, stored them like seeds against a hungry winter, and set about casting my strongest spell.

I danced just for Lorca that night. I had started to dance with my little cousin Manuel who had come to live with us earlier in the year. He was only eleven years old, but already had the deep rhythms of the *duende* in him. I rattled my castanets and started to click my heels to the rhythms of my brother's guitar. Manuel grabbed his *panderete* and joined me. I could feel Lorca's eyes on me as I moved. In truth, he was as mesmerized by Manuel's movements as by mine, but his eyes, those dark fathomless eyes in which I had drowned as surely as if I had fallen into one of the wells of the city, his eyes were like black brandy emptying into mine, and I used every power that I could summon to plumb the depths of his heart.

What pain I saw! I doubled over with his pain, my heels stamping on the boards the staccato of his aching love. He wanted someone more than his life. Not me, not any woman, I saw that clearly. Not Manuel, either, for he was just a boy, though the secret was in Manuel's body and in my brother Moisés' yearning voice and in the keening strains of my brother Elías' guitar.

"Take me," I told him with my eyes, *zapateando* near his chair. "I will give you what you need."

I swung my hips in front of his face, reached for a *chirimoya* from the bowl of fruit my mother liked to keep on the table in the middle of the room, and handed it to him, still clacking my heels. Then I turned my backside on him, felt the thumping of his heart like a drumbeat in my own blood. With my eyes closed, I danced around the table and worked him with my mind.

"Lover of Gypsies," I said, "be my lover. Take me like this fruit." A final rattle from Manuel's tambourine, a flurry of wrists and castanets. *Eppah!* I opened my eyes to see if he had fallen under my spell, but his chair was empty. He had left.

The next day, it was a Friday, I remember. Two days before the Feast of Santiago, I received a gift, a sewing basket lined in pale green linen. It was filled with sewing items: a box of pins, another of needles, a leather thimble, several spools of colored thread, a pair of scissors, a pincushion in the shape of a heart. The kind of gift a young man would give to the girl he wants to marry. On the bottom of the cushion, he had pinned a note, this note that I have kept stashed in my prayer book for more than seventy years. Here, let me read it to you, but you will have to translate it for yourself, Child. I will not spoil Lorca's words by changing them to English.

Gitana,
Hoy me comí la chirimoya que me diste,
Today I ate the *chirimoya* you gave me,
la carne dulce como labio de niño,
the flesh sweet as a boy's lip,
fresca como la noche que yace oscura en tus ojos,
fresh as the dark night in your eyes,
semillas negras que quiero sembrar
black seeds I want to plant
adentro de tu jardín, cáscara vieja que flota
inside your garden, old skin that floats
cual el recuerdo por las aguas frías del Darro.
like memory in the cold waters of the Darro.
Atrás de la Alhambra, en un matorral
Behind the Alhambra, in a thicket
de juncos y zarzamoras, al lado de la cascada
of cattails and blackberries, beside the cascade
te espero bajo la luna verde de la noche de Santiago.

I wait for you under the green moon of Saint James night.
—Federico (1923)

None of what happened later would have occurred if my mother hadn't gone to see Chorrojumo. She never forgave me for betraying my husband, you know. Told me Chorrojumo had foreseen that I would pollute myself with a *payo*, a non-Gypsy, and that I would become a pariah to my own family. Chorrojumo predicted my offspring would be cursed for eternity unless I returned to the Sacromonte and buried my shame in the right place. None of it made any sense to me, then, but I knew I was doomed.

You see, I was carrying Lorca's child, but my mother put a curse on it, and it never came to term. When she found out I was pregnant, she was enraged, and beat me with my dead father's belt. She paced up and down our *piso* in the Albaicín, pulling at her hair, yelling off the balcony that her daughter had been shamed, that misfortune had found us, but to me she hissed, "I know it's your fault, I know you worked your magic into him somehow." She ordered my brothers to find him. "Go and bring that *hijo de la gran puta* to me!" She said she just wanted to talk to him, but I knew it was revenge she desired for the disgrace he had brought to our family.

My brothers found him in his usual café, drinking absinthe and reading a book. For once, he was alone. Either he had not believed the rumor that *los* Vargas were after him, or he didn't care. They say he came willingly, jauntily, some said, as if daring my brothers to avenge the family's name right then and there.

He got only as far as the vestibule in our building before my mother descended upon him with all her fury.

"My daughter is carrying your child, Señor Lorca," she declared, and I had never seen her look more venomous. "You had your fun, now you must meet your obligation."

"Señora, I took your daughter to the river, thinking she was a maiden," he said defiantly, "and it turned out she was just an unfaithful wife. That child could be anybody's."

His own venom when he looked at me weakened my knees.

"No, Señor, my daughter was a decent woman, and a widow at that, until you kidnapped her heart and contaminated her body with your *payo* seed. I curse you, Señor Lorca. By the name of Chorrojumo, King of the Gypsies, I curse your offspring. May they all die before they see the light of day. May their hearts shrivel just as you have withered my daughter's and my family's heart."

Lorca laughed and laughed. Even when my brothers, all three of them, dragged him out to the courtyard, kicking and beating him, he didn't stop laughing. My mother threatened to inform his parents, to expose his indiscretion. But that was the end of it. The curse was enough. Lorca disappeared after that. There were rumors that he was writing Gypsy ballads, and later that he had gone to Barcelona to visit with a friend named Dalí, the one who became a famous painter of twisted clocks and severed heads.

Already the troubles were starting with the government, and my brother Nahum was forced to join the army, but I cared about nothing. I wanted Lorca to love me, to marry me, to be a father to my child. But he was gone, and by then my child was cursed. I could feel it dying month by month. And then its heartbeat stopped completely.

Over a year later, I saw Lorca again at the café on the Alameda, where I had rented a table for my fortune telling, since my mother had banned me from working in our tavern. He was drunk and desolate as usual, still yearning for Paris. By then, I hated him. I wanted him to be miserable the rest of his life. With the excuse of helping the owner's wife clear the tables, I picked up his glass, swirled my finger inside it and licked it, knowing that in this way I could read his cards as though he himself had drawn the spread. The cards showed me his wretched fate. I saw a short life ahead of him, filled with fame and controversy and travel, but in the end, too brief, and then his body lying in a heap with others. A bonfire and then ashes.

That same summer, guided by a dream, I took my cards to the bullring in Ronda on the Feast of Corpus Christi. That's where I met your grandfather, Benito Rivera. El Criollo, they called him, because he was born in Mexico. He had a special way of doing the *chicuelinas*, his tall figure pirouetting around the bull like a ballet dancer. To me, he was a mirage of Mexican beauty, much more beautiful than

Lorca. Like all bullfighters, he was a superstitious man. He wanted me to read his palms, he had no faith in the cards (in truth he feared them), and I remember the jolt I felt when my hand touched his, like an electrical current running through my body. I read the lines of his palms, but by then I already knew that he would be my husband. He was from Mexico, and I already knew that I would fulfill my outcast's destiny and break my mother's heart by leaving Granada. But she had cursed me, cursed my child, and I never forgave her for that. I guess you could say I wanted to pay her back. I hope you have not inherited this Gypsy folly for revenge, Child.

Years later, after she had forgiven me for abandoning my people, as she put it, when she learned I had given birth to a son, she sent me a letter dictated to one of my nephews, telling me all about Franco and the Falangistas and how sweet Nahum's life had been sacrificed and how at least I was safe in Mexico because Spain had lost its mind. Never once did she mention Lorca.

But I was not meant to be happy in Mexico. For the first twelve years of our marriage, my body refused to conceive, and your grandfather was very distressed. Doctors told me I had an intestinal obstruction, that this was preventing me from conceiving. Others thought I had a cancerous tumor. Some claimed it was a large kidney stone that had somehow become embedded in the tissues behind the vagina. But it was none of these. It was my mother's curse, and I knew it. But I also knew that Benito would never believe such a thing. I couldn't tell him the cause of the curse or that I had ever been pregnant. His pride would have made him divorce me, Catholic and in love with me though he was. He preferred to believe I was fallow and that his good seed was going to waste, and so he took to finding other women with whom to father his children.

What could I say? Had your grandfather been a Gypsy, he could have deserted me after the first year for not giving him a child. That would have been his right as a man. Could I blame him for wanting a family? After my fifth miscarriage in six years, the doctors determined that I was barren. I was twenty-seven years old, my husband, thirty-five, both of us young, still, and yet our marriage was pronounced sterile. The shame of it drove your grandfather away.

We got news of the death of one of Benito's half-sisters in New York. His father insisted that he had to accompany him to the funeral and stay to take care of his other sister, the twin of the one who died. It was a bad time to be in New York because of the Depression, but your grandfather didn't come back for five years. Can you imagine? Five years I waited for him to return, to send me word of where he was. I know his father came back to Mexico because I saw him and his wife several times at Mass in the Cathedral, but they refused to talk to me or answer any of my messages. The truth was, they hated my dark skin, despised that their green-eyed, *güero* son had gone and lost his heart to a *gitana.*

I sent telegram after telegram to his sister's address in New York, but like his mother, he never responded. And then I dreamt a horrible accident. I saw a trolley car crash into a kiosk and the bodies of children lying in the debris of wood and newspapers, their bodies broken like puppets. I saw your grandfather in the dream, wearing his matador's suit of lights, weeping over a dead boy whose head had split open like a watermelon. I knew, then, that something had happened to him, and that his family did not want to tell me.

I sought the help of his lover, Cleotilde, who had become my best friend during the time that he was in New York. At first, it broke my spirit to see the children Benito had fathered with Cleotilde, two boys, green-eyed like your grandfather, blonde like Cleotilde; and a little girl, daughter of Benito and Cleotilde's maid, with black hair, black eyes and skin the color of hot chocolate. Good-hearted woman that she was, Cleotilde was raising the girl as her own. I remember they had the strangest names: León and Lobo were the boys' names, and Araña was the girl's, which Cleotilde later changed to Araceli.

Cleotilde and I looked for your grandfather in all the hospitals and clinics across the capital. We called his manager in Toluca, and he helped us contact every bullfighter and *banderillero* who had ever worked with El Criollo. But they all knew nothing, and his family said nothing. At last I had to accept that your grandfather had run away from his barren wife. And his second family. It was this more than anything that bound Cleotilde to me.

Five years later, when he knocked on my door, I didn't recognize him. He had grown so gaunt and had the look of Lorca in his eyes, the green glint of his gaze replaced by a tragic darkness. I stood in the doorway and asked him what he wanted (though inside I could hear tambourines fluttering in my heart, and I wanted to cry out in Gypsy joy—*¡Viva Dios!*—that he'd returned), but he didn't answer, just stood there and shrugged his shoulders like a shy boy, so I let him in.

For weeks, that's what he became, a child who needed constantly to be consoled. He would start sobbing for no reason, and the nightmares that woke us both in the middle of the night brought on the worst headaches, made him vomit and become dizzy and confused. Migraines, the doctor called them, and all he could do was lie in a darkened room with a poultice of alcohol on his head and the tears running down his face.

He left again. He said he loved me, still, but couldn't live with himself and that he wasn't a man or a husband and didn't deserve all the love and caring I was giving him. Who knows what secrets he harbored. Once a week he came around to give me money and sleep in his own house. He took up with Cleotilde again, for which I was glad because Cleotilde told me everything, and at least he had his children to give him comfort. In fact, it was Cleotilde who told me about Lorca. You see, she was an actress and often played at the Bellas Artes.

It was 1936, and by then, Lorca's plays were being produced all over Mexico, and even in places as far as Argentina and Cuba and New York. In Mexico, his books of poetry were being sold at all the best bookstores, and even in the stands in the Zócalo. That spring, a few months before his death, as it turned out, one of his plays came to the Palacio Bellas Artes. Cleotilde told me that an actress from Spain, the one whose first name was the same as mine, Margarita Xirgu, was going to star in that play, and Cleotilde was going to be her understudy. *Yerma*, the play was called. Cleotilde asked me if I wanted to go, and that she could get me free tickets in a private *palco*, no less. I guess she saw something kindle in my eyes at the sound of Lorca's name. I went, of course, dragging the teenage son of my maid to accompany me because it was not acceptable for a woman of society to attend plays by herself. Don't think I'm putting on airs, Child. As the wife of Benito Rivera (Mexico's beloved El Criollo), I was by right a woman of society.

At the *teatro*, I wept openly at what I saw. The stage was barren, befitting the title of the play, a wasteland, an empty box, like the woman named Yerma who cannot marry the man she loves, who longs more than anything to bear a child. But her husband cannot have children, so she remains barren. I knew, then, that Federico had not forgotten me. I was Yerma. And the Old Pagan Woman was my mother. Lorca had written a play about my mother's curse.

Other plays followed, sad tales mostly, about unrequited love, cuckolded love, doomed love: *The Shoemaker's Prodigious Wife, The Love of Don Perlimplín and Belisa in the Garden, Blood Wedding, Doña Rosita the Spinster*—but none were as morbid as *Yerma*. Of course, I saw them all, several times. Lorca's name seemed to jump out at me from the marquees of the city. I was once again, you see, obsessed with Lorca. Cleotilde laughed at me. She did not know what my obsession really meant. And then I read an article in the *Excelsior* announcing the arrival of the eminent playwright and poet, Federico García Lorca, in Mexico City at the end of August. I fainted when I read the news.

On the afternoon of his arrival, there was to be a reception for him at the house of Margarita Xirgu, and Cleotilde fixed it so that I received an invitation. "I think you're hiding something from me," she would say. "You're a *paisana* of his, both from Granada. You must have known him or heard of him, Margarita."

Know him? I shook my head and bit my tongue, knowing she would run with the story to your grandfather.

As you can imagine, I was terrified of seeing Lorca again. Over and over I kept dreaming of that evening in the blackberry thicket behind the Alhambra. The walls of the old castle glowed like burnt blood under the full moon. He wanted to watch me, he said, and I felt him touching me with his eyes, tasting my skin. I unbuttoned my blouse and shook my hair loose from its combs. Then his hands grabbed my breasts; his lips hovered over my neck as he whispered a poem to me. Even now, after all these years, I still remember the strength of his thick body between my thighs, the stain of blackberries on my petticoats.

Don't blush, Child. Your Grandma Maggie was not always such an old woman. She had a body as young as yours once, full of Gypsy passion. I thanked the Virgin of the Gypsies that your grandfather was not at home to witness my thrashing about in the bed at night, calling out Lorca's name in the dark.

The afternoon of the reception, we found out that Lorca had not been on the train, as expected. It seemed he had missed his flight altogether, but La Xirgu went ahead with the reception, in his honor. Suddenly the attention was on me, for Cleotilde told everyone that I was a great fan of Lorca's and had seen every one of his plays. She told them I was from Granada, an authentic Gypsy, she said, and everyone knew how Lorca felt about Gypsies.

"She probably even knew Lorca," said Cleotilde, narrowing her eyes at me. "I bet we can get the secret out of her if we try."

"Tell us," pleaded the young actor sitting beside me. "Did you ever meet the great Lorca?"

Their prodding forced me to reveal that he had come once or twice to my family's tavern in the Sacromonte and that he loved to sing the *cante jondo* with my brother Moisés and drink until daylight.

"I remember you," said La Xirgu, and for an instant I was filled with dread.

"We've never met, Señora," I said.

"You're of the Vargas family, aren't you?"

"That was my family name, yes."

"Of course. I remember Federico talking about you, the *gitanita* daughter of *los* Vargas who stole his heart. He wrote a poem for you, did you know? It's dedicated to some woman he met in Cuba and her black maid, but he told me it was really about you, '*Casada Infiel*,' it's called. We used to tease him for courting a married woman."

"I was a widow by then, Señora," I had to say. I couldn't have them thinking I'd been an unfaithful wife. "And he never courted me. He liked my brothers."

Cleotilde raised her eyebrows and made a face at me. "You sure had it hidden," she said, and I knew then that all hope of keeping the story from your grandfather was lost.

"But isn't he one of those?" asked somebody in the room. "You know, an invert?"

"You heard her. She said he liked her brothers."

"I heard he was Dalí's lover," someone else said.

"And Buñuel's, too."

"Certainly not Buñuel. Buñuel hates fags."

"What about Dalí?"

"Dalí does have a thing for rear ends."

"No, no, no. The great love of Lorca's life was that young sculptor, that Emilio character who ran off with a woman and broke Lorca's heart."

"I thought it was that bullfighter who got gored to death."

"No women anywhere."

"Except in his plays. You realize he's the doomed lady in each of those dramas!"

"I don't know about that," said La Xirgu, winking at me across the room. I opened my fan and pretended to be indifferent to the conversation. But inwardly my heart was racing.

"There was a girl he was in love with as a young man," La Xirgu continued. "María Luisa, I think her name was. Then, after he gave his heart to my *tocaya* here, there was a Dutch woman he was very close to. They met on the ocean liner to New York, and of course he courted her with his poetry. Although she was from the Netherlands, she could speak perfect Spanish. They stayed together for the full journey, but then, they parted for some reason when they got to New York."

"He had many women friends," I said.

"No, this one was special he told me. I believe she was going to have his child."

My heartbeat stopped for an instant. My mother's curse came back to me in a rush of blood to my face. I felt myself swoon.

"Señora," said the young man beside me. "Are you not well?"

I shook my head, embarrassed that they would think I had had too much Manzanilla sherry. I could not tolerate hearing about Lorca any longer. But still, I had to know.

"So, he had a family?"

"Oh my, no," said La Xirgu. "She wrote him from Holland a few years later to say that the baby had died. Good thing, too, poor woman. Federico had no intention of turning into a family man. Said he'd been cursed by an old Gypsy woman from the Sacromonte for failing to marry her daughter after an indiscretion."

Everyone's face turned toward me, and again I swooned.

"Poor Federico . . . " La Xirgu could not be stopped. " . . . always such bad luck in love. After the sculptor's betrayal, he got into such a depression. It scared us all, we expected him to cut his veins at any moment. That's why his family sent him to New York. His father wanted him to have a change of air."

"What year was that?" someone asked.

"1929. I always joked with him that the Great Depression resulted from his arrival in New York."

I had to get out of there. "*Dios mío*, look at the time," I said, nudging Cleotilde. We got to our feet.

"Must you leave so soon?" La Xirgu asked me, stretching out her hand as though she expected me to kiss it. "Won't you dine with us? We're having *gazpacho* and *tortilla*."

"The children," said Cleotilde, "they get so sad when we are late getting back." She started kissing everyone in the room goodbye.

"Thank you, Señora," I said to La Xirgu, shaking the tips of her fingers. "It was a privilege to meet such a marvelous actress, and one from my own country. You must allow me to return your hospitality one day."

"Come see me backstage next time you're in the theater," La Xirgu said, dimpling. "I'll be sure to tell Federico you said hello."

Before I could protest, she turned toward Cleotilde. "I am completely thrilled that you brought Lorca's old friend to entertain us, Cloti. From what I heard, she used to be quite the dancer. And a teller of fortunes, too. I think she was much too modest with her stories." She turned back to face me. "Maybe next time you can regale us with a performance of your own."

"It would be my pleasure, Señora. Good night everybody!"

"Goodnight, Doña Gitana!"

In the taxi on the way home, Cleotilde kept badgering me with questions, but I refused to say any more about Lorca and promised to hate her if she dared breathe a word of it to your grandfather. But I was lucky. Lorca never arrived in Mexico. The Falangistas in Granada killed him on the very day he was supposed to have arrived in Mexico. The story appeared in all the newspapers and was reported on all the radio stations.

Federico García Lorca Assassinated!

An odd thing happened when I read the headline. I noticed that my heart did not quicken at the thought of Lorca's death, but my womb did. I felt it very distinctly stir back to life, as if the news of his death had released me from my mother's curse.

I burned cinnamon that night, threw ice into the corners of each room and swept out the house. On the day of your grandfather's regular visit, I washed my hair in henna and scented my skin with sandalwood. I wore my red silk skirt and all my bracelets. I put kohl around my eyes. I lit red candles to the Virgin of the Gypsies. I wanted to be a Gypsy again, and charm him as I had when we met outside the bullring in Ronda. And it worked. He never went back to Cleotilde's bed, though I insisted that they move in with us in that big house he bought for me in Coyoacán. I told him he had to provide for his children, that if he could not give them the legitimacy of his name, at least he could give them a family and a good home. Cleotilde and I became closer than sisters. Her children thought of me as their Tita Margarita.

I was pregnant within a month of Lorca's death with your uncle Benjamín. Benjamín Nahum, I named him, after your grandfather and my dead brother. Your mother was born two years after that, whom I named after my mother and grandmother, as was our custom. Thanks to them, I have grandchildren and great-grandchildren, and Benito Rivera's line lives on. But remember this, my child. None of you would be here now if Federico García Lorca had not died. His death meant my resurrection.

After Benjamín's birth, I stopped going to the bullfights. I did not trust leaving my child with one of the maids. Without me to bewitch the bull from my shady perch in the box reserved for the matadors' families, your grandfather truly believed that he was cursed each time he walked into the bullring. The usual problem was that he could not kill the bull in the first attempt, although sometimes, when his bravado had been strengthened with too much wine, he would dance too close to the bull's head and get a rib broken or a hip gored. Poor sad Benito, always blaming me for his scars. Even for the cancer that started on his nose and spread down to his mouth and chin, until the operation that removed the cancerous flesh left a map of gouges on his face.

When your mother was born a year later, we hired a Mayan nanny to help me care for both the children, but I still could not bring myself to leave the house without the three of them in tow. Our section in the *contrabarreras* box became a spectacle of its own: the gypsy wife (as I was known) casting my evil eye on the other bullfighters (or so it was rumored), the Mayan nanny in her colorful *huipil* and the children crying for the bleeding bull proved too distracting for everybody, especially the judges. Your grandfather stopped asking me to the bullring in Mexico City, but he would beg me to accompany him on his long flights to Spain, where he followed the circuit from Madrid to Sevilla and Málaga to Valencia. You probably think I would have jumped at the chance of going to Spain again and seeing my family, but the truth is, I was still afraid of the power of my mother's resentment, of how my brothers' envy might cross the ocean and affect my children's lives while I was not there to protect them. And then, one day, I received an Air Mail envelope from Madrid with nothing but that newspaper clipping. Go ahead *m'ija*, open it.

El Criollo Dances His Last Faena in Las Ventas, I remember the headline exactly. I almost vomited from the sudden panic that gripped my entrails. But thanks to *la Virgen*, he wasn't dead. He had gotten gored in the bullring in Madrid, almost as badly as Manolete, the bull's horn missing his aorta but by a few centimeters, and he would be recovering for the next month in the hospital. His mother begged me to accompany her to Madrid to be with him during his recovery, but the children had no passport, and I would not leave the children in the care of the nanny, and so she took Cleotilde, instead. After a few weeks, I got a telegram that they were sailing home with Benito. Clearly, he had lost the battle with his mother. Benito Rivera had no choice but to retire from bullfighting.

His family wanted him to remain in Mexico City and help manage the theater they owned in Polanco, but he wanted to pursue a career in the newspaper business that he had invested in some years earlier. It was run by a friend of his who lived in the north, in a border town named Ciudad Juárez, where we all eventually crossed over and became *americanos.* Just as I had gladly left Spain, never to return, I was happy to leave Mexico. I wanted nothing to do with my past as a barren woman, or with the ghost of Lorca's curse.

But the truth is, I've been fooling myself all these years. I know this is going to sound unbelievable, but I promise you, everything I am going to tell you next is true. Do you believe me? You must believe me. And you must accept that strange things happen that only God understands.

Do you remember that obstruction I had in my stomach when your grandfather and I were first married and the doctors could not explain why I wasn't able to get pregnant? It was no tumor or kidney stone, but the petrified fetus of Lorca's child that never came out of me. You see this bulge in my stomach? It is still in here. Petrified inside me. It died, yes, but it never left. I found out about it more than twenty-five years ago, though it has lived inside me for eighty years now.

You were still in primary school, but maybe you remember coming to visit me in the hospital. You brought me *chirimoyas* because you knew it was my favorite fruit. That's when the doctors found I had this growth inside me that they determined from the x-rays to be a petrified fetus. They were going to operate on me to remove the growth, but your mother and uncle Benny would not let them. I was too old, they said, and there were too many risks. I wept for the doctors to take it away. I had been living with that curse inside me for too long. But your mother was afraid I would not survive the operation, and the doctors said my body had adapted to that petrified thing in my stomach, and that since it wasn't life threatening, I could keep my product, they called it. *I don't want to keep it*, I wept, but as an old woman, I had no say over what happened to my body. And so they left the petrified thing inside me. Do you know what that means? It means the curse is still alive, even now as I lie here on my deathbed. My mother's curse will not die until Lorca's child is laid to rest in the appropriate place. That was Chorrojumo's prophecy.

Don't be frightened, Child, don't look at me as though you doubt my sanity. I might be a hundred years old, but I haven't lost my wits yet, just my teeth and my will to live. You must believe me. I know you have heard that Gypsies lie, but Grandma Maggie would never lie to you, much less about this.

Look. It's all here in this envelope, in that other clipping from *El Diario de Juárez*. Read it for yourself so that you can see I am telling you the truth. I have waited all these years to show it to you. Your mother didn't want me to tell you. She is so afraid of what she doesn't understand. But you're different, I know you are. You are the eldest of my grandchildren, my *consentida*. And, though you are not related to Lorca in the least, you remind me so much of him, the way your heart bleeds for a kind of love you think is impossible. Yes, I've always known this about you, the way this secret has marked your choices and filled your eyes with a sadness I find very familiar. And you're not the only one like Lorca in this family. Sometimes I think that was the real curse of Lorca's I passed on, this doomed love for those of your own kind.

That is why you, my eldest granddaughter, are the only one I trust to help me bury my secret, to take my ashes back to the Sacromonte in Granada and bury my mother's curse once and for all. You must take my ashes to the cemetery in the Albaicín and spread them over the grave of Chorrojumo. Only then will the family be liberated of Lorca's ghost.

Go on, Child. Read the clipping. It confirms everything I've told you. And if you still don't believe me, if you still judge me a liar or a madwoman, ask your mother, then. She won't like it, but she'll tell you that everything it says in that newspaper story is true.

What nobody but you knows is that this petrified being that I carry inside me is all that is left of Lorca's seed. He never married me, and I never gave birth to his child, but they are both dead within me. And that poor Dutch woman in the story, she must be the woman Lorca enamored when he sailed to New York, the one that Margarita Xirgu said was carrying Lorca's child, who never gave birth, either. You see, my mother's curse on Lorca's offspring, that they would never come to light, it touched the Dutch woman, too. It's my mother's fault that I became Lorca's widow.

The Octogenarian with the Petrified Fetus Finds Herself in Good Health

El Diario de Juárez
November 2, 1984

The 88-year-old woman who became pregnant in 1923 and who to this day carries the mummified product in her womb is in good health today, now that the digestive problem that took her to the IMSS has been ameliorated. But the matter of the petrified fetus, which was discovered coincidentally, remains unresolved. Due to her advanced age, it has not been decided yet whether to perform a surgical operation to extract the fetus.

Doctors seem to think that the most prudent course of action would be for her to continue carrying it in her body under constant medical attention.

"In reality it is a very rare case for contemporary medicine," said the hospital's director, Doctor Roberto García, "for a woman's body to carry a mummified fetus for 61 years. In antecedents and statistics of similar cases, only one to three percent of pregnant women can retain the product after its death; usually it is expelled after a time, but to retain it for over half a century without any organic complications or discomforts is even rarer."

"What caused the arrest of the fetus' development is unknown," added Doctor García, "because all we have are the details provided by the patient. However, according to the x-ray taken of the woman's womb, we have deduced that the product ceased to exist at 27 or 28 weeks of gestation; after that period, it died, and, since it was not exposed to the environment, it became mummified."

According to the doctor, there are multiple and variable causes for why the body failed to expel it, such as an illness or perhaps some organic disorders of the woman's body.

The state of mummification is a natural process similar to the one utilized in medicine to conserve a body from decomposition. The difference here is that this occurred without man's intervention.

The patient in question was examined because of supposed intestinal obstruction, which turned out to be the dead fetus. It is a condition known as "fetal death before birth." At first, x-rays produced a diagnosis of a tumor. After she was diagnosed as carrying a dead fetus, she was transferred to a hospital clinic, where doctors discussed the method of extracting the dead product of her pregnancy.

"We have to evaluate the patient's health before we can decide to practice a surgical operation to remove the product," said Dr. García. "However, her advanced age impedes us from doing so since such intervention implies mortal risks, even for a much younger and stronger patient."

The doctor went on to say that the patient is in good health and her mental state is normal, and that no medical intervention would be necessary, as long as she remained so and her intestinal discomfort did not worsen.

In 1979, the Dutch newspaper *De Telegraaf* reported on a similar case of an old woman, who in 1929, initiated a pregnancy that she maintained for more than half a century. The woman, like the patient in Ciudad Juárez, complained of pains in her womb. As in the Juárez case, she was diagnosed with a uterine tumor, and surgical intervention was ordered. On the operating table, the surgeons discovered a pregnancy of little more than four months. The fetus was also mummified and showed no signs of decomposition.

The same patient remembered that fifty years earlier she had become pregnant but did not recall having given birth.

Curse of the Gypsy

His official nickname in the bullring was El Criollo, son of Mexico but with a Spaniard's pride. He had become famous not only for his bravado but also for his ability to dance *chicuelinas* around the bull, pirouetting on the bloody sand in his bullfighter's slippers, until he mesmerized both the spectators and the beast. Among the women in his circle, he was known as Sweet Hands Benito Rivera, Benito de las Manos Dulces. His face wasn't so pretty to look at, scarred as he was under the chin where a bull had gored him in Guadalajara, and on the face, where part of his upper lip was missing from the cancerous mole that had been cut out by a barber in Toluca. But those hands—his women, and all those others who longed to be touched by him, couldn't stop talking about those sweet hands. The long slim fingers that held the *banderillas* with such grace, the strong and supple wrists that he liked to show off during the different passes with the cape. He was the only ambidextrous bullfighter of Mexico who could kill a bull with either hand. Not to mention what he could do, with both hands, to a woman's body.

By the time he arrived at the Plaza de Toros in Ronda, the famous bullring just outside of Málaga, Spain, and met the Gypsy who would become his wife, Benito Rivera had conquered all manner of bulls and women. That's exactly what it was for him, whether in the bullring or the bedroom, a conquest, and every time he set out to do either, he reenacted in his mind the greatest *conquista* of all time. He became the great conquistador, Hernán Cortés, and the bull or the woman he was courting became either Moctezuma falling at his feet with the sword stabbed delicately in his heart, or La Malinche begging to be saved again and again.

What happened with Margarita was that she conquered him. Without fanfare or trumpets, without a cape or a sword, but with a simple stroke of her fat little thumb across his palms, Sweet Hands Benito lost his touch. He knew it the minute that first bull from Salamanca charged through the gate and ran enraged around the ring. Part of the animal's bravura, he knew, was that the bulls were injected with adrenaline just before being released from their pens, and it hit them like a dart of energy and rage in the middle of their skulls so that as soon as the red gate was lifted, the animal burst into the arena ready to kill any man in its way, matador or *banderillero*. But the other part was just fear, because the animal knew instinctively that it was going to die that afternoon in the bullring. Only the bravest of bulls, stoic and strong enough to withstand the matador's goading, the picadors' drilling, the insistent stabbing of six *banderillas*, a bull who kept his poise and magnificence despite relentless torture, could win the crowd's heart and be deemed worthy of sparing, his valiant seed used to sire brave new bulls for the ring.

Benito had never gotten a bull he couldn't dance to its graceful death, but this one, this one looked like he was going to do whatever it took to be spared. Benito could see it in the bull's eyes, a fierce determination not to die. It was the first time in his twenty years as a matador that Benito felt the trickle of fear in his veins, the slow and deadly leak of doubt, even though the Gypsy woman who had read his palms outside the ring earlier had told him he was going to have the best *faena* of his life.

He wasn't dressed in his costume, yet, so there was no way for her to know he was one of the matadors arriving two hours early at the plaza. He remembered the way her short and fat little thumb—more appropriate for a midget or a little girl than a grown woman reading fortunes in the street—moved across his palms three times. The way she fixed him with her black eyes. The way her dark plum lips moved when she pronounced his fortune: "You will have the best *faena* of your life, Señor," she said, "and then you will marry me."

That part terrified him. He laughed and crossed her little table with several pesetas before she told him that her hands could not touch coins, only paper. He then took out his wallet and handed her the first bill he found, not even bothering to check the denomination.

"You're good," he said, meaning he was impressed at how she had gotten him to pay for something that could be his fate or just a sentence hanging in the hot air of Ronda.

"It is not over," she said. "I will be watching you."

"How did you know I was a matador?"

"Señor, I have seen the lines in your hand. I know everything about you."

He laughed again and walked off into the shade of the plaza, but the whole time that he was preparing, going through the motions and the routines that had become as indispensable to his art as the cape and the sword, he thought about the Gypsy. She had done more than read his palms. He could feel it.

Just before the musicians broke into the *pasodoble* that announced the beginning of the *corrida*, he had looked down at his hands and saw that his palms were sweating. The Gypsy had hexed him somehow, he was sure. He swung his cape over his shoulders and tried to dispel the thought as he made his entrance with the other *matadores*, followed by the *banderilleros* and then the *picadores* on their padded horses. In his red and green suit of lights, his white silk cloak brocaded in gold filigree and decorated with the Mexican eagle in gold sequins, a gold Virgen de Guadalupe amulet pinned to the inside of his jacket, Benito felt his confidence coming back, at least for the minute it took to walk across the arena in the opening *paseo*. At the head of the procession, riding Andalusian black stallions in ribbon-festooned manes, the *alguaciles* wore the regalia of ancient knights. Each one shook hands with the president of the bullring, who then handed one of them the key to the gate from where the bulls were let out to fight. That signaled the official beginning of the bullfight, and the trumpets blared.

His manager had not told Benito that the other two matadors he was going to be fighting with had only recently taken their *alternativas* and moved from apprentices to full-fledged bullfighters. This made Benito Rivera, "El Criollo" as he was billed on the *carteles* plastered all over the city, the senior bullfighter that afternoon, which gave him the right to kill the first bull. He hated going first, especially in a ring he had never been to and in a foreign country. No chance to observe the bull or the crowd, to see how the shadows of man and beast moved over the sand. *Already starting on the wrong foot*, he thought. Then the bull charged into the ring, and for a moment he looked up and thought he saw the Gypsy watching him above one of the gates on the sunny side of the plaza. Remember la *conquista*, he told himself. His father had always told him that they were descendants of the great Hernán Cortés, and that bull pawing at the sand in the arena is nothing but the savage standing in the way of glory.

That first bull was a disgrace. He fought well enough at the beginning, and together they had drawn a few spirited *olé's* from the crowd during the first movement, but the *picadore*s had gored him too much from their horseback perches, digging their lances deeper and deeper into his back; and then the *banderilleros* took their turn, their short harpoons placed perfectly together on the weakened withers of the bull, streamers dancing colorfully in the afternoon light, and the bull's blood running in red streams off his hide.

After the last pair of *banderillas*, the fear won over the rage in the animal, and Benito could not get him to respond, to follow him in the dance of his death. Instead of paying attention to Benito's insistent *epa, toro, epa!* or to the cape the animal walked in the other direction and stood there pawing at the dirt as if challenging the grey planks of the *barrera*. They still had the third movement of the *faena* to finish before the kill, but the bull was useless to him, now, and not worth the energy it took to keep the animal focused or to dance around him in his signature series of pirouettes. Besides, the animal was making him look bad in front of all these Spaniards, who were hooting at him and yelling obscenities about second-rate Mexican bullfighters. Without waiting for the trumpets to signal the moment of the kill, he decided to forego the rest of the choreography with this bull and get to the end of it.

He took off his hat, saluted the four directions of the bullring and walked over to the *barrera* to where his sword handler waited for him to exchange his pink fighting cape for the red *muleta* that signaled the bull's upcoming death, and his cape sword for the killing sword with its curved tip. He took the sharp sword out of its case and inserted it into the seam of the red cape and returned to the center of the bullring to finish off the poor beast.

The Gypsy was wrong. It was not the best *faena* of his life, but the worst and most humiliating. For thirteen years, in every one of his bullfights until now, he had killed the bull in one stroke, the sword stabbing precisely in the small cleft between the top of the shoulder blades where the curved tip could glide smoothly between muscle and bone all the way down to the animal's heart. For every good kill, he had earned at the very least one of the bull's ears; a good kill and a good performance on the sand usually netted him two ears; daring theatrical showmanship full of vulgar displays of *cojonismo* always earned the highest reward in the ring: both ears and the bull's tail. That gypsy-cursed bullfight earned him nothing but shame and ridicule. The bull did not die in one stroke. No matter how hard he concentrated on the imaginary target between the bull's shoulder blades, how swiftly he tilted his weight forward from back foot to front foot, spinning the red cape in front of the bull's dazed eyes and plunging the killing sword down into the bull's bleeding flesh, Benito could not find the right spot. Each time he thrust the sword, he managed to get the blade halfway into the bull's flesh, but the placement was wrong, and he had to pull it out and try again. After three attempts, the wound on the bull's back looked like ground meat. The first bugle sounded, warning him that ten minutes had passed since he had started the kill. It was as if the animal, though terrified and weakened by all the blood it had lost, refused to give up its life to this second-rate, Mexican bullfighter. By the time the second bugle rang out, the shouting of the crowd was unbearable. He had come to Spain, homeland of matadors, conquistadores and his own ancestors, only to lose face.

The bugle called out the third and last warning, and the bull was still alive, head lolling like an old cow's, long grey tongue dragging on the sand. The bullfight had moved now from mockery to torture. The *alguacil* called out the *puntillero*, and a man dressed impeccably in white pants and shirt marched out into the arena, his short knife gleaming at his side. His job was to bring a quick end to the poor bull, the cheap way, the easy way: three short jabs to the back of the head. Some called the *puntillero* an angel of mercy, but for Benito, he was no better than a barrio butcher. The bull's blood splattered all over the butcher's white shirt. Benito watched the animal stagger under the realization that it was dead.

Benito stalked out of the ring and wept into his cursed palms. He wept for his own misfortune, for the shame he had brought to his reputation, but most of all, for the stupid beast who would not surrender to its fate, even with Benito's clumsy sword dangling from the deep gash in its back. The trumpets flourished again, and he knew it was the second bullfighter's turn to take the ring. He wished for his flask of tequila. He could use a quick shot of Mexican courage.

The image of that woman's thumb kept haunting him, that absurd little thumb that had brushed over the lines of his hands like a curse. It was the Gypsy's fault, he reasoned, and his own, too, for having allowed her to read his fortune when that had never been a part of his ritual. *You're a stupid man*, he told himself, *letting that pinche gitana touch you.* The only thing he could do now was wait for his second turn and perform the Mexican daredevilry that never failed to cast a spell on the audience and the arena.

And suddenly he heard her voice again: *you will have the best faena of your life, and then you will marry me*. It was the conviction in her statement that had frightened him, that had caused him to lose his concentration, but he had focused mainly on the last part. Now he had to believe the first part was true.

The second bullfighter, a left-handed *madrileño*, did reasonably well, but he slipped once on the bloody sand and nearly lost his footing, leaning on the arm of a *banderillero* to keep from landing on his ass. He was awarded no tokens for his efforts. The third bullfighter, a young man native to Granada, had the crowd's full attention and Andalusian love. *Olé!* they shouted at every move he made, as though he were the great Joselito himself. He was a native son, after all, thin and tall and Moorish looking with tightly curled black hair. When time came for the *banderillas*, he took the first set and planted them in the bull's back himself, gracefully arching his back like a bow. The tip of the bull's horn hooked on the flap of the young matador's jacket, and for a moment the crowd heaved in fear that their boy had been gored. The boy ran his hand quickly over his sash, then held it up for the crowd to see he had not been touched. A rumble of *olés* and bravos shuddered through the arena. A man's voice cried out clearly: "That's a real matador, not a *mamarracho* from the colonies!"

Benito's face reddened with shame. Now he was a clown of the colonies. The one thing he could be thankful for was that his father had not come to witness his son's humiliation. Not that his hidalgo-minded father ever attended one of his bullfights, disgusted as he was at his son's choice of career.

The Granada boy did not plant any more *banderillas*, obviously still shaken from the close call of the bull's horn. His final stroke hit the target at an angle, so that the *banderilleros* had to huddle around the beast, swishing their pink and yellow capes in front of the bull to make him dizzy and bring him to his knees, at which point the boy reached down and sank his sword deeper into the animal and only then managed to kill the beast. Benito was not surprised when the president of the bullring awarded the boy the trophy of one of the bull's ears for his valiance.

The afternoon sun was sliding towards dusk when Benito's second turn came around. Already the full arena was in shade and the round patch of sky above the plaza was turning a purplish blue. The air smelled of rain. While the body of the third bull was dragged out of the arena and the ocher sand raked smooth and tamped down again, Benito clasped his Virgen de Guadalupe amulet and said a quick prayer to the patron of his homeland. *Bless me, virgencita,* he said, *and help me prove myself to these high and mighty gachupín sons of bitches.* He walked out into the ring again and pretended not to hear the catcalls and the booing, and instead lifted his cap to the president of the bullring, kissed it and threw it up into the covered box of the *ayuntamiento*, where the officials of the city council sat with their women. He'd show them the difference between a boy's nuts and a man's *cojones*.

The first movement was flawless. The bull—a big brown and white one from Pamplona, much younger than his first one—stayed at his side like a pet, obeying every command and following every flourish of the pink cape. Benito executed a series of *olé*-inspired passes: *verónicas, medias-verónicas, paso de pecho, paso alto, paso bajo, paso natural, a mariposa* and even a *cambio de rodillas* where the bull charged at him while Benito waited on his knees.

In the second movement, the *picadores* came out on their blindfolded horses, their lances ready to poke deep into the bull's flesh. Benito stopped them after the first lance. He would not allow them to cow the animal with their drilling. "That's blood, not petroleum," he shouted at them, "*¡Fuera!*" waving his hands to indicate he wanted them out of the bullring.

Now his squad of *banderilleros* stood at attention, each one grasping his pair of bright paper-covered *banderillas*, ready to dash out into the ring to insert them into the hump of the bull's neck, making a show of how narrowly each escaped the bull's horns. Benito took the *banderillas* from their hands, broke them in half to make them shorter and more dangerous, and inserted them, himself, all three pairs, not just one. First the red ones, then the white ones, and last, the green ones, the colors of the Mexican flag streaming from the animal's back as it ran in enraged circles around the ring. He knew, then, that he had conquered not just the bull, but the crowd.

For dramatic effect, Benito whistled at the bull and brought him to the middle of the ring with a swirl of his cape. He stood square in front of the bull, right arm stretched out, hand hovering just above the left horn, then knelt on one knee and brought himself eye to eye with the animal. The last time he had done that, the bull had lunged at his face and gored him under the chin. But this bull, he trusted, would not move, would hold his stare as long as Benito wanted. The crowd erupted into wild cheering. *So fickle*, he thought, *aficionados can be worse than a woman.*

He rose to his feet again, slowly, making sure he was positioned exactly between the bull's eyes, then turned his back on the bull. Dragging his pink cape behind him in the sand, he strutted over to the *barrera*, chest puffed out like a rooster, hips and belly pulled tight, to exchange his cape and sword. Someone threw a wineskin into the arena and he caught it in midair, uncapped it and let the warm wine arc into his mouth in a thin red stream. He threw the wineskin back up into the stands, and then returned to where the bull was still waiting for him in the middle of the ring, pawing at the ground.

"*¡Epa, toro!*" he called. "*¡A bailar se ha dicho!*"

The final movement nearly broke his heart, it was so perfect. The best *faena* of your life, the Gypsy had said, and he never dreamed he could be so good at this choreography of death. First, standing so close to the bull, he got the animal's blood on his sash, he danced the red cape in front of the bull's eyes like the skirt of a *folklórico* dancer while slowly turning the animal to face the four directions of the plaza. Next came the waltz as he stretched out his arms and legs and dragged the cape like the train of a long cloak over the horns and the short *banderillas* still quivering in the bull's back. Finally, a ballet of *chicuelinas*, Benito's signature move, as the cape wrapped around his own slim hips like a crimson shroud while he pirouetted from one end of the bull to the other.

When the trumpet announced that it was time to dispatch the bull, he made sure the bull was standing squarely on all four hoofs, took his position, standing sideways like a fencer between the bull's horns. He balanced himself on the balls of his feet, placed the *muleta* low to the ground to keep the animal's head down and his gaze fixed on the red cloth, and aimed the point of the sword at the imaginary crosshairs between the animal's shoulders and spine. He made one final entreaty to the Virgin, then plunged forward and sank his *estocada* right into the sweet spot. It was one continuous motion, the furling of the cape with the left arm, the thrusting of the sword with the right, his body at a perfect right angle between the bull's horns, his weight shifting forward on his left foot. He felt the blade sink past muscle and bone, the curved tip lodging in the dense mass of the animal's heart. The bull dropped at his knees, as if bowing to his conqueror.

The same crowd that had earlier been yelling epithets about his colonial genealogy got to its feet and cheered as though he had suddenly become their national hero. The president of the bullring gave him the highest trophy. Benito took his time walking around the ring, the pair of ears in one hand, the tail in the other, letting himself be adulated for his victory, as flowers, ladies' shoes and wineskins were thrown down into the arena. He told his *mozo* to gather up the flowers in his cape. He kissed the toe of each lady's shoe and threw it back into the stands. From each wineskin, he took a generous swallow, letting the wine spill over his mouth and into his collar. From the box of the *ayuntamiento,* a lady threw down his cap, a rose and a fifty-peseta note tucked inside.

The Gypsy had been right, after all, about both things.

She was waiting for him, long past the end of the *corrida*, by the door where the bodies of the bulls are butchered and sold for meat to the poor. Standing under a street lamp against the henna-colored façade of the building, her red skirt, black hair and copper bracelets on both arms made her seem like something out of a fairy tale. She saw him coming and her black-lined eyes creased as she smiled.

"Are you waiting for me, Negra?" he said, handing her the makeshift bouquet of the drying flowers his servant boy had collected in the ring.

"Only if you don't mind being seen with a cursed woman," she answered.

He couldn't tell if she was challenging him to believe her or just testing his sense of humor. "Negrita," he said, smiling down at her, "you could be cursed by the Pope himself, and I would still want to invite you for a coffee."

She laughed. "Señor, you may be a mexicano, but you have a Gypsy way with women."

Already he was in love with her voice, the directness of her stare, her silly little thumbs. "Have you ever been to México?" he said, offering her his arm.

"Not yet, Señor, but I see in your very near future a short trip to my hometown of Granada."

They were married a week later in the church of an old abbey in Granada, her mother, her long-haired brothers and Benito's manager the only ones attending. Her entire clan showed up for the celebration in a whitewashed cave in the Sacromonte that belonged to her family, her troupe of cousins providing the flamenco entertainment. Her mother—a sharp-chinned, wide-waisted little matriarch named Doña Fatima—resented that Benito had not asked her for her daughter's hand in marriage, but since Margarita was a widow, not a virgin, her family's permission to marry was not necessary. What Doña Fátima could not forgive was that Benito was taking Margarita across the ocean. Without her family close by, there was no telling what dangers could befall Margarita. "I shall put the evil eye on you, Benito Rivera, if you dare to mistreat my daughter," she had threatened, smiling the whole time. She had her ways, she said, of finding out if he was being true to his word. Benito kissed the woman's hand and swore he would be true, "*por mi madre*," he said—never an oath to be taken lightly. The wedding celebration lasted three days, and by the third night, with Benito still standing under the influence of jeréz and cante jondo, Margarita's brothers had all accepted him as their *payo cuñao*.

Of course, Benito did not believe his wife when she told him she had been cursed by the old king of her tribe, and that her mother was somehow responsible. He didn't care that she had been married before, that she was a soldier's widow and not a virgin. Nor could he be bothered with worrying what his arrogant, light-skinned family with their aristocratic airs and fake coat of arms might say about his dark bride. It was her scent of sandalwood, the way her eyes and teeth gleamed behind the gossamer fabric of the veil she wore on their wedding night, it was the way her hips and belly undulated when she belly-danced for him in private, the way her wrists moved while she played the castanets, the way she surrendered to him so completely—that's what he cared about, that and the Spaniards' respect for him as a matador. Curses and threats, scandals and cultural differences—Benito feared nothing. He returned to Mexico City with two ears and a tail from his first *faena* in Spain, and a woman who adored him. How fortunate could a man be?

From Madrid, he had cabled the news of his wedding to his half-sisters, Yolanda and Zenaida, who lived in the Lower East Side of Manhattan. He knew better than to let his mother and father know ahead of time.

You married a Spanish Gypsy?! Papá is going to have a heart attack! Have you lost your mind?

Benito regretted having read the telegram aloud to his bride.

"Why?" Margarita asked. "What is wrong with your father's heart?"

He shook his head and folded up the telegram into the inside pocket of his jacket. "Nothing. Papá is perfectly healthy. They don't know what they're talking about. I'm sure they're dying to meet you."

He managed to steer the conversation to the topic of his sisters, of how they were the product of his father's *casa chica*, and how his mother refused to acknowledge them as members of the family. Of course, Margarita understood perfectly. To her people, Benito was the outsider, and her mother and brothers had no faith that he would be able to make her happy.

Benito chose not to tell Margarita that he had had to bribe the captain of the ocean liner they were sailing on back to Mexico to allow his wife into the first-class cabin that Benito's manager always reserved for him. The morning they boarded the ship, he made a point to shake the captain's hand and thank him for his open mind.

"Just be sure you keep her under lock and key," the captain warned, ogling Margarita at the same time.

"Do you think I would let my new wife wander about the ship, Captain? I will be needing her services in the cabin, don't you worry."

But his sisters' telegram worried him. It was true that their father flaunted the superiority of his Spanish genes, but what they didn't know was that his mother, although a half-breed mestiza herself, felt the same way. She had always insisted Benito attend private schools, associate only with light-skinned friends, go out with girls of their own *alcurnia*, class. His mother had been even more horrified than his father at their son's choice of career. *You might as well have become a cirquero*, she had said. *Do we look like a circus family?* Although his sisters and his mother never spoke, or so he had been led to believe, the news of his gypsy bride had spread quickly from Manhattan to Mexico City.

No one met them at the Port of Veracruz, and Benito had to hire a car to transport them all the way to Cuernavaca, where his family's home was located. Instead of welcoming him home with her usual fanfare and a delicious spread of all his favorite dishes, his mother hugged him stiffly, barely glancing at his wife and motioning with disdain for the maid to carry up their luggage. His father was reading the newspaper in his study and would not be joining them until lunch. In the back patio of the house, the long cedar table had been laid out with the Talavera plates his mother only used for informal occasions, but she led them past the patio into the more formal living room and directed Margarita to take one of the stiff leather armchairs while she settled herself next to her son on the leather divan.

"May we get something to drink, Mamá? We are both very thirsty from the long drive."

His mother rang the servant's bell on the end table, and Profunda, the Indian cook who had been with the family since Benito's childhood, stepped into the living room, smiling at Benito. He got up to give her a hug.

"Bring us a pitcher of *agua fresca de tamarindo*, por favor, Profunda," said his mother.

"*Al niño le gusta de jamaica*," Profunda pronounced.

She had not lost her native lilt, even after all these years of working in his family's kitchen. In her old eyes, Benito was still the boy following her around the kitchen, wanting to taste everything she made.

"*El niño*," his mother started sarcastically, "can drink hibiscus tea somewhere else. Today you will serve us *tamarindo* tea with our lunch."

Profunda shrugged and left the room. His mother had dictated her orders, and everyone knew better than to contradict her.

Benito did not complain. Maybe Margarita liked the tart drink of the tamarind seed. His father had taught him how to pick his battles with Mamá, and this one was clearly not one he could win.

"So, tell me, Benjamín, what new scandals have you gotten yourself into in Spain, aside from marrying this Gypsy, I mean?"

"Did you not hear the news of my glory in the bullring, Mamá?"

"How could you have done this to us, Benjamín? How could you have gotten married in Spain without telling us about it? And to a *gitana*, of all things? Have all those bullfights made you a complete idiot, or did this woman cast a spell on you, superstitious as you are?"

Margarita turned to gape at Benito. He shook his head slightly to keep her from taking his mother's bait.

His mother's harangue continued. "First, you embarrassed us with this vulgar bullfighter business, then you invest our money, your father's money, in some crazy newspaper scheme in El Norte, now this. Why do you want to ruin the family's good name, Benito? Your father will write you out of his will. You know that, don't you? You will end up stealing on the street, alongside your little Gypsy woman."

In his heart, Benito was cursing his mother's arrogance and narrow-mindedness, but he was afraid to speak the words out loud for fear that the emotions raging inside him would betray the deep humiliation he felt in front of his wife.

Profunda returned with three blue-rimmed glasses of tamarindo tea and a bowl of candied limes, Benito's favorite snack. She winked at him and smiled kindly at Margarita before leaving the room.

Benito reached for a glass, passed it to his wife and took another for himself.

"Have you ever had a candied lime, *cariño*?" he asked Margarita, and savored the sugar-crusted snack. Margarita stared down at her glass of *tamarindo* water and shook her head.

The butler stepped into the threshold of the living room and announced that lunch was ready to be served.

"*A comer*," said his mother, getting suddenly to her feet. "If you don't want to discuss this *barbaridad* that you've committed, Benito, let's eat. What are we having today, Sergio?"

"Cream of asparagus soup, Señora, and *tortilla española*."

"Cook knows what I like, Mamá," said Benito.

"The bathroom is over there," his mother said to Margarita, the only words she directed at his wife that afternoon. "Please, wash your hands before coming to the table."

Benito shut his eyes, wincing at the mean bite of his mother's words. He was too ashamed to say anything and escorted Margarita to the bathroom instead, where they both washed their hands without looking at each other.

When they took their places at the outdoor table, he hoped his father and grandmother would at least be civil to Margarita. But he was wrong. His father, who had once played chess with José Vasconcelos when he taught at the University of Mexico and fancied himself a member of the new education ministry, tried a more indirect affront on that first and only evening they shared a dinner table, asking Margarita if she had ever read the Vasconcelos treatise entitled *La Raza Cósmica*.

"She's a Gypsy," his grandmother had quipped as she took a delicate spoonful of her cream of asparagus soup. "You can't expect her to be cultured, poor dear."

Margarita ate nothing that night, just sat there with her eyes on her lap as Benito's father gave her a private lecture about the benefits of purifying the race.

"Vasconcelos argues that we are a mix of the four major races of the world—the white, the black, the red and the yellow—and that their mixture will produce a fifth race—a bronze race, he calls it—that will be more beautiful, more intelligent and more powerful than any other in the cosmos. But before we can become that powerful cosmic race, we must purify the blood and try to breed out the dark influences as much as possible."

"How many times must we hear about Vasconcelos, Papá?" said Benito. "Nobody cares about *la raza cósmica* these days."

"Who would you prefer to talk about, then, Cantinflas? Tin-Tan?" his father sneered.

"Yes," said Benito. "That would be much more interesting than all these *tonterías* about some stupid cosmic race."

"Your father is trying to explain something important," his mother said. "This marriage of yours is a great jump backwards."

"Maybe his kids will be from the *no te entiendo* caste," added his father, laughing.

They were saying all of this as if Margarita were not sitting at the table. He never realized that his family could be so rude and so cruel.

"*¡Ya basta!*" Benito had exploded, pounding his fist on the table so hard he tipped over his wine glass, staining the lace tablecloth with the Rioja he had brought back from Spain. "I am tired of your insults, Papá. Of your rudeness, Mamá. Margarita is my wife and you will all respect her as my wife and the future mother of your grandchildren or we will go away from Mexico and you will never hear from me again."

"Think of your inheritance, Benito?" his mother entreated. "Why compromise your inheritance by marrying *una prieta gitana, ¡por Dios, hijo!*"

"At least she's from Spain," his grandmother added, dabbing the corners of her mouth with a cloth napkin. "It could be worse. She could be an Indian."

"Your mother is a wise woman," said his father, pausing to take a sip from his wine glass. "I don't understand how she gave birth to such an imbecile."

Benito stood up from the table, pulled the chair out for Margarita and fixed his angry gaze on his father.

"*Ya basta, Papá. Soy un hombre, no tu pinche escuincle para sermonear. Mamá, cómo me has decepcionado. Nunca pensé que podrías ser tan cruel. Me duele decirles que ya no voy a regresar a esta casa. Y a mis hijos ninguno de ustedes los va a conocer.*"

For the first time, he had stood up to his father, man to man. He was no longer a child to be preached to. He would leave his father's house forever and none of them would ever know the children he brought into the world with Margarita. That last bit had made his mother's eyes tear up. His grandmother just shook her head.

His father's sarcastic laugh followed them to the front door. "*Oye*, Criollo, remember the money you owe me for your trip to Spain," his father's voice boomed out.

Benito wanted to shout back what his father could do with his money, but Margarita pressed her little thumb against his lips and shook her head, her eyes like velvet on his bruised manhood. At the threshold, Benito picked up his Gypsy bride and carried her out into the afternoon drizzle. She placed her arms around his neck and kissed him with a reverence he had never felt from any woman.

Benito ordered his driver to take them to the finest hotel on the *zócalo* of Mexico City, but even there, although the place was surrounded by Indians selling their goods on *petates* under the arcades, they were turned away because of the color of his wife. Finally, they found lodging near the Palacio de Bellas Artes in a beautiful colonial house, said to have once been the residence of a great *cacique*. They lived there until his bullfighter's fortune bought them a good house in Coyoacán.

Benito looked forward to settling down and starting a family, with or without his father's inheritance. The only relatives that he communicated with were Yolanda and Zenaida in New York City, and they would write to him often, inviting him to bring Margarita to visit them before she got busy making babies. But there were no babies, and the harassment about having married a Gypsy, and a barren one at that, continued, now from his friends.

Pobre pendejo, his friends joked with him at the country club, and one of them even composed a stupid rhyme about his situation. *You were bewitched and now you're hitched and she's nothing but a Gypsy witch after a man who's rich.* Hard to believe, they said, that a man who had so many women chasing after him, who could have had any woman in the capital, including a stage actress that everyone knew had a crush on him, would stoop so low.

Benito de las Manos Hechizadas. Once he had been known as Sweet Hands Benito Rivera. Now he was Cursed Hands Benito Rivera, and he had no lucky amulets in his matador's repertoire to woo this crowd. The worst part of it was that, deep in his heart, he was starting to believe that he really was cursed. Or, that at least his marriage was cursed, because even after six years of conjugal life, his wife could not bear a child.

Benito separated from Margarita on their sixth anniversary and took up with that Mexican actress, with whom he fathered two sons and a girl with the actress's maid. Finally, though, the pain in his wife's eyes each time he returned home for clean clothes, the shame he felt each time he ran into his parents at an Easter or Christmas Mass in the Cathedral, with Cleotilde rather than Margarita on his arm—all of it was too much for him to bear, and so he left his *casa chica* as well.

A year later, his sister Zenaida died of tuberculosis in New York City, and Benito insisted his father accompany him to the funeral.

"I cannot be the only one in the family to care about your daughters, Papá," Benito said. "You have been completely indifferent to them. I'm the one who has corresponded with them all these years, sending them birthday cards and whatever money I could spare. The least you can do is attend Zenaida's funeral."

It was June 1931 and the Mexico City airport had just been inaugurated two weeks earlier. Benito convinced his father to purchase flights for them to New York City. The trip took three days longer than expected, and they landed on the day of the funeral. They had to hire a cab to take them from La Guardia to the funeral home in Queens. When she saw Benito walking in, Yolanda collapsed into his arms in all her grief.

"Benito! I thought you weren't coming," she wept. "I didn't know how I was going to get through this by myself."

She took no notice of the older man who accompanied her older brother. According to his father, the last time he had seen them, the last time he had been in New York City, was in 1902. They had been little girls, maybe three years old, dressed exactly alike, in red sweaters and beanies, waving goodbye to him as he climbed the bridge of the SS *Esperanza,* the steamship that was taking him back to Mexico.

"Yolanda, this is Papá."

Immediately, Yolanda composed herself. She wiped at her eyes with a handkerchief, smoothed her hair down and crossed her arms.

"It's nice to make your acquaintance, Señor. It's so sad you weren't able to meet the other daughter you abandoned."

Their father was too stunned to speak. He had removed his hat to greet her, and his whole head reddened and broke out in a sweat. He was not used to being remonstrated by a woman.

"I'm going to pay my respects," Benito announced. He had no desire to be caught in the middle of those two intractable wills. There were only a few people in attendance, women mostly, with hard faces and dye-stained hands. No doubt they were workers at the same textile factory that the sisters worked in. He approached the coffin and seeing Zenaida lying there so peacefully in the embroidered silk mantilla he had brought her from Spain broke his heart. He made the sign of the cross, kissed his thumb, clasped his hands and muttered a few Hail Marys.

"You must be her brother, the bullfighter she told me so much about," said a soft voice behind Benito. He was dazed from the long trip, the lack of food, the loss of his favorite sister, so there was nothing to protect him from falling under the spell of the most cerulean blue eyes he had ever seen. She shook his hand with her fingertips.

"I'm Charity, Naida's nurse. I was with her when she passed."

"Naida?"

"Nobody in the hospital ward could pronounce her name so she said to call her Naida."

Benito felt a tug in his bowels and knew that it was too late. He had been conquered again, this time by a shy, American nurse who did not speak Spanish. Already he could tell that his life would never be the same. He sent his father back to Mexico alone.

In September, Benito and Caridad (as he called her) were married in City Hall, and seven months later she gave birth to their son, Samuel. Finally, Benito had a legitimate son of his own, a beautiful yellow-haired boy with blue eyes like his mother and a cleft chin like his father. Even his relationship with his mother went back to normal, and she would write him long letters about everything going on Mexico and what new financial ventures his father was investing in and what gossip she heard of either *la gitana* or the actress who was raising his three illegitimate children. Benito never shared these letters with his American wife, and she never asked about them, so he was free to pretend he was the happiest man in the world, now that he had everything he had ever wanted.

It was his sister Yolanda who snuffed his pipe dreams. Benito and Caridad had moved into Zenaida's room after the wedding, and this helped everyone pay the rent in their two-bedroom Lower East Side flat. But once the baby came and kept everyone awake with his loud cries, Yolanda started to resent first Benito, then Caridad and finally the child.

"I don't know why you two don't find yourselves your own apartment. I'm sick and tired of that screaming brat," Yolanda would grouse instead of saying, "Good morning."

Finally, Benito asked her what was wrong. Surely, she could not hold crying against a baby.

"I can't do it anymore, Benito. Why do I have to carry your guilt? I don't even know your Gypsy wife, and she keeps haunting me in my dreams."

"Keep your voice down," Benito hissed. "Cari doesn't know anything about the Gypsy."

"Has she learned Spanish, finally? Do you think she will understand the word, 'bigamy'?"

"For God's sake, Yolanda. Shut your mouth!"

"You better tell her about it, then, Benito, or I will."

Benito's heart was pounding and he could feel a livid heat rising into his neck and face. He knew Yolanda was right. His marriage to Caridad might be legal in the United States, but his first wife, his only wife in the eyes of God, would always be the Gypsy he had brought back from Spain. His cursed union with Margarita was the only marriage recognized by the Church.

When his American son was killed in a trolley car accident in Times Square, he knew the curse was not in his Gypsy wife, but in his own two-timing soul, so much like his father's. He knew, as well, that it was time to return to Mexico and do right by his marriage.

Everything was different when Benito returned to Coyoacán. His mistress, Cleotilde, was now more loyal to Margarita than to him, for they had grown closer than sisters in his long absence, and now formed a family of sorts as together they were raising Benito's three children. But the real difference was in his wife. She had started teaching belly-dancing lessons to support herself while he was away, and somehow Margarita had become more sensual and more attractive during his years in New York. Once again, she was the dark vixen that had so enchanted him outside the bullring in Ronda.

A year after his return to Mexico, Margarita gave birth to a son, whom they named Benjamín Nahum, and two years after that, to a daughter, Fátima Dolores. Half Mexican, half Gypsy, each had green eyes like their father and dark skin like their mother.

By the time his legitimate children were born, Benito had little left of his bullfighter's fortune, but at least his father had not disowned him completely. The shares his father had bought in the Mexican Eagle Oil Company on Benito's tenth birthday, a decade before the Mexican Revolution, paid off handsomely during the Second World War, when Mexico became the leading supplier of oil to both the Allied and the Axis forces. At the end of the war, Benito sold his shares to the government, and took his Gypsy wife, his mistress and their five children to the border city of Ciudad Juárez. There, he would work in the advertising department of the binational newspaper, *El Fronterizo*, and see the births of his thirteen grandchildren, five born Mexican, all the others born in El Paso, Texas, before a cancer that had started eating at his face metastasized into his liver. One afternoon, listening to his favorite grandson playing Gypsy music on his violin, he collapsed while planting peach trees in his backyard.

The Bullfighter's Last Confession

"Bless me, Padre, for I have sinned. It has been thirty, no, maybe forty, years since my last confession. I can't remember any more, but it was after my last bullfight. I have carried this secret for many years, Padre, thinking I could drag it with me to my grave, but I see now that God will not take me from this world, nor save me from this flesh-eating disease, until I have purged my soul of this sin."

"Cleanse your conscience, my son."

Benito wiped his handkerchief over his brow, careful not to disturb the bandages from his latest surgery, the removal of another cancerous mole on the side of his face. Not knowing how to start, he unbuttoned his collar and removed his hat. Cleared his throat. Dabbed the sweat beading thickly around his neck. A voice inside his skull was urging him to flee the confessional, fearing not God's wrath, but the priest's judgment. You are a matador, the voice chided him, stop acting like a *maricón*.

"Proceed, my son," the priest encouraged him.

Benito made the sign of the cross and got straight to the point. "Six years after I married my wife, Margarita, I went to live in New York City and got together with another woman and had a child with her, a beautiful yellow-haired boy that I was crazy about, my American son, Samuel, until he was killed in a horrible accident. He is the secret I have carried in my heart all these years."

"Did your wife know about the other woman?"

"She must have guessed. How could she not, being a Gypsy and knowing me as well as she did. And I think she probably suspected about the boy, because, you see, my wife was barren, at least she was, for the first six years of our marriage. No matter how much we tried, she could not conceive. Doctors were consulted, they drew our blood, and we were both told we were healthy, but for some reason her body refused to become pregnant. We had second and third opinions, and always it was the same diagnosis. Since our wedding night, my wife had told me she had been cursed by her Gypsy mother, but I never asked her about it, not wanting to hear any of her Gypsy superstitions. All I wanted was a family, Father. I know that is no excuse for infidelity, but it was stronger than me, this desire for a family. I wanted a son, even a daughter, a piece of myself to leave in the world. I know my wife did, too, and it was breaking her heart not to give me what I most wanted.

"We fought constantly. She was never one to keep her mouth closed when she had something to say, or when I lost respect for her and treated her badly. Then one day I received news that Zenaida, one of my half-sisters who lived in New York City, had died of tuberculosis. Yolanda, her twin, sent me a telegram insisting that I go to her immediately, as she had no money to pay for the hospital or the funeral. As bastard daughters of my father, they had never expected anything of him, but of me, their half-brother. They imagined it was my duty to provide filial support. They were my chosen family, after all. I did better than comply with Yolanda's request. I took our father with me to pay his last respects to a daughter he had abandoned long ago, and to seek forgiveness from the other. After Zenaida's burial, Yolanda begged me not to return to Mexico City with our father. It was just the two of us left now, she said, and we needed to be together. I paid the rent in arrears of her flat in the Lower East side and stayed for five years. Margarita did not come. Truth is, I did not invite her. I told her it was going to be a difficult time and that my sister Yolanda needed all my attention. I had already retired as a bullfighter by then, and there was nothing forcing me to stay in Mexico. I guess you could say I had no intention of returning."

"Is that where you committed adultery?" asked the priest.

"No, not adultery, Father. She was not married to anyone else."

"But you were, my son. Hence, you committed adultery."

"My sister Yolanda called it bigamy."

"That is another name for the same sin," said the priest.

"I know it was a sin, Father, but I did not intend to fall in love. How was I to know that this little American woman who had been Zenaida's nurse in the hospital, who sat with Yolanda night after night, praying the rosary for the novena, who helped us so much during the wake, and cleaned out Zenaida's room, and even made meals for us, would steal my heart?

"During those sad first weeks after my father left, taking half of Zenaida's ashes with him to be buried in the family crypt in Mexico City, Caridad and I fell in love. After we married, Caridad and I moved into Zenaida's room in Yolanda's flat. Cari could not work in her condition, so she took in ironing to make extra money for the rent. I looked for work everywhere, but every employer that interviewed me wanted me to know English. Finally, I got a job as an elevator operator in one of the big hotels near Central Park, where the most I had to say in English were *good morning, good afternoon, good evening and what floor please?* When my son was born, I wept, Father, like a child who finally gets his deepest wish. I felt like a new man, like a real man, with a wife and a family, just like I'd always wanted. I wanted more children, of course, but Caridad had had a difficult labor with Samuel and wanted to wait until the boy started school before giving him a sibling. She took birth control, Father, but I had nothing to do with that decision. As an American woman, Caridad had her own ideas about motherhood.

"Occasionally, Margarita visited me in my dreams, and I would wake up terrified that she had followed me, and that she was in the room. I swore to Caridad that I could smell sandalwood, that I could hear the jangling of Margarita's bracelets when I closed my eyes. I could not lie to Caridad about Margarita, but you see, she thought we were divorced. Being an American, that was her conclusion. How could I tell her that, in fact, I had two wives, though Caridad, as the mother of my child, was my legal wife, and Margarita, barren though she was, and a Gypsy, was the only wife recognized by the Church?

"The boy grew quickly and I loved him more than my life, Father. He was tall for his four years, and had learned to speak in complete sentences. On his fifth birthday, the boy begged me to take him with me to work, he wanted to ride the elevator all day and sit on my stool and push the buttons to make the car go up and down. I agreed, and Caridad dressed him in a little suit, with a little cap and even a pair of white gloves—a miniature version of his father.

"'This is not a game, Samuel,' I cautioned him as we walked to the hotel. 'This is my job, if you misbehave, I will lose my job and we will all starve to death.'

"He nodded solemnly and took his job very seriously. *What floor please, mister or ma'am,* he would ask, and *How are you today*—and it was a good day for tips because of the boy's charm. I gave him a quarter for his work. He was very pleased with himself on our way home, could hardly wait to tell his mother about all his rides in the elevator that day. But I had to make my nightly stop at the kiosk in Times Square and check the dailies from Mexico. Instead of staying beside me, the boy wandered off to buy a balloon from the vendor on the other side of the kiosk. If we had not stopped, we would have made it home that night, but who can explain God's will?

"For some reason, the lights went out over Times Square and people started to run like chickens without heads in the dark. There was so much chaos and shouting. I ran around the kiosk, calling out for the boy, when suddenly a horrible sound filled the air, the screeching of metal wheels against metal tracks. In slow motion, I watched the trolley car jump its tracks and swing directly into the newsstand. It killed my five-year-old son, standing two feet away from me.

"Caridad blamed me for our son's death. The grief was driving her crazy, and her anger at me for having taken the boy with me that Saturday turned into maniacal rage. One night I woke up to find her standing over my bed with a kitchen knife in her hand. It was terrifying Yolanda and me, both. Finally, her family committed her to the Creedmoor Asylum in Queens. I had nowhere to go but back home to Mexico, to Margarita if she would still have me. It was Yolanda who persuaded me to go back. She said that maybe God had punished me for my bigamy, and maybe I should go back and be with the woman I had married in God's house. I couldn't afford the airfare back so I booked passage on the first steamship going to Mexico. It wasn't until my ship docked in Veracruz that I remembered the old Gypsy woman, Margarita's mother, warning me to be true to her daughter. I wasn't true, Father, and even when I returned, I did not tell Margarita the truth of what my life had been like those five years in New York."

"That is a terrible burden to carry all these years, my son. All those lies, all those secrets. It's no wonder that your heart is heavy."

"Margarita accepted me back without a word, acting as though I'd just stepped out of the house to buy cigarettes. I never told her a word about Caridad or the boy, but some nights I cried like a child in her arms, and she soothed me with her hands, suckled me with her breasts and reminded my body that I was a man and she, my *mujer*. But I couldn't forgive myself, you see, not for what had happened to my family nor for what I had done to Margarita. Sleeping with her became such a torture to my conscience that I was unable to perform my husbandly duties after a while. I moved out again and within a few months took up with Cleotilde, the widowed actress with whom Margarita and I used to play canasta in the old days.

"Of course, I still loved Margarita. It was myself I deplored, myself I wanted to hurt and humiliate. Cleotilde was just a companion, and somehow, she stayed friends with Margarita through the whole affair. They shared a passion for plays and poetry, especially the poetry of that Spaniard who was Margarita's *paisano* from Granada, that poet by the name of García Lorca. I think they compared notes behind my back. Sometimes I even suspected Cleotilde and Margarita were making a fool of me, which only contributed to my depression.

"I'm not sure when the change came, when she started dressing in her Gypsy clothes again and casting her spells on me, but one morning, after my weekly overnight visit to Margarita, she told me she was pregnant. Twelve years had passed since we'd married, that's how long it took for my seed to take root in her body.

"When the war with the Nazis ended, we moved north, taking only what we could pack into our luggage, and started over again as a family. Margarita and our two children, as well as Cleotilde and the three I had fathered in her house came, too. I bought a modest house near the bullring in Juárez. For a few years, I even worked as a *banderillero*. I had the paunch and the bald spot of an old bullfighter, though no one remembered me as El Criollo. I guess the reputation of Benito Rivera did not extend to the border. I did not stray after the birth of my legitimate son, Padre, but I never told my Gypsy wife the truth about the little skull I always put on her altar on Day of the Dead, the skull of my first legitimate son, Samuel. Will God forgive me for all these sins, Father?"

"God forgives all, my son. It is your wife's, the Gypsy's forgiveness, that I cannot promise."

Day of the Dead

Who did La Lupe think she was, anyway? Just because she'd once been crowned the prettiest girl in the Second Ward didn't make La Lupe anybody's boss, and certainly not Chole's. Lupe was only ten months older, but pretended it was a whole decade between them, the way she liked to push around Chole and the boys. She even acted like the boss of their own father, once their mother went away for good. La Lupe was only fourteen years old, Chole thirteen, when their Tarahumara Indian mother, María de los Ángeles, went to visit relatives in the Copper Canyon and never came back. Since then, La Lupe acted like she was the one in charge of the family.

Why does Lupe always get to wear the guns? her little brothers would ask their father. *Can't you be the sheriff for once?*

Papá Lobo would just shake his head, shrug his bony shoulders and keep on reading his book or newspaper. He was a quiet man, unlike his rambunctious brother León or his wild sister, Araceli. He had married an Indian woman for a reason, he liked to say, but nobody knew what that reason was. If his eldest daughter took the reins of the family, menaced everyone to do their chores and keep the house running smoothly without their Mamá, Papá Lobo wasn't going to stop her. It was his fault, really, that Lupe believed she was *la mera mera*.

After forty years of letting Lupe play the sheriff, letting her believe she was better than everyone in the family, Chole had had enough. She was going to take matters into her own hands. It was their father's father who was being honored on this year's Day of the

Dead altar. Chole had insisted it was her turn to host the Día de los Muertos celebration at her house, because it wasn't fair que La Lupe always got to do it at her place every year. Chole was going to go all out. She was going to show that bossy sister of hers that she wasn't the only one who knew how to build a Day of the Dead altar.

"*Ay, sí*," La Lupe had scoffed when Chole announced she was taking a trip to Oaxaca—land of the cult of the dead, place of the best altar-making materials on the planet. "Is the Juárez *mercado* too good for you, now? Why you got to traipse all the way down to Oaxaca, Chole, you big show-off, like it's really going to make a difference?"

Even her husband, Vicente, thought she was crazy. But Chole wanted the authentic stuff, not the cheap replicas they sold at the Juárez Mercado: sugar skulls made in China and plastic reproductions of *pan de dulce*. Chole had a vision, inspired by a documentary she had seen on TV about the Oaxacan tradition of *ofrendas* to the dead. She wanted sugar skulls confectioned in a Oaxacan bakery with the names of each of her brothers and their wives and their children, one for Papá Lobo with his droopy mustache, one with a crown of flowers for their absent mother, Sabina, and a special one wearing a bullfighter's cap for their honoree, Don Abuelo Benito, who had once been a very popular and beloved bullfighter of Mexico. She wanted real *zempaxuchitl* garlands that she could drape like curtains from the ceiling to the floor around the altar, and *papel picado* cut into three-dimensional *calavera* patterns before her very eyes by the Zapotec girls selling it on the cobblestone streets. A lace altar cloth from the convent of Santo Domingo. Candles bought in clumps from the candlemaker on the plaza, wrapped in newspaper with their wicks uncut. A fifteen-mystery rosary blessed by the Bishop of Oaxaca. Fresh *copal* incense brought down from the mountains. A gilt-framed image of her namesake, the Virgen de la Soledad. Little clay pots filled with tart *tamarindo* candy for the kids. Chole could see it all. Her *ofrenda* for Abuelo would be the best one the family had ever seen. Even La Lupe would have to admit it.

The idea of going to Oaxaca fell into place by pure coincidence. Her *comadre*, Marina, in Los Ángeles, was sending her three daughters on a pilgrimage to visit their grandmother in a little town on the coast of Oaxaca, and Marina had called to ask Chole to please pick them up at the bus station in El Paso and give them a ride to Juárez for their connecting bus. Chole could do better than that, she told Marina. How about if she went with them on the trip? Three girls traveling alone on a bus in Mexico was asking for trouble. Marina explained the girls had a chaperone already, a retired schoolteacher neighbor of hers that she was entrusting with her daughters' lives.

"Is she a *gringa*?"

"*Ay sí,* Comadre. Why would I send a *gringa* with them? She's Mexican American, like we are. Well, maybe a little *pocha*, but she's good people. Very responsible, Comadre. *Es una* schoolteacher."

"I tell you what, Comadre," Chole said, "I think I'll go along anyway, just in case. Your goddaughter, Sofía Lorena, has just been suspended for ditching school, so I'm going to take her with me. And I'll make my brother Pancho come with us, too, because you know it's best to have a man at your side when you travel on a bus in Mexico, even if all he does is sleep, eat and fart."

The truth is, Chole knew Vicente would never let her go without a male escort. Pancho would go anywhere, as long as she paid his way.

"The small problem is, Comadre, that I'm only going to Oaxaca City to buy the things I need for my altar. I can't stay for the *Día de los Muertos* celebration. It's my turn to build our family's *ofrenda* for Day of the Dead, so I only have a few days. I would love to stay longer and witness the real thing, but what can I do? It's a family tradition. And we've never celebrated it at my house."

"*Pues*, I can't lie, Comadre. It would make me feel less *ansiosa* if you and your brother could accompany the girls and Miss Agnes on the bus. My mother lives in La Subida, about an hour outside Oaxaca City, and they will have to take another bus to get them there. Why don't we say that the girls can visit with their grandmother for a couple of days, and then they have to come back to Oaxaca City to meet you at the bus station for the return home?"

The plan was perfect.

"If bus tickets for three people is what you want to spend your retirement money on," Vicente said after she told him her plans, "that's your business, *vieja*. I can't help you."

"Nobody's asking you for help, *viejo*. Just make sure you take care of the *barbacoa* and build the platforms for the altar for me in the garage. This is going to be the best *ofrenda* the family has ever seen. I want four platforms, not just three. And I'm going to hang a frame from the ceiling at the very top, so put in some hooks in the ceiling with some fishing line."

"When is this rivalry you've got going on con La Lupe gonna stop, Soledad? Is it really so important that you have a better Day of the Dead altar than your sister? I can't believe you're willing to waste good money just to go shopping in Oaxaca when the Juárez market has the same stuff."

"*Mira*, Vicente, you don't understand any of this, and it's none of your business, anyways. Just do your part, and have everything ready when I come back, *me oíste*?"

"If you want people standing in the garage, I'ma have to put a heater in there, *o se van a* freeze to death *toda tu familia*."

"*Cómo que* 'freeze to death'? You're sounding like my *comadre* in California. *Todo pocho*."

"*Mejor pocho que pobre*, like you're gonna be, *vieja*, dirt poor but speaking good Spanish." Vicente chuckled as he ambled off to play with the dogs in the backyard.

"I think that's them, Mom," said Sofía Lorena, excited to be meeting some girls her age from what she called the coolest place on earth, L.A. It wasn't difficult to spot Marina's daughters as they unloaded their luggage from the Los Angeles to El Paso Limousine Service bus. *Puras pochas*, all three of them, mixing English with Spanish *sin vergüenza* and without apology. The puffy-eyed, bedraggled older woman standing with the three teenagers was probably the schoolteacher, but in her stained hoodie, tight jeans and running shoes, she didn't seem proper enough to be a teacher. Chole tried not to stare, but she couldn't help frowning at the girls' clothes. *What was Marina thinking? Didn't she have any control over these girls?*

One looked like she belonged in one of those vampire movies that Sofía Lorena loved to watch, all dressed in black—black raincoat, black pants, black tenis—her black lipstick and black nail polish making her skin look ghostly white. The other was a hippie in a loose skirt and *chanclas*, her long *greñas* looking like she hadn't run a comb through her hair in days. The youngest one, a *marimacha* for sure, with a flat-top haircut like Pancho's, wore military shorts, a Dodgers T-shirt under a plaid flannel shirt and purple combat boots. With her heavy backpack hanging off one shoulder, the teacher had the carefree attitude of a woman who has never been married and never raised a child. *What kind of a Mexican mother would let her daughters go on a bus to Oaxaca with a woman like that?*

I guess that's the influence of California, thought Chole, thankful to have brought up her own family close to home on the border.

The schoolteacher herded Marina's girls toward Chole. "Hi, I'm Agnes." She stuck her hand out, but Chole didn't shake it.

"Hi, Agnes," said Pancho, reaching out to shake the teacher's fingertips.

"I guess you know who they are," the teacher said, trying to make a joke. The truth is, Chole hadn't seen Marina's family since Doña Maggie's funeral years ago.

"Diana," said the vampire girl, waving.

"Gina," said the hippie, waving.

"Little Jay," said the *marimachita*, thrusting out her chin like a boy.

"I'm Sophie," piped up Sofía Lorena.

"How was the trip?" asked Pancho.

"Not bad," said the teacher. "We had good seats at the front of the bus. They slept the whole way."

"I like your bag," said Gina to Sofía Lorena, admiring the tooled leather purse Chole had bought her at the Juárez mercado. "I can't find any like that in L.A."

"You can have this one," said Sofía Lorena. Chole gave her one of her looks. "I mean, you can find one like this one at the Juárez market. This one was a gift from my mom," she added, rolling her eyes.

"So what part of L.A. are y'all from?" asked Pancho, acting all eager to start a conversation.

"El Sereno," said Agnes, as if that meant anything to anybody. "East of East L.A."

No wonder, thought Chole. All the movies she had ever seen about East L.A. didn't paint such a pretty picture of Mexicans in Los Angeles. Bunch of hoodlums, illegals and homeless.

"So, are we cousins or something?" said the youngest girl. "Is that why you guys are going with us to Oaxaca?"

"No blood relation," said Chole. "Your mother is my comadre, she baptized Sofía Lorena."

"She did? How come she's never mentioned you guys before?"

"We're going to meet our grandmother in Oaxaca," offered the middle girl.

"Chole's competing with our older sister," Pancho offered an explanation. "She's going all the way to Oaxaca to buy Day of the Dead stuff."

"Seriously?" said the teacher.

"It's an important tradition in our family," said Chole.

"Yeah, it's huge in L.A. too," said Diana.

"*Bueno*, we better get going. Vicente's waiting for us in the car. He's driving us over to the bus station in Juárez."

"Right now?" asked the teacher. "Our bus doesn't leave until 5 pm." She looked at her glow-in-the-dark watch. "That's still ten hours from now."

"I like to be early," said Chole. "I want to make sure I get tickets for the same bus. I promised Marina I'd watch over these girls."

"Ms. Agnes is watching over us," said the little one, linking her arm through the older woman's and staring up at her with baby-soft eyes.

"We're starving," said the teacher. "These girls ate everything as soon as we passed 29 Palms."

"They sell food at the bus station," said Chole.

Pancho was half-dragging, half-carrying the two heaviest pieces of the girls' luggage, one in each hand. *Who's he trying to impress*? thought Chole.

"We're not gonna fit," he said, out of breath.

"Yes, we are," said Chole. "Remember, we're traveling light."

"Sorry about all this stuff," said Gina. "Ma made us bring gifts for the whole town, it feels like."

They piled into Vicente's old station wagon, their luggage stacked on their laps and squeezed between the spare tire, the toolbox and an old lamp Vicente had probably found on the street. Luckily, at this hour of the morning, the southbound traffic at the bridge wasn't too bad, but poor Vicente was going to get stuck in at least an hour-long line on his return to El Paso.

I don't like her, thought Chole, *that teacher lady. I don't like the way La Juanita hangs all over her, either*. It would be best not to talk to them. Not to let Sofía Lorena spend too much time with those girls, either. She didn't want her daughter to come back sounding like a *pocha marimacha*.

"Why are we doing this, Ma?" Sofía Lorena had been fidgeting in the seat next to her all day, fussing with her music, bored with her videogames. Nothing was keeping her attention. "You're making me miss school and everything."

"*¡Ay, ay!*" said Chole, pinching the girl's leg. "Two weeks into the new school year, and you're already in trouble."

"Ma! I wasn't ditching. I needed to get a notebook for school."

"*Sí, ¡no me digas*!" Chole huffed. "Since when do you go buy notebooks at Cielo Vista mall when we live five minutes away from a 99-cents store?"

"*Cállense el hocico*, you two," grumbled Pancho from the seat behind them. "You guys aren't letting me sleep."

"*Ya cállate tú*," Chole said over her shoulder. She was not about to let anybody push her around on this trip, especially not that lazy brother of hers, no matter how much bigger he was.

Chole kept an eye on Marina's girls. They were still asleep. Only the teacher was awake, writing in her notebook. She'd been writing almost the whole night. Somehow, they had managed to get the first two rows behind the driver's seat again, while Chole had been given three seats near the toilet.

"I'm hungry," moaned Sofía Lorena. "Is it time for lunch yet?"

Chole had made a *tortilla española* for the trip, an omelet pie thick with potatoes, onions and chorizo, browned perfectly on both sides and cut into four big wedges that she had learned to make from Doña Cleotilde, her father's mother. Pancho said that was dumb food to take on a bus. Burritos and *tortas*, that's what people take on bus trips, he said, not some hoity-toity potato pie wrapped up in aluminum foil. Chole paid no attention to him. If he wanted to buy greasy, slimy burritos and *tortas* from the vendors who climbed on the bus at the different stations, she wasn't going to stop him. *Menos burros más olotes*, as her mother used to say when any of the kids didn't want to eat whatever food she'd put on the table. Chole prided herself in providing healthy and delicious food for her family. It was one of the things La Lupe envied most, Chole's cooking skills. That and her intelligence. Lupe might have been the prettiest girl in El Segundo Barrio a hundred years ago, but she sure wasn't the smartest. That talent fell to Chole. Which is why she'd gotten a scholarship to attend Lydia Patterson Institute for high school and New Mexico College of Agriculture and Mechanical Arts in Las Cruces. Chole was the first one on both sides of her family with a college degree. A Bachelor of Arts and Sciences in History. *History?* she remembered La Lupe scoffing.

"*¿Qué vas a hacer* with a diploma in History, Chole? You won't be able to teach. Who's gonna hire a Mexican teacher, with your accent? At least get a degree in Home Economics. Do something useful with your college education."

Chole ignored her. She wanted to set an example to her brothers Oscar, Mario, Sergio and Pancho. Maybe one of them would want to go to college, too. But no, she was the only one, until La Lupe's daughter, Carmen, graduated from the University of Texas at El Paso nine years ago with, guess what, a degree in History. Like godmother, like goddaughter.

Pinches historians, was all La Lupe had to say about that.

"I'm gonna get me a snack," said Pancho, heaving his big belly past the seat.

"Get me some, too, Tío," Sofía Lorena called out.

The bus had pulled in to the station in Villa Ahumada and an older woman with gold-capped teeth and blue eyes had climbed aboard to sell quesadillas.

Pancho took six quesadillas for himself and bought two for Sofía Lorena. Chole looked out the window. It's not that she didn't like a good chunk of Menonite cheese melted into a freshly made corn tortilla, but she didn't want to spoil her appetite for her *tortilla española.* Maybe she should offer some of it to the teacher, since neither Pancho nor Sofía Lorena were going to have any.

A pair of Tarahumara women, each with a baby slung on her back and carrying a pile of hand-woven palm baskets on her head, paraded their goods back and forth between the buses. Chole stared at their paisley skirts, their dark *rebozos* and bare feet. To think her mother was a Tarahumara. Had she lived like this, Chole wondered, selling baskets in bus stations, carrying their baby brother or sister on her back, the baby she was bringing to term in her belly when she left the family? Maybe one of those women out there was her little sister. She'd be almost thirty-five by now. Her name would have been María, of course, as their mother was María de los Ángeles, as Chole and her sister were María de la Soledad and María Guadalupe. She stared more intently at the Indian women's faces. Which one could be her sister? The taller one with the chiseled jawline, or the shorter one with hazel eyes staring out from a copper-colored face? *Hazel eyes,* she thought. *Didn't our mother have light-brown eyes that sometimes looked tinged with green in the right light? Her name would be María Candelaria, just because her eyes looked like candle flames in a dark church.*

"Ma? You okay?" Sofía Lorena was tapping her on the shoulder. "You want a bite of my quesadilla? It's yummy."

"What? Oh, no thanks, *m'ijita.*" Chole shook her head and blinked her eyes quickly.

"Are you crying, Ma?"

"What would I be crying about? Just stared into the sun too long," said Chole.

It was not something she or her siblings talked about, their absent mother, an agreement they'd come to long ago. And nobody's kids knew that their grandmother had been a Tarahumara woman. Papá Lobo had invented a story about how his Indian wife had died in childbirth with their sixth child, and everyone stuck to it. *Stop wallowing in tonterías*, La Lupe would be chiding her right now. *What good does it do to torment ourselves with memories of a woman who left us? She cared more about her Indian relatives than her own six kids. She can go to hell, as far as I'm concerned. I was the Mom of this family, and you, Chole, were the big sister.*

The bus pulled away from Villa Ahumada and Chole settled in for an afternoon nap, bunching up her sweater against the window for a pillow. She wasn't hungry anymore. There was a smell of fart in the bus and she tried not to focus on it.

"*¿Quién chingados se está surrando*?" the bus driver yelled out.

"Ma, did the driver really just ask if someone had taken a shit right now?"

"Don't listen to him," Chole muttered. The man's bad manners were a disgrace.

Chole awakened with a start to cold air on her face and an intolerable stench in the dark bus.

"Oh my god!" Sofía Lorena had her face buried in Chole's belly. "Ma! It stinks! It's so gross!"

There were children crying and people shouting.

"What's going on?" Chole's eyes had still not adjusted to the darkness. She pinched her nostrils tight.

"*Cabrones, cochinos. ¿Quién se está peyendo tan feo allá atrás?*"

"Someone's been farting the whole way," whined Sofía Lorena. "Couldn't you smell it, Ma?"

"Is someone in the toilet?" Pancho called out.

"The toilet doesn't work," someone said.

"*Pues, con razón*. No wonder. Do they expect us to hold it the whole way?"

"*¡Parece que andan podridos, culeros!*" the bus driver was still cursing. "You assholes are rotting back there."

"Open all the windows."

"They are open."

"It smells like something died in here. *Huele a muerto.*"

"*No, hombre. Huele a pedos de muerto*."

All three of the *pochas* cracked up.

Farts of the dead, very funny, thought Chole. It was probably Pancho after pigging out on six quesadillas.

The bus pulled over. "Everyone out!" barked the bus driver. "I want to check the bus. One of you *marranos* must have taken a dump in the bus, and I'm going to find out who it was. Out! *¡Todos! ¡Bájense, cabrones!*"

Slowly, people got to their feet and started to file out of the bus.

"*¡Apúrense, hijos de la chingada*! And you better not wander off, *se me quedan aquí*!"

Chole didn't want to get down without her purse, but it was stashed inside the *mercado* bag in the overhead storage compartment.

"What if someone takes my purse?" said Chole under her breath.

"Don't worry," said Pancho. "We're just going outside. We'll be right back."

"Come on, Ma! I'm gonna puke if I don't get some fresh air."

Outside, the obsidian sky was pocked through with millions of stars.

"Where are we?" she heard *la marimachita* asking. "Is this, like the end of the world?"

The cold blade of the wind sliced into Chole's flesh. Parked on the side of a deserted mountain road, the Estrella Blanca bus looked like a huge petrified rabbit. The only light came from the headlights of the bus and the driver's flashlight going row by row inside the bus.

"*Ay, qué pinche frío*," someone whined.

"Is that man crazy?" the teacher came up and asked Chole. "We're going to catch our death out here."

"Better to die out here in the clean air than inside that latrine!" Chole retorted.

"I can't believe you made me come on this trip, Ma. Jesus! Talk about a third world country."

"Don't be so rude." Chole pinched her daughter. "Look at the stars. Have you ever seen so many stars in your life?"

"They look like diamonds, don't they?" interjected Agnes.

"Do you have any idea where we are?" Sofía Lorena asked the woman.

The woman held up her cell phone. "No signal," she said. "No clue."

Chole shrugged. "Somewhere in the sierra, I guess."

"*Culo del mundo*, it looks like to me," muttered Pancho. "Look it! We're not even on the highway."

"Do you think we're being hijacked, Ms. Agnes?" said *marimacha* girl.

"Anything's possible in a third world country," said Pancho.

"That's a very problematic remark," the teacher said to Pancho. "Especially since you're talking about your own people."

"Snap!" said *marimachita.*

"Whatever," said Pancho. "I'm just saying it's dangerous in Mexico, with all the murders and everything."

"Don't try to scare us, Uncle Frankie!"

"How long is this gonna take? I'm freezing my nipples off," said hippie girl, huddling with her sisters.

Chole shook her head at their language. *Ay, Marina, if you only knew*, she thought.

"I told you guys it was going to get cold," said Agnes, pulling the hoodie over her head. "But nobody listened to me."

"Our baby's going to freeze to death" a woman with a sleepy toddler in her arms called out to the bus driver. "Can we get back on, now?"

The bus driver came out holding the flashlight in one hand and a mercado bag dangling from his outstretched hand. "Who does this bag belong to?" he called out, shining the flashlight in each of their faces. "This is the shit that's been stinking up the bus," he said. "Something rotted in here. Whose is it?"

"Isn't that our bag, Ma?" Sofía Lorena whispered.

Chole gulped, nudging her daughter with an elbow.

"It's the stupid *tortilla española*, I bet you," muttered Pancho. "I thought it smelled like rotten eggs. *Híjole*, Chole, I told you not to bring that shit on the bus! You didn't even eat the shit and it spoiled!"

"*Cállense los dos*," ordered Chole.

"If it doesn't belong to anybody, then I'm going to have to throw it the hell out," the bus driver warned.

"Isn't your purse in there, Ma?"

Chole was too embarrassed to move. How could she admit the bag was hers, that she was the one causing all this *escándalo* with the *pedos de muerto?* She couldn't understand what could have happened to her beautiful potato pie. How could it have spoiled?

The flashlight shone over Chole's face. "Señora, this was over your seat. Is it yours?"

Chole shaded her eyes against the glare, pursed her lips and tilted her chin defiantly, but didn't say anything.

"There's a purse in here, Señora. Are you sure you want me to throw it out?"

They could drag her under the bus, but she would never admit the bag was hers.

"Let me see that," said Pancho, yanking the bag from the bus driver's hand.

Chole couldn't speak. Silently, she was praying for the earth to open and swallow her. She watched her brother walk to the back of the bus, remove her black patent leather purse and throw the mercado bag down the embankment. He came back and handed Chole her purse. Chole took it without a word.

"*Ay, señora, qué chinga nos ha metido*," the bus driver said, shaking his head at the big problem she had caused. "Bueno, party's over. Everybody better take a shit or a piss right now before they get back on the bus!" the bus driver ordered. "I'm going to have to drive *cómo loco* to make up for the lost time. I'm not going to stop for anything or anybody. *¡Ándenles! A cagar o a mear* right here. Anybody does it on the bus, and I'll kick your ass off."

"This man is out of his mind," said Agnes.

"*Doña Pedos de la Muerte*," Pancho muttered behind Chole. "You're welcome!"

Finding our sister Sabina deranged, we raised our prayers to the Holy Virgin of Guadalupe and begged her to restore Sabina's health. She heard our prayers. For this great favor, we published this retablo.

October 1925, Rosa María y María del Refugio

The Sacrament

Bless me, Father, for I have sinned. It has been one month since my last confession. I am writing you this confession because I smell bad, and I don't think you will forgive this dirty smell, Father. I have not been to church or washed myself or cooked for my father or swept the house in a whole month.

Let me tell you something about my sisters, Rosa and Refugio. They think I'm deranged. Can you believe that, Father? They think I've lost my mind just because I tell them the truth. I can't marry that *muchacho* who is the cousin of Rosa's husband. He keeps coming by the house to leave me little love notes and *regalitos* on the windowsill. One of these days my father is going to find out and beat me for being a flirt, even though it's Rosa's fault because she's the one who's encouraging that *flaco* to come around.

I tell my sisters they can wait till they're dead to see me get married. They're horrified. They tell me that marriage is a sacrament, a commandment from God, and that if I don't get married, I'm going to burn in hell. Is that true, Father? Will Doña Herminia and Doña Esmeralda, the *solterona* spinsters who run the *tortillería,* burn in hell when they die?

Does it count if my father has been showing me the ways of a husband since Mamá died, Father? He ordered me not to tell anyone that I am his lover and he my true and only husband. I know there's nothing I can do about Papi, that he will always be my father and I must obey him, no matter what, as that is one of the ten commandments. Will I still burn in hell if I don't get married, but my father is my husband? This business with sacraments and commandments is all very confusing, Father.

I tried to explain it to Rosa and Refugio, and that's when they decided I was deranged. They've been to the church every day this week, to prostrate themselves to the Virgen de Guadalupe and plead for her intercession, that Our Lady might illuminate my heart and heal this mind that has become estranged from everything that is good and holy.

They think I'm lying, you see, Father? They think our father is a saint and that he would never do anything to hurt any of his daughters. Did I say he was hurting me? All I said was, "What do I need a husband for if the man who is our father eats my food and opens my legs like any husband? I can't get married, so stop trying to fix me up with *fulanito* and *manganito*."

You wouldn't believe how crazy they went, Father. Rosa slapped me till my ears rang and my nose bled, screaming curse words at me like a drunk. Refugio just sat there and howled like someone was stabbing her in the gut.

Now they're saying I'm suffering from *enajenación mental*, as if my mind has been taken over by aliens from another planet. They're saying I'm crazy, Father. They took me away from my father's house and put me into this convent, where the lunatics live. As a protest, I don't speak or wash. Rosa and Refugio say they won't take me out of here until the Virgin grants their *milagro.* So until then, all I can do is write you this confession, Father, and maybe you'll get it and maybe you'll go and talk some sense into my sisters whom I will never speak to again as long as I live. And maybe God will forgive me for breaking the sacrament of marriage.

Your humble servant,
Sabina

The Tattoo

It was one of those neon-blue late July days on Venice Beach with no clouds in the sky and sailboats bobbing on the horizon, the smell of pot and patchouli emanating from the locals who had set up shop along the boardwalk. Somewhere in that boardwalk madness of joggers, skateboarders, rollerbladers, dog-walkers, Hare Krishnas, tourists and homeless people, Little Jay De La Torre knew that her sisters Diana and Gina were probably looking for her. She had escaped from them over an hour ago, and she expected them to be totally pissed at her, but she didn't care. She was on a mission to get a good henna tattoo, and had finally, after comparison-shopping between several booths, decided on the Indian man across from the House of Ink. All of them charged the same, but his designs were cooler—mendhi, he called them—and his booth smelled of the sweet incense he sold.

Little Jay climbed into a high director's chair under a red umbrella, and texted her favorite cousin/soul-twin/BFF Remy with one hand, while Mendhi Man worked on the peacock design she'd chosen on her other arm.

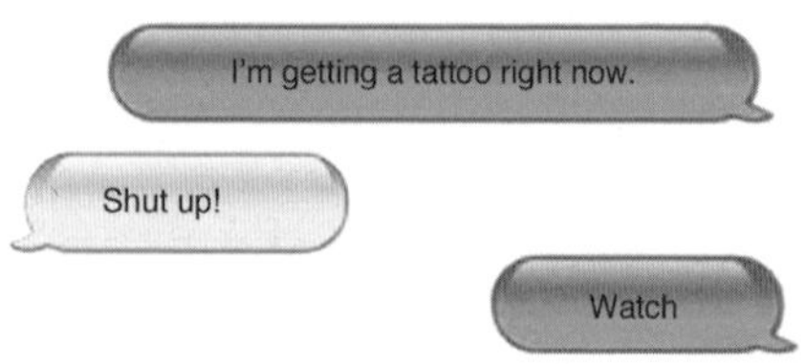

I'm getting a tattoo right now.
Shut up!
Watch

She took a picture of the bearded tattoo artist in his white toga-like outfit, a white beanie on his head, his long, wild hair billowing in the ocean breeze, scrolling a dark paste over the inside of her arm. She texted the picture to her cousin.

That's just a henna tattoo
Don't you think it's kool?
Not as kool as a real tattoo
Do you want my mom to throw me out?
So what? Ur coming to live with us anyway. My dad won't care.
Oh shit. D and G found me. B4N.

D and G were her sisters. One Saturday a month, Diana drove Gina to Venice Beach to sell her hand-embroidered denim handbags and cell phone holders that she made from recycled jeans and peddled under the label L.A. Gypsy on the boardwalk. Gina had made a deal with the lady who sold papier-mâché crucifixes and calavera heads, to watch her booth for a few hours so that the lady could do something with her little girl. In exchange, Gina got to set up her handmade goods and sell them without having to pay rent on a space. Little Jay didn't usually tag along, but since Gina had invited her friend Bethany to join them, and since Diana couldn't stand shopaholic Bethany, her older sister had given in and agreed to take Little Jay, on the condition that she promise not to wander off on her own.

Little Jay promised, of course, but as soon as they hit the boardwalk, and she took one look at the beach, Little Jay knew she wasn't going to be able to keep her word. All those folks playing in the waves, walking barefoot on the sand, throwing Frisbees and body-surfing, little kids running back and forth between the water and their sand castles, everyone else having fun and doing what they pleased, enjoying their Saturday afternoon freedom—it just wasn't right that she had to stay tethered to her older sister. Besides, summer was ending, school would start soon, and it would be too late for a henna tattoo. Little Jay knew she had to escape Diana's eagle-eyed supervision ASAP.

"Tell me you didn't!" Little Jay heard her older sister Diana yelling out. Diana was only nineteen years old but she acted like she was older than Mami sometimes. Her thick black eyeliner made her black crow eyes look like they were popping out of her head. "What do you think you're doing?"

"Get over yourself," said Little Jay. "It's just henna. It washes off." Little Jay's nose twitched over the tang of essential oils emanating from the henna paste.

"I told you she wanted to get a tattoo," said her middle sister, Gina, wheeling her suitcase of handmade goods behind her.

"You're gonna get it, Little Jay," Diana threatened. "Mami's gonna kill you!"

"I think it's cute," said Gina. "I mean, in a Bollywood kind of way."

Little Jay rolled her eyes. "Whatever."

"He's doing your fingers, too? *Pinche loca*," Diana swore at her little sister. "I guess you want to give Mami a heart attack. Or maybe you think you're all high and mighty now cause you're going to that St. Rigor Mortis School."

"It's Saint Wilgefortis, okay? Stop calling it 'rigor mortis.' Is it my fault I got a scholarship to one of the top private schools in Los Angeles?"

Little Jay and Remy had both been accepted to the exclusive Westside private girls' school, St. Wilgefortis Leadership Academy. They had both landed diversity fellowships, but Little Jay's 4.0 GPA and 98% score on the Independent School Entrance Exam had also earned her the Latina Leaders of Mañana Scholarship that would pay for the full tuition in her first year and was renewable each year if she kept her grades up.

"You call that a scholarship? Mami cooking for the school in exchange for part of your $28,000 tuition?"

"That's only if I don't get the scholarship again next year."

"You better get it, *cabrona*. I don't want poor Mami dragging her bones all the way over to the west side once a week to work in the cafeteria just to pay for your ridiculous tuition, little punk. Don't you think she works enough as it is?"

"Gawd, Diana, can you be a little more bitter?" said Little Jay. "Just 'cause *you* didn't pass the GED doesn't mean I'm gonna flunk out of school."

"Hey, you guys," Gina's friend Bethany called out from the shop across the way, her face dwarfed under a huge pair of gawdy sunglasses, "aren't these shades sick?" She was carrying several plastic bags of other stuff she'd already bought, but she was still on the hunt for the perfect pair of knockoff shades.

"Bethany!" Gina called out to her friend. "Girl, get over here. Come see what Little Jay is doing. She's, like, getting a big 'ol tattoo all over her arm and hand."

Bethany paid for her purchase and approached them, the D&G knockoffs riding high on her head like a tiara. She scrutinized the situation with her blue-contact-covered eyeballs. "Oh my god, Little Jay! You're gonna be in so much trouble," she said, pursing her cherry-glossed lips and shaking her head.

"Our mom's gonna flip, huh?" Gina said.

"Duh!" said Diana.

"Actually, my mom's gonna flip even more," said Bethany. "My little sister's party's in two weeks, Little Jay. And all the girls in the court have dresses with short sleeves. Will that thing come off by then?"

"The henna will peel off in ten days or so, no worries, my friend," said the Indian man, now scrolling henna paste around Little Jay's arm, from elbow to wrist, in the shape of a peacock tail.

"It's called a mendhi," said Little Jay, admiring the intricate feathering of the design.

"Wedding mendhi," said the Indian man. "Very powerful."

"Like for getting married or something?" said Little Jay, not realizing she'd chosen a wedding design.

"Peacock mendhi is sacred to the goddess, my friend. Will bring longevity in love, fertility and good luck. You will get married young. Rich man."

Little Jay gulped at the word fertility. What had she gone and done?

"Did he say she's gonna marry a 'young rich man' or that she'll get married young to a rich man?" Gina said to Diana.

"Shut up, Gina," said Little Jay.

"If it doesn't come off by the party, my mom won't let you be in the court, Jay," said Bethany, lowering the sunglasses over her face. "Oh well. Your loss. Come on, Gina. Let's go see if we can get a table at Jodi Moroni's. I saw some hotties at Muscle Beach."

Little Jay's head started to throb. She didn't care about not being allowed to be one of the seven girls in Bethany's sister's stupid *quinceañera* court. She'd never wanted to do that anyway. The thought of having to wear that Pepto Bismol-colored satin dress with a huge bow hanging off one shoulder, and having to dance with one of the seven guys in the court gave her nightmares. But her mom had promised Bethany's mom that Juanita (Little Jay's horrible given name) would be "so honored" to be in her daughter's court. Whatever. It was the dumb tattoo and what it would do her body that worried her now. Why hadn't she asked what the design meant? The guy could have told her what it symbolized and she'd have gone for something else, a fire-blowing dragon image with her name in the flames or even the Dodgers logo. All she needed was some guy asking her to get married at Bethany's sister's *quinceañera* because of this dumb wedding mendhi design she'd chosen. Made her want to puke. She thought they'd all like the tattoo. What a dork.

The drying paste was making the pale skin of her inner arm itch. She turned her face toward the ocean and a gust of wind blew sand into her eyes. She squinted against the sand, against the injustice of having to be only fourteen years old and under the collective thumb of two big sisters and a mother who didn't see her for who she was.

"Earth to Little Jerk!" Diana snapped her fingers.

Little Jay wiped her eyes with her free hand, ignoring Diana. For a second, she felt a slight tremble under the chair. She'd been feeling it off and on all morning, a slow quivering in the ground, like an aftershock to a big earthquake, only there hadn't been a big earthquake in Los Angeles since the day she was born, January 17, 1994. Just her luck to have been born the day of the Northridge quake.

"Did you feel it?" she said to Mendhi Man. "There was a tremor just now."

The man scowled at her and shook his head. "No, I don't think so, my friend. Please to sit still. I am almost finished."

"We're gonna go get some hot dogs at Jodi Moroni's, alright, fool?" Diana was talking to her. "You meet us there as soon as you're done here. Don't you dare go running off again. We gotta get back before Mami gets home."

Little Jay shrugged. "Whatever."

"Don't 'whatever' me, Little Jay. I mean it. If we're not at the hot dog stand meet us back at the car. Okay?" Diana grabbed Little Jay's chin and forced her little sister to look at her.

"Okay, already. Let go of me!" Little Jay yanked her chin from Diana's grasp and wiggled her jaw back and forth.

"Your sister, she's bossy, eh, my friend?" said Mendhi Man when Diana and Gina had gone.

"She's a big biatch," said Little Jay, staring at the back of Diana's long black raincoat, her glossy goth hair flapping back in the wind. From that angle, she looked like something out of a zombie movie. "Always getting in my face. Not even our mom does that. I don't know who told her she was the big shit, but that's what she thinks. Hey, how'd you know she was my sister?"

"Intuition, my friend," smiled Mendhi Man, his teeth long and yellow like piano keys.

"Anyway, it's your fault," Little Jay said, narrowing her eyes at the guy. "You could've told me this was a wedding design. I'm a dyke, okay? I'm not gonna get married unless it's to a girl, got it?"

Little Jay glanced over both shoulders, suddenly terrified that one of the other customers in the booth had overheard her. You did not just come out to this Mendhi Man, Remy would have said. She half expected lightning to strike out of the clear blue sky.

"Wedding mendhi brings your heart's desire, my friend. Girl or boy, mendhi brings equal opportunity good luck." The man stood back to admire his work. "Twenty dollars, please."

Little Jay jumped down off the high director's chair with her tattooed arm in the air and reached into her back pocket with her other hand to pull out the last two tens from the lawn-cutting money she'd saved just for a tattoo.

"Don't get it wet for at least a day," Mendhi Man said, tucking the bills into a wad of money in his fanny pack. "And use some olive oil on the skin every night for two weeks. Olive or coconut. Keeps the skin supple."

Yeah, right, thought Little Jay. Like my mom would ever let me put that expensive oil on my skin.

"Namaste," said Mendhi Man, putting his hands together in front of his chest and bowing slightly.

"Nama-what?" said Little Jay, but just then, she felt it again. The earth very definitely rolled under her feet. The umbrella swayed over her head and the plastic tote box of his supplies slid back and forth across the surface of the table. Little Jay clung on to Mendhi Man for balance.

"Are you feeling dizzy?" he asked.

"That was a big one," she said. "Did you feel that?" Even the waves had gotten stirred up, and for a second, she was sure she saw a shadow in front of the sun.

"Maybe you got up too fast."

"Oh come on, you didn't feel that earthquake?"

"No earthquake, my friend. You just lost your balance, I think."

"Look at the waves," she said, pointing toward the beach, but the water seemed calm again. The sailboats on the horizon sat perfectly serene on the still water.

"Go home now. You have been out in the sun too long, I think."

"Give me a break," said Little Jay, turning to talk to an older lady in a purple Lakers cap and a young girl in a Beatles baby tee who were standing there contemplating a Ganesha tattoo. "Did you all feel the earthquake just now?" she asked them.

"There was an earthquake?" said the young girl, gazing at Little Jay over the top of her heart-shaped white sunglasses. "Cool." The girl dug her ringing cell phone out of her Mexican beach bag. "Dad, guess what," she said into the phone, "there was an earthquake just now."

"I didn't feel anything," the Lakers cap lady said to Little Jay.

"Drink some water, my friend," Mendhi Man called after her. "I think you have a hydration problem. It's a hot day."

Little Jay didn't mention the earthquake to her sisters and Bethany, who were all huddled at a little table next to the Jodi Moroni stand, stuffing the last of their hot dogs into their mouths and leering at the guys lifting weights in the Muscle Beach gym.

"Hey, Little Jay," said Gina, offering her a fried corndog. "I got an extra one for you, but it got cold. You took too long, dude."

Little Jay gobbled down the corndog in three bites and took the last swig from what was left of Gina's Cherry Coke. She was still thirsty, but didn't want to spend her last two dollars on a bottle of water. Bethany and Diana kept harassing her about the tattoo but she ignored them.

"Nice work," said Gina, admiring the finished tattoo. "That would make a cool pattern to screen on one of my bags."

"Don't you have an Open House at your fancy school next week?" said Diana. "Some scholarship girl. All tatted up. Mami's gonna die of embarrassment when she sees that thing."

"Get over it," retorted Little Jay. "I told you, it's not permanent."

As they ambled back to Diana's car parked off Washington Street, two blocks east of Venice Pier, Little Jay felt troubled, like she'd forgotten something important. The dried henna was already starting to peel off her arm, and she suddenly wanted nothing more than to run over to the shoreline and dip her whole arm into the ocean to wash off the stupid wedding design. What a waste of twenty bucks! Bethany was rattling on about her little sister's *quinceañera* dress and the matching dresses of the court, and how her mom had to remortgage the house (whatever that meant) just to pay for the party. They were almost to the car when Little Jay realized what she'd forgotten.

"Oh shit," she said aloud, "I left my backpack."

"Are you serious?" said Gina.

"Goddammit!" said Diana. "What's wrong with you?"

"I've gotta go back where I got the tattoo," said Little Jay.

"It's going to take you twenty minutes to go all the way back there and come back," whined Bethany.

"No way, Little Jay. I am not letting you out of my sight again," said Diana.

Little Jay had already spun around in her Chucks and started running down the boardwalk. Behind her, she could hear Diana yelling at her to fucken hurry up or else they were gonna leave her ass behind and she'd have to take the bus home.

"Don't threaten me with a good time," Little Jay muttered.

She ran all the way back to the House of Ink where Mendhi Man had set up his booth, but the booth was deserted. No sign of him or his tattoo pictures or his umbrella or anything. Just an empty table in the sun, wedged between the tarot card reader's table and the guy making sand sculptures on the asphalt.

"Have you all seen the tattoo guy?" Little Jay asked them, panting.

"He just left," the tarot card reader told her.

"Did he have a Guatemalan backpack with him?" she asked, starting to panic.

The tarot card reader shrugged. "He had a lot of stuff," she said. "He put it all into a shopping cart, like a homeless guy."

"Maybe he did, maybe he didn't," said the sand sculpture guy, finishing the breasts on his mermaid sculpture.

"Really?" Little Jay stomped her foot. "Come on. Which way did he go?"

"That way, I think," said the tarot card reader, pointing north toward Santa Monica.

"No, that way," said the sand sculpture guy, pointing east away from the beach.

"Thanks a lot," said Little Jay.

She went north, figuring that the tarot card reader probably had a better view, considering the other guy had his back to the boardwalk. There were four things in her pack that she could not lose: her new smartphone, which had cost her a summer's worth of hard work peeling wallpaper and sanding walls over at the neighbor's house, for a group home the neighbor was going to open for homeless girls; her journal, which told everything about what she was and who she had a crush on; her insulin pen; and the lucky 50-peso coin she'd found on the bus to Oaxaca last year, which was imprinted with an image of the Aztec warrior goddess, Coyolxauhqui, whose name meant Bells on Her Cheeks.

Remy's Dad, her Uncle Andrew, a History teacher and expert on all things Mexico, had told Little Jay the legend of Coyolxauhqui, who was the eldest child of Coatlicue, the mother of the Mexica gods and goddesses. The legend, as it was recorded in the codices, tells that Coyolxauhqui was angry that her mother was going to give birth to Huitzilopochtli, the god of the sun, who would also be the god of war. The birth of Huitzilopochtli signaled the end of the Fourth Sun of Plenty and Abundance, and the beginning of the Fifth Sun, the sun of mayhem and destruction. Coyolxauhqui conspired with her 400 siblings, the 400 Southerners, to attack their baby brother at the time of his birth and so prevent war and bloodshed from ruling the world.

On the night of his birth, instead of a baby, they found a full-grown god in armor rising out of their mother's ancient womb, wielding a fiery serpent-shaped sword in his hand. With the speed of a hummingbird, the youngest brother killed most of his 400 siblings and sliced off his sister's head, chopping up her body and hurtling the pieces down the blood-stained steps of the temple. From then on, to immortalize the daughter's rebellion against the mother, the sister's uprising against the brother, to remind enemies of the price of insurgence, Coyolxauhqui's severed body and head had solidified into stone. This stone was used as the base for the pyramid of the Templo Mayor where all the sacrificial victims to the god of war would land after their hearts were removed by the high priests of the temple and used to feed the great god Huitzilopochtli on ceremonial days. It was this legend and the 1978 discovery of the Coyolxauhqui stone in the excavation of the Templo Mayor site in Mexico City that this coin commemorated.

"It's obsolete, now, mi'ja," Uncle Andrew had said, "and that makes it a collectible. You could sell it on Ebay one day. You're lucky to have found it."

That's when it became her lucky coin. Now she'd gone and lost it because of this stupid henna tattoo that was going to give her mom a heart attack.

"How could I be so stupid?" she muttered, dashing between tourists and baby carriages and dogs on leashes, scanning ahead of her for a long-haired Indian man in a white beanie and a white toga pushing a shopping cart. *How hard could it be to find him?* she thought. Even in this motley crowd of weirdoes and winos, somebody like that would stand out. For a second, she felt another shudder in the earth and she stopped cold. Someone ran into her from behind.

"Hey, it's you again," said the girl in heart-shaped sunglasses she had seen earlier at Mendhi Man's booth.

"Oh, hey," said Little Jay.

"Look at my tattoo." The girl showed off the Ganesha image hennaed to the inside of her arm. "My Nina got one just like it. Nina, show her your Ganesha."

The lady in the Lakers cap held out her own arm.

"Can you take a picture of us?" asked the girl, pushing her iPhone into Little Jay's hands.

Flustered, Little Jay took the picture. "Like mother like daughter tattoos," she said lamely.

"Cute, huh?" said the girl. "But she's not my mom, she's my godmother."

"Did you happen to see a backpack when you were there? I think I left it by the chair."

They shook their heads.

"Oh no!" said Little Jay, her voice breaking. "I lost my bag. I'll never find it now. Shit."

She was about to let loose some tears like a big crybaby, but the Lakers cap godmother touched her shoulder and told her to stay calm.

"Look, if you concentrate real hard, you can bring it back to you. I do that all the time, and whatever I've lost always comes back. If it's meant to, that is."

"How?" said Little Jay, desperate enough to try anything right now.

"Close your eyes, concentrate real hard on whatever it is that you need to come back to you. Your thoughts can work like a magnet if you try real hard. Go sit over there on that bench, and visualize whatever it is that you want to draw back to you. You'll feel a surge when you're doing it right. That's the universe telling you it worked."

Little Jay did as she was told. She found an empty seat on a bench next to a homeless lady in dreads smoking a joint and sat down to concentrate. She took a deep breath and closed her eyes, focusing on the black and purple stripes of the pack. She had bought it at a vintage clothes place in Pasadena, and it was small enough to use every day but sturdy enough to use as a book bag for school. She saw the torn seam of the zipper on the front pocket and wondered why she hadn't asked Gina to fix that yet. She focused on her phone next, all the texts between her and Remy about THE BIG SECRET, all her friends' phone numbers stored inside it, her music, her games and pictures. But she didn't feel any surge. All she was aware of was the smell of the pot wafting over her head and sneaking into her nostrils. She inhaled again, certain that she was starting to perceive the effects of second-hand marijuana smoke. Next, she visualized her journal. The entries in which she talked about liking girls, missing Remy who was the only one she would ever trust with this information, the crazy dreams she'd been having about kissing Selena Gómez. Little Jay felt a definite surge over that.

"Hey, stop bogarting my smoke," the homeless lady next to her said, smacking her arm.

"Huh?" said Little Jay, opening her eyes in time to see the lady pushing off on her rollerblades, her dreadlocks flying behind her like Medusa snakes.

Little Jay felt weird, almost like she'd been transported somewhere else, to a parallel universe inside a funhouse mirror where things looked stretched out a little and people seemed to be much closer than in the real world. She got to her feet and tried to remember what she was doing, where she was going, and it was as if she could see herself walking without feeling her legs moving or even her body leaving the bench.

Little Jay felt someone staring at her from behind. She turned around and saw a disabled man lying belly down on a skateboard approaching her. He was missing the lower half of his body; he had only his head, trunk and arms and he used the skateboard to push himself around the boardwalk.

"You looking for a bag?" he said.

"What? Yes. How did you know?"

"What color is it?"

"It's Guatemalan."

"What's it got inside?"

"None of your business."

"There you are, my friend," said a familiar voice.

Mendhi Man had reappeared with his shopping cart full of stuff and her Guatemalan backpack hugging his skinny spine.

"Hey, what's going on? That's my bag."

"I was trying to go after you," he said, smiling with his piano-key teeth, "but you were walking too fast for me, so I lost you in the crowd. I asked my friend Colibrí here to try to catch you."

Colibrí saluted her with one gnarly hand.

"Here you go, my friend." Mendhi Man removed the pack from his shoulders and handed it to Little Jay.

Your thoughts can work like a magnet if you try real hard, the godmother had told her.

"That's awesome, dude," was all she managed to say.

It felt like it took her forever to make it back to the car on Washington Street. Diana was having a hissy fit waiting for her.

"You know what, Little Jay," said Diana, pasting her face so close to Little Jay's that the bits of relish and hot dog trapped in her older sister's teeth came flying out of her mouth. "This is the last time you're coming with us anywhere, you hear me? You're such a royal pain in the ass, getting lost, getting tattooed, forgetting things, taking your sweet-ass time, making us wait on you like we ain't got nothing better to do. Just 'cause you're going to that college-prep school don't mean we gotta wait on you. I'm sick of it, Little Jay, okay? You hear me? I'm sick of it. Grow up once and for all, *cabrona*."

"Let's go already," called Bethany, fixing her make-up in the back seat. "You can yell at her in the car. Gina wants to stop at the Staples Center to buy her Morrissey tickets."

Strapped in her seatbelt in the passenger seat, Gina had her eyes closed, her headphones on, singing out the lyrics to a My Chemical Romance tune to block out Diana's high-pitched tirade.

"Get in the car, Little Jay," Diana ordered, pulling on the strap of the backpack. Little Jay resisted, and Diana pulled harder.

"Stop yanking on me, Diana, you're gonna tear my pack."

"I said get your skinny ass in the car."

Diana pulled even harder, on the front pocket this time, and tore the already frayed seam of the zipper. Little Jay watched as all the stuff she had in the pocket fell out. She reached out with both hands to catch her lucky 50-peso coin, only it looked much larger, almost the size of her hand, and she could clearly make out the goddess's body parts carved in relief, the disarticulated arms and legs, bare breasts and torso, feathered helmet on the head. In slow motion, Little Jay watched the coin fall to the sidewalk and roll down into a storm drain. She tried to stop it with her foot, but it was too late.

Immediately the earth shifted, a movement so definite even Diana felt it, her mouth hanging open as she looked around at the undulating cars of the parking lot.

"What the fu . . . "

Her words were swallowed up in the melee of people bolting out of their cars, their screams mixing with the wild barking of dogs running free of their leashes and the roiling of sea water gathering up into a vortex between the shore and the sky. Storm clouds thickened over the beach. Rocks and planks and glass panes catapulted through the air as one tsunami-sized wave hovered over the pier like a gigantic dark green hand tipped with foamy white fingers. Little Jay was yanked, slapped and probed by the cold wind, but she stood her ground, transfixed by the giant hand about to demolish the pier.

Instead of crashing down, the tsunami vortex opened wide and something rose straight out of the sea, like in one of those B movies that Remy loved so much. It looked like a wall of red stone rising from the sea, a huge round stone at least fifty feet in diameter, carved with shapes that made no sense but that seemed to be separate body parts: a leg and foot, an arm and a hand, a torso of breasts and loins, a head wearing a feathered helmet. The parts were scattered across the stone, like a body that had been dismembered, a woman's body cut into pieces, trussed with snakes and wedged with skulls. Little Jay realized then that the stone rising out of the sea had the same markings as the Coyolxauhqui figure embossed on her now-lost-forever 50-peso coin.

"It's the moon goddess," Little Jay heard herself say aloud, mesmerized as the colossal stone rose out of the sea on Venice Beach that July afternoon and came to life. The severed body parts started to move toward each other, the legs to the loins, the arms to the shoulders, the head to the neck, and suddenly she was whole again. The dismembered goddess, the mutilated sister, in one piece, her golden breasts gleaming in the sun, long quetzal feathers standing out from a crown of marigolds. Her skin an ocher yellow, her armor a deep aqua blue, a tattoo of bells on each cheek, Coyolxauhqui stood fifty feet tall, the Venice pier jutting against the skull heads at her kneecaps. She wasn't translucent like the 50-foot woman in the movie, but solid as stone.

Little Jay fell to her knees.

"Can you believe this kid?" a sharp voice brought Little Jay back to earth. Someone was shaking her shoulder and poking her in the face.

"I cannot freaking believe this kid!" Diana was staring down at her, her black-lipstick mouth pursed like a prune. "Wake up, *cabrona*! You're gonna drive me out of my mind!" She was shaking Little Jay's shoulder hard enough to sprain something.

"What happened?" said Little Jay, sitting up. She was still on the same bench in front of the House of Ink next to a Legalize Marijuana booth. She must have passed out.

"Seriously?" said Diana. "You're taking a nap while we're over there waiting for you for almost an hour?"

"Diana, I swear, I thought I'd gone back there. After the Mendhi Man gave me back my pack . . . " She looked down at the bench and saw that she'd been using her pack for a pillow. " . . . I swear I walked back to the car and you were yelling at me and then this weird thing happened. . . . "

"Yeah, it's called an earthquake," Diana interrupted.

"No, that's not what I mean. I know it was an earthquake, I kept feeling tremors all day. It was more like a tsunami."

Diana frowned at her. "There wasn't no tsunami, what are you talking about? It wasn't that big of a quake, 5.5 they said on the radio. In Chino Hills."

Little Jay kept talking. "But then this huge round stone came out of the sea and turned into a giant goddess in blue armor with long feathers in her headdress." She opened the zippered compartment on the pack as she spoke, and there it was, her Coyolxauhqui coin, still in the pocket. It hadn't rolled out, after all. "Oh my god, Diana. It's still here." Little Jay was so relieved, tears came to her eyes.

"What's wrong?" said Diana, the furrows between her brows deeper now as she pressed her sweaty palm against Little Jay's forehead. "I knew it! Your sugar's low. Look at your eyes. They're all glassy and shit. Hold out your hands."

"Diana . . . "

"Hold out your hands, goddammit!"

Little Jay's hands were shaking.

"Damn, Little Jay! What were you thinking? Running back and forth on the boardwalk all day without any food. In an earthquake? What are we gonna do with you?"

"I don't know what happened, Diana. Honest. I passed out, I guess."

Diana opened her blue Razor phone and dialed a number.

"I found her. She says she passed out. . . . Looks like it, it's right here. No, I gotta get her a drink. Her sugar's low. Order something for her at Mao's. Hurry. She needs to eat."

Nothing had changed. Venice Beach was still buzzing with weirdoes and winos, the air still smelled of pot and patchouli, sailboats still dotted the horizon, and her sister Diana still thought she was a hopeless loser whose only mission in life was to mortify their mother to death. For no good reason, except maybe she was emo, Little Jay started to cry. Crying, crying, crying like a lost kid trying to find her way home.

Diana took her by the hand and led her to the nearest store, bought her a bottle of Orangina and made her drink half of it before they returned outside. The sweet fizzy drink and the overhead fans of the store cleared the hot fog in her head. Her hands stopped shaking.

" . . . with your diabetes," Diana was yammering on and on as they treaded people on the boardwalk, "you could die, Little Jay. That was a really stupid thing to do. Why don't you ever think of the consequences? One of these days you're seriously gonna give Mami a heart attack. Is that what you want, huh? You wanna kill Mami?"

Little Jay was staring at her henna tattoo while Diana finished scolding her and saw that the skin around the black crusty lines of dried henna paste was bright red, as if the sun had seared the tattoo into her arm. Only instead of the elaborate tail feathers of the mendhi that she'd paid twenty dollars for, the image had morphed into the full-bodied image of Coyolxauhqui, wearing her quetzal-feathered helmet and loincloth of knotted snakes.

Artemis House

In her fifty-two years, Agnes de la Cruz had never been to a gay club. If it hadn't been for her tarot-card-reading friend, Hazel Eaves, who outed her at the first reading, Agnes would never have gone to the Palms in West Hollywood that night, would never have met Queta and would never have had her heart broken. But pushy white woman that she was, Hazel had practically dragged Agnes out that November night, and Agnes was terrified that she'd be recognized by somebody from the district or, worse, one of her own students. High school students were always finding ways to get fake ID cards so they could get into clubs.

"Oh come on, Agnes. I thought you were such a feminist," Hazel had prodded her.

Agnes had wrapped a thick woolen scarf around her neck, wore a knitted beanie and kept her coat and sunglasses on, thinking she'd be both incognito and insulated from anybody's attention. Boy was she wrong. Everyone turned to look at her when they walked in. Everyone seemed to be talking about her. Everyone who knew Hazel stopped at their table and gawked at her. One queeny guy in a beard and top hat actually laughed in her face.

"Halloween is over, honey."

And then this other guy in a black leather bomber jacket and a loose pair of fatigues came up to the table, his short dark hair slicked back behind the ears. Agnes felt a muscle spasm between her legs, and she was startled by her reaction. Since when did men turn her on? She turned her face and gazed at the dance floor, feeling hot and ridiculous in her disguise, but unwilling to expose herself.

"*¿Quieres bailar?*"

It took Agnes a moment to realize the guy had spoken to her.

"Excuse me? Did you say something?"

"Yeah. Do you want to dance?"

The deep dimples in that smile made Agnes feel faint. The skin on his face looked pockmarked from acne. The boy could pass as one of her own students at University High. He couldn't be more than eighteen years old.

"Sorry, I don't dance. I'm a teacher."

Why had she said that? The dimples deepened, and the boy leaned his head back and started to laugh. Agnes saw gold-capped teeth. The bomber jacket fell open exposing a pair of small breasts and dark nipples under a tight white sleeveless T-shirt, what her students called a "wife-beater."

"Oh, you're a woman," Agnes said stupidly.

The woman held out her hand. "Queta's the name, and getting *chulas* out of the closet is my game."

Queta had done more than get Agnes out of the closet. She'd introduced her to a whole new world of passion and sensuality that explained to Agnes why she'd never been aroused by men. She loved Queta's masculinity, hard on the outside, lean and strong, gruff and blunt, but the softness and tenderness in her lovemaking was something Agnes had never experienced with a guy. She and Queta had stayed together twelve years, until she found out about the other woman in Memphis, where Queta had gone for basic training. A white trailer-trash type named Winona with a little girl named Sunny. Queta carried a picture of the three of them tucked between her license and medical card in her wallet. On the back, written in a woman's scrawl that was not Queta's handwriting, it read: *Winona, Sunny and Daddy Q.* They were all posing in front of a bright blue doublewide trailer next to a Memphis Realty sign that said SOLD.

When Queta came back from her second tour of duty, Agnes was gone. She'd taken her retirement money out in one lump sum, bought a fixer-upper in the hills of El Sereno and decided to open a group home for homeless girls, licensed by the State of California and serving the County of Los Angeles. The three good things that had come of her relationship with Queta were: a) her own coming out; b) the community of women that took her in and cared for her during her loneliest hours and; c) the way that all that great sex had helped anchor Agnes to her own skin.

The buzzing iPhone startled her. She didn't realize she'd drifted off again into memory lane, where infidelity didn't matter. She was late picking up the call. She scrolled to the list of recent calls and recognized the number immediately.

"Hi, Agnes, this is Marcia Rodrigues, calling from the Department of Children and Family Services," said a tired voice. Agnes recognized the tone of a beleaguered social worker at the end of a long day. "I know you're probably tired of hearing from me, but this time it's a little different. I'm wondering if you might have a vacancy for a 14-year-old female who says she knows you? Please call me back if you do."

After she'd retired from LAUSD two years earlier—retirement had been her fiftieth birthday gift to herself—Agnes threw herself into volunteer work. She taught ESL night school classes at All Saints Church, led poetry workshops for the human trafficking victims of the Children of the Night Shelter and offered GED tutoring for the Downtown Women's Center's Literacy Program. She had also been recommended to serve on the Advisory Board of St. Wilgefortis Academy by her friends at the Liberty Hill Foundation, who wanted to make sure their investment in the school was being put to good use in the service of LGBTQ youth. It would be a lifetime appointment, a dubious honor that she quickly declined as she wanted to remove herself from high school politics altogether. All the volunteer work absorbed most of her time and energy during the week and, most importantly, kept her from obsessing about Queta and her other family. But the weekends were murder. Every single thing she liked to do on Saturdays and Sundays reminded her of Queta: brunch or dim sum with friends, a matinee, a visit to LACMA or the Getty museums, a picnic in Griffith Park, a concert at the Hollywood Bowl, a Dodgers game, a Lakers or Sparks game—these were what she and Queta indulged in whenever Queta came home on leave. She needed something else, something that would absorb all her time, 24/7.

When all the madness about the sex offenders populating El Sereno started, the *El Sereno Voice* publishing lengthy articles about it every month, Agnes found her mission. She wanted to do something proactive, get involved, make a difference. She wrote letters to the editor of the *Voice* and the *Los Angeles Times*, started an email campaign to the El Sereno Councilman and County Supervisor Gloria Martínez (none of which helped) and even went door to door in her neighborhood for a couple of weeks to bring attention to the problem. Finally, Agnes realized nobody was going to do anything about the sex offenders themselves; despite Megan's Law, the police didn't give a shit that so many sex offenders were living in halfway homes located near schools and day care centers. But she could do something about all the homeless girls in their community who were putting themselves in harm's way just by living in the streets as fodder for all those sexual delinquents. That's when the big idea occurred to her. Why not convert the Spanish-colonial fixer-upper she had just bought with her retirement money into a group home for homeless girls?

She had not known when she started on this adventure last summer what a rigmarole it would be to open a group home. First, she had to take six weeks of classes through the Department of Children and Family Services or DCFS to become a certified caregiver, even though her "clients," as the social workers she was working with called the foster care wards, were going to be teenagers. She had to get finger-printed, get a background check and take a certified CPR class at the Red Cross. Then her home had to get licensed, but before the licensing could take place, she needed to renovate the five-bedroom, three-story house to use the entire second floor for the living quarters of the residents, upgrade the bathrooms and the kitchen, convert the ground floor into one big great room where she could keep an eye on the girls while she cooked dinner and they did whatever they liked to do for their leisure time. She also needed to convert two-thirds of her three-car garage into a classroom space, for Artemis House would not be just a safe hang-out space; she would be teaching some self-empowerment techniques and feminist principles to all. For all the renovation to take place, she needed to apply for a home equity loan, and the red tape on that had been ridiculous: the credit checks, the home inspections, the repairs, the appraisals. Only after she received the official license from the state of California could she open the doors of Artemis House to her clientele: runaway girls, homeless girls and girls who had been thrown out of their homes for being gay. This last bit she had not advertised as such in her home equity application, but simply targeted girls who had severe conflicts at home that caused them to suffer domestic abuse or get evicted by their families.

Although she had never operated any kind of shelter or group home before, Agnes had worked thirty years in the Los Angeles Unified School District. She had taught high school English for eight years at Garfield, six years at Roosevelt, two at Lincoln High, served five years as Assistant Principal at Woodrow Wilson High School and the remaining nine as Principal of University High School. In those thirty years, she had seen her share of extreme behavior—everything from students with guns to school walkouts, teen suicides, mascot controversies and phone stalking. She felt well prepared to handle at-risk girls, and she had already secured two volunteers to help her run the educational component of Artemis House. Hazel Eaves was on board for computer literacy. Hazel's poker buddy, Ivón Villa, herself a PhD and part-time lecturer at UCLA, would be offering what she called Shadow Beast workshops, based on the theories of Gloria Anzaldúa. Agnes would run the daily Morning Circle meetings and the after-school homework workshops.

As soon as Artemis House opened—she had named it Artemis House after her patron goddess and lineage of Abby-tabby cats—not a day went by when she didn't get a call from DCFS looking for a vacancy. Obviously, there was a big need in Los Ángeles to house homeless youth, and the LGBT Center no longer provided housing for their underage clients. Artemis House was fully occupied, so she didn't bother calling Marcia back. She'd taken in her last girl three nights ago, and her license was limited to eight residents. *Sorry, no more beds*, thought Agnes. She was about to trash the message, but the fatigued sound of the social worker's voice triggered her empathy. She listened to the message again, and this time paid attention to the "who says she knows you" part. Maybe this was one of her former residents who had gotten kicked out again.

She dialed Marcia Rodrigues's number. She knew it by heart.

"Hi, Marcia, Agnes de la Cruz, from Artemis House."

"Thank you so much for calling back. Please tell me you have a vacancy."

"Actually, I don't. All eight of my beds are filled. But I'm wondering if the girl is one of my previous wards?"

"She says she knows you, but I can't tell you who it is, Agnes. You know the regulations."

"Exactly," said Agnes, annoyed with herself for having called back, "and the regulations are I'm licensed for eight beds and they're all full."

"She's really scared," Marcia whispered into the phone. "Her mom got deported today. Can I bring her by? Maybe you can talk to her and calm her down while I find her a placement."

If there was one other issue Agnes was devoted to other than homeless girls, it was undocumented youth with deported parents. Agnes looked at her watch, almost 9 pm on a Friday. She had a 9 pm curfew, and any girl that was late lost her bed. She had two girls still out.

"You do remember this is a house for girls who are homeless, gay or transgendered, right?"

"So you've told me. But it just shows up on our computers as a group home for teenagers."

"And the girl knows what kind of home this is?"

"She seems very familiar with the place."

"Okay, then, come on by. I'll make us some coffee."

Agnes hung up and filled the kettle with water from her reverse osmosis faucet. While the water boiled, she took her French press from the shelf, spooned in eight scoops of good Cuban coffee from the Bustelo can she kept in the freezer and set out two, no three, of her Fiestaware mugs, just in case the girl wanted some coffee as well. Wait, was it allowed for teenagers to drink coffee? Probably not. She picked up and stowed the third cup in the cupboard. The water had not even boiled yet, before the doorbell rang.

"What the hell," said Agnes out loud, nearly tripping on her Russian Blue cat, Luna, as she stepped away from the counter. "Goddammit, Luna, you're going to make me break my neck one day. Can you stop being underfoot? It's too early for your treat!"

Her other cat, Artemis IV, watched them placidly from her perch on top of the fridge. Nothing ruffled Artemis IV, and she was the epitome of calm and collected. Calm and collected—that was the motto Agnes developed for herself as the facilitator of Artemis House. She had not had time to change out of her home clothes, so she would just have to receive them in her black terry-cloth bathrobe, pink-and-black-checkered pajama bottoms and hot pink Crocs.

She looked out the peephole and saw the youngest of her neighbor's daughters, Little Jay. *What is she doing here at this hour?* Agnes asked herself. She unlocked the door and opened it a crack.

"Hi, Ms. Agnes."

"It's late, Little Jay. What do you need?"

"She's with me," said a familiar voice behind the girl.

Spotting Luna, the girl pushed the door open and stepped into the foyer without waiting to be invited. She hefted a heavy duffle bag off one shoulder.

"Marcia?" said Agnes.

"I know," the social worker said. "Kids these days, huh? No manners."

Little Jay dropped her bag on the floor and squatted to pick Luna up in her arms, cuddling her like a baby.

"No, I mean, what's going on? This is my neighbor's girl."

"I know. I was next door when I called you."

"You could have said so," said Agnes. "What happened?"

"All we know for sure is that the mom got deported this morning. Nobody has seen or heard from her two older sisters."

"I don't have any sisters," Little Jay uttered quickly. "It's just me and my mom. Those two girls are just renting a room from us." The girl gave Agnes a knowing nod. "Right, Ms. Agnes?"

Great, thought Agnes, *now I'm supposed to lie*. It would be best to redirect. She certainly didn't want to risk exposing the girl's sisters as undocumented, but she didn't appreciate having to lie to a social worker. She could hear the kettle whistling in the kitchen.

"Put the cat down and come here, Little Jay," Agnes ordered. "Tell me exactly what happened."

The girl did as she was told. There was an urgent earnestness in her dark eyes. "I don't know exactly what happened, Ms. Agnes. I got home late from the bowling alley and found our apartment door had been busted open. Nobody was home. I thought Mami had gone to work. But when I called the lady she cleans for, she said Mami hadn't shown up and hadn't even bothered to call. The lady was pissed. I didn't know Mami had been deported until I read the note. I called my . . . uh, my cats but couldn't find them either. Whoever broke in took our laptop, our boom box and all Mami's jewelry. They also took the money we were saving for our trip."

"What note?" asked Agnes.

"This," said Marci, handing Agnes a corner of today's *L.A. Times*, a few words quickly scrawled on the upper portion. *Mami deported. Uncle's house*.

Obviously, the note had been written by one of Little Jay's sisters, but Agnes wasn't sure if it meant their mom had been deported from their uncle's house or that their mom had been deported and they had gone to their uncle's house. Probably the latter.

The kettle continued to whistle.

"Do you mind turning off the kettle for me?" Agnes asked Marcia.

"No problem," said Marcia. "Do you need me to do anything else?"

"Sure, if you know how to make French press coffee."

"I think I can handle it."

"Great. After you pour the water in, please set the timer for four minutes."

"Got it. I sure could use a good cup of joe right now."

Luna followed Marcia into the kitchen, trotting behind like a puppy.

Agnes lowered her voice. "What uncle, Little Jay? I didn't realize your mom had any relatives here, other than you guys."

Little Jay made a face at her like Agnes was spilling the beans already.

"Don't worry. She can't hear us. Where did they go, your sisters?"

"Diana didn't say. Wanna read her text?" She scrolled through her phone until she came to the message she wanted to show Agnes.

> LJ where U been? Mami got ICEd. Its UR fault, cabrona. I told you old FF was going 2 get back at us. G and me are on the DL. Go to Remys.

"Why is it your fault?" Ms. Agnes asked, handing the phone back to Little Jay.

The girl shrugged. "I didn't report her. Maybe they think it was my fault Mami broke up with FF, or FuckFace, which is what we called Mami's boyfriend, Mr. Courts. But he was trying to hit on me, so I told Mami about it. Is that wrong, Ms. Agnes?"

They heard the timer go off in the kitchen.

"That's ridiculous. That old geezer that I kept seeing walking with your mom to the Food 4 Less, that's Herman Courts?"

"Yeah, he was acting all helpful and everything. Carrying her groceries. Bringing her flowers and taking her to bingo and Saturday night dances at the Senior Citizen Center. He even proposed to her on Valentine's Day, in front of all of us. It was a hot mess!"

"He proposed? How strange that your mom never said anything to me about this."

"Yeah, Mami don't talk about her personal life. But old Fuck-Face was all moved in and everything, until I found him in our bedroom one morning feeling up my legs."

Agnes shook her head. "How awful, Little Jay! Is that all he did?"

"Hell yeah. I sleep in the top bunk, so I kicked him in the face and ran out of there. Mami had gone to work and Diana and Gina were watching the news in the living room. They said Mr. Courts was just trying to wake me up so I wouldn't be late to school. They said don't make a big deal about it, don't tell Mami for sure. But for sure I told her. I know what he was doing. He wasn't waking me up for no school."

"I hope it's okay that I served us," said Marcia Rodrigues, coming out of the kitchen with two mugs of black coffee. "I didn't know how you took it," she added, handing Agnes her cup.

She liked it with two cubes of brown sugar, but she wasn't going to be picky right now. "This is fine," said Agnes, taking a small sip of the bitter black coffee. Somewhere in the back of her mind, it occurred to her that for the first time since Queta had lived with her, there was another woman making coffee in her kitchen.

"So this uncle of yours, you were saying . . . " Agnes prompted Little Jay to return to their previous conversation.

"He's my dad's sister's brother-in-law," said Little Jay. "Lives in Lennox. He's my cousin Remy's dad."

"So does this note mean your mom was taken from your uncle's house, or is that where . . . "

"I don't know, Ms. Agnes," Little Jay interrupted. "Maybe I'm supposed to go to Uncle Andrés' house. I guess that's what it means."

"We tried calling the uncle's number already," said Marcia, "but we don't get an answer. Lennox is a long way to go if nobody's home."

"Remy would probably be home," said Little Jay.

"But you said she's your age," said Marcia. "We can only leave you in the care of an adult."

"Remy's brother, León, is an adult. I think," said Little Jay. "He lives there, too."

"Is he over 21?"

"I don't know. I could text Remy and ask her," said Little Jay, texting as she talked.

"This coffee's so good," said Marcia.

"Bustelo," said Agnes. "I used to buy Peet's when I lived in Santa Monica, but there's not even a Starbucks in El Sereno, much less a Peet's."

"Bummer," Little Jay muttered at her smartphone. "Remy says León's only 19."

"Where's your uncle?" asked Marcia.

"M.I.A., says Remy. Sometimes he goes off to Vegas, he's a gambler."

"I thought you said he was a history teacher," said Marcia.

"I guess he gambles in his spare time," said Little Jay.

"It happens. In fact, teachers can be big gamblers," added Agnes. "I'm a Texas Hold Em fiend myself. I even belong to a poker club."

"I don't really need to know that," said Marcia. "Anyway, it doesn't look like I'm taking you to Lennox, young lady."

"Ewe, don't call me that," said Little Jay. "I'm no lady."

"Excuse me, sir," said Marcia.

Last summer, when she'd employed them to help clean up and repaint Artemis House, Agnes had had a hunch that both Little Jay and Remy might be gay. It wasn't only their haircuts—LJ with her buzz cut, Remy with her Justin Bieber bob—but the way they walked, the way they acted like such tomboys together, the dorky crushed-out way they acted around her, competing for her attention and approval. In her thirty years as a teacher, Agnes had had her share of tweenie crushes, boy and girl.

They were still standing in the foyer, the front door open, when one of the girls Agnes was expecting by 9 pm showed up on the porch at 9:02, her pink-streaked blonde hair in disarray and carrying a Hello Kitty backpack.

"There she is," said Agnes. "Glad you could make it, Crystal."

"May I come in?" said the girl. "Sorry I'm a tiny bit late, Ms. Agnes, but the bus . . . "

Agnes raised her hand. She had no desire to listen to a long-winded explanation. "Is Olga with you?"

"We went to Barnes and Noble together, but I didn't see her after that. I told her to meet me at the front of the bookstore at 8 o'clock sharp, but she wasn't there and missed the bus."

At Artemis House, there were two girls per room, and roommates who had earned the right number of credits by doing their weekly chores and getting good grades on their homework could go out one Saturday a month to one of the approved educational places—a bookstore, a museum, a college or university campus—but they had to return together before curfew. If someone failed to return, she forfeited her bed. Agnes motioned for Crystal to come in and go up to her room.

The girl rushed in, gave Agnes a tiny peck on the cheek and took the stairs two at a time.

"Well, I guess you're in luck, Little Jay," said Agnes, "one of my beds just opened up."

Calaveras in the Closet

My little brother David and me are littermates, as my dad likes to say. We were adopted when I was five and David was three, and since then, we've been Delilah and David Cunningham. I know it sounds kinda like an Anglo name, but we're one hundred percent Mexican from el Segundo Barrio, as my aunt Ximena is always telling us. And she's a Cunningham, too. And the one who saved us from what she called "foster care roulette."

David and I were living in the projects in south El Paso with Doña Tacha, who moved around on crutches but took good care of us just the same. She used to be the neighbor of the people who were supposed to be our mom and dad, but when our mom disappeared and our dad was arrested right there in our kitchen one morning while he was fixing our breakfast, Doña Tacha took us in.

The neighbors said someone in the building must have said something to somebody, cuz suddenly these two police ladies and a nurse showed up at the door along with Aunt Ximena (who wasn't our aunt yet, just some nosy social worker asking too many questions). Her and Doña Tacha talked for hours while the police ladies asked us stuff about our mom and dad.

David and me were scared at first cuz we thought Doña Tacha was going to get taken away, too, but they didn't. They just wrote things down, took some pictures and the nurse drew some blood from David and me. A few weeks later, this man with a ponytail and the nosy social worker were coming over to visit us every weekend. And then suddenly, Doña Tacha was packing our stuff into paper bags, and the ponytail man came to pick us up and brought us here, to Grandma Fátima and Grandpa Michael's house. Turns out ponytail man was gonna be our dad.

David cried at first cuz he missed Doña Tacha, but I didn't cuz I'm older and happy to be living practically next door to a public swimming pool in this big house that sits right on the edge of Memorial Park. That was, like, six years ago, and since then, we've been part of this HUGE crazy family.

I didn't know how big the Cunningham family was, or how many branches it had, like the Riveras, the Moraleses, the Espinosas and the Villas, until the funeral of Double Great Grandma Maggie, Grandpa Michael's mom, a Gypsy from Spain and the oldest lady on the planet, according to my cousin Gaby. By then, I'd already studied the family tree, more like a maze than a tree, and knew just about everybody and how x connected to y connected to z. But no one had ever told me about the XYZ Club. And I had no idea there were so many big secrets.

The day of Grandma Maggie's funeral, they arrived, all nine of them packed in Uncle Patrick's VW van. Not all of them were from out of town, but seeing all those ladies together like that, filing into the house according to some weird logic of age or height, made even the familiar ones seem like strangers. They could have been Menonites or martians, for all I knew.

According to my favorite cousin Irene (who's the assistant editor of the family newsletter that Aunt Ximena sends out every year and knows all the *chisme*), the four oldest were from the original XYZ Club: Aunt Ximena (my dad's older sister, the same social worker who came to talk to Doña Tacha); Great Aunt Lulu's twin daughters, Aunts Yazmín and Yesenia (who lived on the east side and showed up with a pair of identical Chihuahuas named Chuy and Chela); and another of my dad's sisters that we hardly ever saw, Aunt Yreina from Las Cruces. Two were from the second wave, Cousin Ysela (who was being raised by Irene's dad, Uncle Joe) and Irene's older sister, Cousin Yvonne from Los Angeles, who'd changed her name to Ivón for some reason nobody liked to discuss. The only one missing from the O.G. club, Irene said, was Gaby's older sister, Uncle Joe's oldest daughter, X. Mary Espinosa who had been living on a train in the Copper Canyon for the last twenty years, tracking some old witch she said was her mother's mother.

There were three others with them that were not members of the XYZ club, but were still part of this fairy godmother madness that suddenly dissolved the sadness in the room. Another of my dad's sisters, Aunt Zulema, also from Los Angeles, the black sheep who'd been banished long before me and my brother came into the family, and her illegitimate half-black daughter (she was the reason Aunt Zulema had been banished, Irene added). Clinging to Ysela's arm like she was blind or scared or something was an older woman about the age of Ivón and Irene's mom that none of us had ever seen, at least not to my dad's knowledge.

The minute those nine fairy godmothers walked into Grandma and Grandpa's house, I knew things were going to be different. First came the big shock. I mean, the first big shock. Aunt Zulema was welcomed back to the family fold in a big old gush of tears. Grandma Fátima would not be stopped. Over and over she kissed Aunt Zulema on both cheeks, hugged her tightly, kissed her again, hugged her again, tears running black with mascara down her face.

Meanwhile everyone hugged and kissed everyone else, and some folks started crying, talking about Grandma Maggie. Someone started to sneeze because of the dogs, and Uncle William took the dogs into the garage. David said all that kissing and hugging was stupid, so he and Uncle William's boys, the little Mormons Billy, Benny and Diego, just hung back and made fun of people till my dad told them to quit being a pain in the wazoo. From the kitchen, Great Aunt Lulu cried out, "I can't come out! I'm right in the middle of the enchiladas!" And the twin aunts, Yazmín and Yesenia, bolted in there to say hi to their mamá.

Grandpa Michael was still waiting his turn to hug Aunt Zulema, but Grandma Fátima wasn't finished working her over with the kissing and the hugging.

"I lost my mother but I got my daughter back," Grandma Fátima was saying. "It's been too long." Smooch. "Gracias a Dios." Smooch. "Thank you, Virgencita." Squeeze.

Aunt Zulema just stood there letting herself be fussed over, but you could tell she felt weird, the way her eyes kept shifting from side to side like flies buzzing over a bowl of menudo. She cast a pleading glance to the light-skinned black girl that had come with her. The girl shrugged like she had no clue what to do. Then she looked at me, and we connected. She was about my age, maybe a little older, maybe a lot older, hard to tell because of her baggies and backward Dodgers cap. She could've passed for Black except she looked so much like Double Great Grandma Maggie, even David was surprised.

"Mami," Aunt Zulema said at last, "I want to introduce you to your other granddaughter, my daughter Zoey." Her Spanish had gotten rusty out in California, and right away Grandma Fátima blinked in that irritated way of hers. She quit her theatrics as if a director had just yelled, "Cut!"

Aunt Zulema nudged the girl forward. "I named her Zoey Vargas Cunningham, after both of her great-grandmothers."

"Where's her father?" asked Grandma Fátima, point-blank.

Aunt Zulema looked down at her yellow and white checked Van's.

"I see," said Grandma Fátima, eyeing the girl up and down and raising her eyebrow just a twitch. She stuck out her hand like she expected the girl to kiss it or shake it. But the girl dropped the bags she was still carrying and threw her arms around Grandma's shoulders.

"Grandma!" she beamed. "I'm so happy to meet you at last."

Grandma Fátima just stood there looking embarrassed, her arms in a suspended embrace.

Then Zoey stepped away from her and reached out to Grandpa Michael. "Grandpa," she said, "my guardian angel."

He took her in his arms and held her there for like a whole minute while Grandma Fátima wiped the black streaks from her face with his hankie.

"You knew about her?" Grandma Fátima asked him.

"Daddy has been sending us money every month," said Aunt Zulema. "I don't know what we would've done without him."

Luckily, Great Aunt Lulu called out: "Who's hungry?" and that brought everyone back to the situation at hand.

Right away, as if they lived there, all the fairy godmothers got to work. I saw arms reaching into drawers and cabinets, and suddenly, magically, the table was set. Someone ladled the beans into plastic bowls. Someone warmed the tortillas. Someone stood at the fridge filling glasses with ice for my dad's famous mojito tea, which was just mint leaves and sweet lemonade. Someone else dragged chairs in from the other room. Great Aunt Lulu placed a steaming enchilada casserole next to the bucket of KFC and the two platters of corn on the cob. All the while stories were swirling like dust devils.

Nobody spoke to her but everyone had their eye on the older woman who had come in with cousin Ysela and who now stood in the living room looking over the wall of photographs that Double Great Grandma Maggie had collected over her hundred years. She wore a black scarf over her silver hair, a black sweater over a black dress embroidered with tiny white roses and black cowboy boots that looked like they'd seen better days. Big turquoise jewelry hung from her ears, wrists and fingers.

"Who's that lady?" whispered Aunt Yesenia as she cut the casserole into tiny portions.

"Oh my God," said Cousin Ysela, wiping her hands dry on a dish towel, "in all the commotion I forgot to introduce you all to my big surprise."

She went to the living room and semi-dragged the old woman into the kitchen. Something about her looked familiar, but I hadn't seen the resemblance yet.

"Doesn't anybody recognize her?" said Ysela, putting an arm around the woman's shoulders. "This is Luz O'Shaugnessy, people. She's my mom, the famous Tía Luz!"

I'd never heard of no Tía Luz, so how famous could she be?

The older folks' jaws dropped, and I mean it literally.

"What are you talking about, Yselita?" asked my dad.

"She was bartending at Caesar's in Vegas. Lucky thing I was covering the Cher show and stopped at the bar. She saw my name on my credit card and asked if I happened to be related to Beatriz Villa. What are the odds, right? *She's my grandmother, I said. I'm your mother, she said.* Really? How come no one ever told me my mom was still alive?"

This was the second big shock.

Great Aunt Lulu dropped the stack of hot tortillas she was carrying to the table and fainted on my dad.

"What on earth!" said my dad, all startled.

"Mami, oh my god," said Aunt Yazmín, fanning Great Aunt Lulu with a tortilla.

"Is something wrong?" asked Cousin Ysela.

"What could be wrong?" said Grandma Fátima, placing a wet dishrag over Great Aunt Lulu's forehead.

"I told you I didn't want to come," the Tía Luz lady said to cousin Ysela. "I didn't want to kick up a fuss. Not at a time like this."

Uncle Patrick jumped up and offered the woman his chair. He had already started to serve himself some fried chicken, so he picked up his plate and stood behind the chair, holding his plate like some big doofus.

"It's okay, I can stand up," said the lady, sitting down. "Hello, everybody, I'm you-all's Tía Luz."

"I remember you!" said Aunt Yesenia, getting up to give the woman a hug. "Don't you remember her, Ivón?"

"How could I forget Tía Luz?" said Aunt Ivón. Was it my imagination or were Cousin Ivón's ears bright red?

Right away, folks started lining up to kiss her on the cheek.

"Someone better call Aunt Lydia," said Aunt Ximena.

"I'll do it," said my dad, picking the receiver up in the kitchen.

"*No seas menso*," Grandma Fátima chided him. "Go call her from your cell phone outside. It's too loud in here."

"Oh, yeah, sorry, I wasn't thinking," said our dad. He was the first son of Grandma Fátima and Grandpa Michael's eight children, and, like Aunt Ximena, he lived with his parents, which is why we lived there, too.

Great Aunt Lulu came to, her hair all pulled out of its bun, and Grandpa helped her to a chair next to Tía Luz. The ladies looked at each other a long time and then for no reason, threw their arms around each other and hugged and cried.

"Oh brother, are we ever gonna eat?" said David.

"Do you know how long it's been since we've seen each other, young man?" Great Aunt Lulu chided David. "I think Lyndon Johnson was still president."

Tía Luz laughed and said, "No, it was after Vietnam, so it had to have been Nixon."

"That's right, you were such an anti-war activist. Believe it or not, kids, your tía Luz actually marched in a big rally in Los Angeles against the war."

"No, I didn't. I had a fight with Rubén that morning, remember, and was hitchhiking my way back home while everyone else was getting beaten up and arrested. It could have been me standing next to him at the Silver Dollar."

"Wow," said Cousin Ivón, "you were there? You knew Rubén Salazar?"

"We grew up on the same street. He went to El Paso High, you know?"

"I know, yes, I teach about him and the Chicano Moratorium against the Vietnam War."

"Can we eat now?" said David. "I'm starving."

"Me, too," chimed in Uncle William's boys.

"Okay, let's eat, everybody," said Grandma. "These kids need to eat."

"Kids in the living room," said Aunt Ximena.

"Irene and Zoey," said Aunt Yazmín, "you guys join the kids, okay?"

I could tell Aunt Zulema wanted Zoey to eat with the grownups in the kitchen, but Aunt Ximena gave her a look that changed her mind.

"Don't get the rug dirty," said Grandma Fátima.

"Can we watch TV?" asked David.

"No TV, David," said my dad. "This is a wake, not a party."

"Coulda fooled me," said David, helping himself to a triple portion of enchiladas.

We all loaded up our plates and headed for the living room. I hung back a little so I could hear what the scoop was with Tía Luz, but my dad was on to me and gave me a nudge.

"No fair," I could hear David whining already. "How come you guys get to sit on the sofa? Just cuz you're girls?"

"No," said Irene, sitting down next to Zoey. "Because we're the oldest."

"But me and Delilah live here," said David.

"Exactly, so we're your guests," said Irene. "If you're gonna cry about it, maybe I should smack you?"

"I'm not a stupid crybaby," said David.

I didn't know where to sit, but Zoey patted the sofa. I sat down beside her.

"What's your name?" she asked me.

"Delilah," I said.

"We're adopted," said David.

"How does it feel to be adopted?" Zoey asked me.

"I don't know," I said. "How does it feel to be banished?"

"I wasn't banished, my mom was."

"In this family, whatever your mom or dad is, is what you are. Like, David and me are Grandma Fátima's favorites cuz my dad's her favorite."

"Nuh-uh," said one of Uncle William's boys.

"What do *you* know about it?" I challenged him.

"Our mom says Aunt Ximena's Grandma's favorite."

"I mean of the kids," I clarified because nobody could deny that Aunt Ximena was #1 for Grandma Fátima. Some folks called Aunt Ximena an old maid, even though her husband had gotten killed in Desert Storm, and she was a widow and all.

"Ever heard of this Tía Luz character?" I changed the subject.

"Nah, I just met her at the airport right now," said Zoey, munching out big-time on a fried drumstick. "It's weird to be around this much family that I don't even know. How do you keep track of everyone's name?"

"This is only half of it," Irene said.

"Hey, Susie, don't you want your corn?" David said.

"Zoey not Susie," she corrected him, "and yes, I do want my corn."

"Stop being so greedy, David," Irene scolded him.

"Zoo-y! Zoo-y!" David mimicked. "Get your tickets to the zoo-y!"

"Does the sound of his voice totally annoy you?"

"He's a pain in the butt," I said.

"And you're a cross-eyed bookworm!" David said.

"You like to read?" Zoey asked me. "What do you like?"

I shrugged. "Mysteries. Nancy Drew and stuff. I like to write, mostly. You know, like, stories." Dumb answer.

In the kitchen, Great Uncle Benjamin was giving Tía Luz a hard time. "All due respect to you, Luz, but somebody should've warned us."

"Ay, sí," said Great Aunt Lulu, "that was almost thirty years ago. I'm sure Lydia's gotten over it by now."

"Gotten over what?" said Ysela. "I'm the one who should be mad at everybody for letting me believe my mom was really dead. Lucky thing I was assigned to cover the Cher show at Caesar's that night, or I would never have known. I've gone my whole life thinking I was an orphan."

"It's my fault," Tía Luz said. "I shouldn't have come. This is not the kind of thing anybody can forget."

"Nonsense, nonsense," said Grandpa Michael. "You're part of the family. It's about time you came back."

"We have to let gone-bys be gone-bys," said Great Aunt Lulu.

I giggled. Aunt Lulu was always changing American sayings like bygones to gone-bys.

"What are y'all talking about?" Ysela asked.

"Ancient history," said Aunt Ximena.

"It's Esperanza I'm worried about," said Grandma Fátima.

"Yikes!" said Great Uncle Benjamin. "How are we gonna explain it to Esperanza?"

"Didn't you call them, William?"

"I did, Ma. They weren't home. They're on their way. You know Aunt Betty doesn't let Uncle Joe talk on the phone when he drives."

Zoey caught my eye, but all I could do was shrug. This was all jabberwocky to me.

Suddenly, Uncle Patrick cleared his throat real loud and said, "I think they're here." Almost sounded like a rooster crowing.

"*Ave María Purísima*," Great Aunt Lulu cried out. "Can someone please do something?"

Just then the doorbell rang in that crazy way that Uncle Joe always rings it, ta-ta-ta-TA-ta-tA-tA, and for an instant, the folks in the kitchen went totally silent, like they were holding their collective breath or waiting for somebody's shoe to drop.

"Luz," said Grandpa Michael, "would you come with me for a minute?"

I don't know where he took her, but when Aunt Lydia and her brother, Uncle Joe, walked in with the old geezers—their parents, Great Aunt Betty and Don Santiago, and Great Aunt Esperanza, the oldest living relative of the whole clan now that Double Great Grandma Maggie was gone—neither Grandpa Michael nor Tía Luz was anywhere in sight. Esperanza was Great Aunt Betty's and Great Aunt Lulu's older sister, and she was known affectionately as Flaca Calaca or Tía Flaca because she was so tall and skinny and always wore black like she was waiting for Halloween every day of the year. My cousin Gaby, Uncle Joe's youngest daughter, staggered in with a plastic market bag full of illegal fruit from the Juárez Mercado: oranges, avocados, papayas and, layered on top, plastic bags full of freshly peeled prickly pears the color of cranberries, my favorite.

"The Espinosas and Villas are here!" David called out, like we hadn't figured that out already.

"Come in, come in," said Grandma Fátima.

"Hey! Look at everybody!" said Uncle Joe, initiating the greeting ritual for a third time as everyone piled out of the kitchen and went through the huggy/kissy thing again. Though this time, it was Aunt Lydia doing the crying and the squeezing and her daughter, Cousin Ivón, squirming around in her arms. I rolled my eyes at Zoey, but I could tell she was fascinated.

"Wow, your family really loves each other," said Zoey.

"Whatever," I said.

"What's wrong with these children?" barked Old Man Santiago, referring to us kids. "Don't they know how to say hello? Acting like a bunch of *gringos cabrones*!"

"Give 'em a minute, Apá," said Aunt Lydia, gesturing at us to give the mean old geezer a kiss on the cheek.

Gaby loved her grandpa to death, but I just found him obnoxious. The whiskers on his face felt like thorns under my lips.

"We brought a snack," said Uncle Joe, hauling in a huge aluminum pan and paper bags that said Moe's Barbecue. "Move over, everyone, this stuff's hot."

"Don't drip on the rug!" cried Grandma Fátima.

"Where do you want this fruit, Tía?" Gaby asked Grandma Fátima, lugging the bag across the floor.

"Girls," cried Grandma Fátima, "Yreina, Ximena, one of you, come out here and help. Take that bag of fruit in the kitchen and wash it for me, okay?"

"I'll go in and help you in a minute," said Tía Flaca.

"You don't have to do that, Esperanza," said Grandma Fátima, a little too loud. "The girls can handle it."

"Who are all these people?" Old Man Santiago's voice always sounded like static on a microphone. "I don't know any of these people."

"*Pura familia*, who else?" said Great Aunt Betty.

"Bunch of good-for-nothings, they look alike to me," the old man grumbled, hobbling over to the sofa where Irene and Zoey had left their plates.

"*Espérate*, Santiago," warned Great Aunt Betty. "You're gonna sit on someone's food."

"*¿Que qué*?" said the old man, about to lower his skinny *nalgas* on a plate of enchilada casserole.

"Take that food offa there!" yelled Grandma Fátima, and Zoey rescued the plates just in time.

"Did you bring the dominoes?" the old man shouted, oblivious to it all.

"I've got it, Santiago, *bájale a tu micrófono*. Nobody's deaf here except you," said Great Aunt Betty.

"What's burning?" said Tía Flaca, twitching her long, skinny nose in the air.

"Smells like someone left the tortillas on the stove," said Aunt Ximena.

Out of the corner of my eye, I could see David grinning from ear to ear as he heaped slices of barbecue on his plate. He snuck a sip from our dad's beer glass and then burped as loud as he could.

"David!" Grandma Fátima scolded him. "*¡Grosero!*"

Tía Flaca was already rolling up her sleeves, grumbling about the new generation of women who couldn't even warm a tortilla without burning down the house.

"Michael!" Grandma Fátima called out in this stressed-out trembly voice, "Esperanza's here. She's in the kitchen. Make sure you keep the garage door closed, we don't want her to catch a draft."

"What's my compadre doing in the garage?" Uncle Joe said, heading in that direction. "Hey Mike, come get some barbecue before these kids gobble everything up."

"Is it my imagination, or is some shit gonna hit the fan right now?" Zoey said.

"Maybe Grandma doesn't want Tía Flaca to see Tía Luz," I said.

"Shut up, you guys," Irene said.

And then Great Aunt Lulu made her move, looking pale as *menudo* tripe.

"Uh-oh, here it comes, I bet," Irene whispered in my ear.

We all watched, and again I had the feeling that everyone was holding their breath for a count of five. Great Aunt Lulu approached Aunt Lydia (being Great Aunt Betty's little sister, Lulu was really Lydia's aunt, but they were only five years apart and had always gotten along like sisters) and all but collapsed in her arms.

"*¿Qué te pasa*? What's the matter with you?" snapped Aunt Lydia.

"You're not going to believe this, Mana . . . " Great Aunt Lulu started to say, but Grandma Fátima told them to go into one of the bedrooms to talk.

"Everybody else, back to the table!" said Grandma. "Food's getting cold."

Suddenly, Uncle Joe yelled out from the garage. "God al-fucken-mighty!"

"Sshh!" several people said.

"I don't believe it!" Uncle Joe's voice boomed out. "What are *you* doing here?"

"Who is she, Dad?" I could hear Gaby asking.

It was like this wild stampede to the garage. By the time I managed to squeeze through all the adults crowded into the doorway, Great Aunt Flaca was keeling over, just like that. No warning or nothing. Just the sound of her long bones thudding to the concrete floor.

Several of the aunts screamed. Grandma Fátima yelled out, "Get the neighbor, get the neighbor, she's a paramedic, hurry up!"

Uncle Joe pulled out his cell phone.

"How many people are gonna faint today?" I heard David ask, and my dad whacked him on the head.

Aunt Ximena knelt over Tía Flaca and touched her neck. I could tell right away that it was too late. Flaca Calaca's eyes were wide open like she'd just seen a ghost, and her skin had gone completely gray.

It wasn't until the funeral that we found out the Really Big Secret. I mean, the second funeral, cuz in the end, we had two services to attend. On Saturday morning, a Mass at Our Lady of Guadalupe Church dedicated to Double Great Grandma Maggie, and then, on Father's Day, the funeral rosary for Great Aunt Flaca at the Mount Carmel mortuary way out on the east side. The urn of Double Great Grandma Maggie's ashes was placed on a pedestal next to the coffin, and David whispered that Great Aunt Flaca looked like the witch in the Wizard of Oz, which got him a pinch on the leg from my dad.

That's when I found out about the XYZ club—the aunts and cousins whose names began with an X, Y or Z. They sat together in the back pew and were the only ones praying along with Father Francis, like a chorus of fairies saying the first- and then the second-half of the Hail Marys. Us kids just sat there watching Tía Luz, Aunt Lydia and Great Aunt Lulu wailing over the coffin.

After the rosary, after the wailing aunts had each been given a sedative from Grandma Fátima's personal stash, the eulogies began. Great Uncle Benjamin spoke about his mom, Double Great Grandma Maggie, choking after every few words. "She was a Gypsy at heart." Choke. "But a Catholic in spirit." Choke. "Now she's up there . . . " Choke. " . . . in that big bullring in the sky . . . " Choke. " . . . with Our Holy Father holding out his cape." Cheesy. Choke. " . . . to bring her back together with her husband."

I had never met Double Great Grandpa Benito Rivera, but my dad told us he was, like, the most famous bullfighter of Mexico until he went to Spain and married Grandma Maggie. After that, folks said he went downhill so fast because his wife had put a gypsy curse on him or something. I bet you anything there's some good secrets I could find out about that.

The whole time Great Uncle Benjamin was talking, Grandma Fátima stood beside him, one hand patting his back, the other dabbing at her eyes with the edges of her mantilla. I got this eerie feeling that they were me and David one day in our future. Brother and sister saying goodbye to their mother. Except, who knows where our real mother is. She might already be dead for all I know.

Uncle Joe took his older sister Lydia's place and said a few words about how Great Aunt Flaca had been his godmother and the godmother of both of his daughters, Xochitl and Gaby, and how, thanks to her support, he and the girls had been able to carry on after the death of his two wives.

Great Aunt Lulu, once she had calmed down—as the sister of Great Aunt Flaca and the daughter-in-law of Double Great Grandma Maggie—had the grand finale. What she said brought tears even to my eyes.

"I want to tell you a story about my big sister, Esperanza," she began. "She was much older than me, seventeen years older, and I grew up thinking of her as my mother because my own mother died giving birth to me. Esperanza taught me to dance. She taught me many other things, but it's the dancing I remember most, how I would be helping her clean up the house one minute, and suddenly she'd turn up the radio and start swinging me around the living room. It didn't matter if it was polka or swing, Esperanza could do it all. When my other sister, Betty . . . " She caught her breath and covered her mouth to keep from crying. "I'm sorry, Betty, it's just that this has been a secret long enough, I hope you forgive me, *hermanita.* Anyways, when Betty had her second baby, she got really sick *con* meningitis and couldn't take care of baby Luz. We didn't think she'd make it, at first, and I remember Esperanza kneeling me down in front of our family's altar to la Virgen de Guadalupe to pray a rosary for Betty every afternoon. Betty's first girl, Lydia, went to live with her father's mother, and it was Esperanza who took care of baby Luz."

At that, every head in the place turned to look at Tía Luz, who by then was weeping into the sleeve of her sweater.

"It was Esperanza who fed her and held her and changed her and told her stories and danced with her all bundled up against her chest. It took Betty two years to get better, but by then, she was pregnant again, *con el* Joe, and baby Luz was so attached to Esperanza, she didn't want to go back home. She wanted to stay with Esperanza. She got an awful fever each time they took her away, and she wouldn't stop crying until Esperanza came to get her. Nothing Betty or Santiago did made her feel better. She could not get used to being without Mami Hope, as she called Esperanza. Finally, her parents decided to let her go back and live with Esperanza, and she grew up calling her real mother Aunt Betty.

"Years later, after Luz ran off with that Irish trucker boyfriend of hers, became a *camionera* herself, and moved to Las Vegas, something terrible, I guess, happened between Lydia and Luz. To this day, I still don't know what happened, and not being a *chimolera*, I never wanted to know. But Luz went away and we never heard from her again. At first, Esperanza wanted to give her time to get over whatever the problem was *que tuvo con la* Lydia. But after three Mother's days, three Christmases and three birthdays passed, and still no word from Luz, Esperanza gave up waiting and started wearing black. She never talked about her feelings, but everyone knew she was *de luto*, you know, in mourning for the girl she raised that she never heard from again. I think Esperanza believed something awful had happened to Luz that nobody wanted to tell her about. So she suffered in silence all these years. And then yesterday, *de buenas a primeras*, Luz appears out of the blue in Fátima's garage after twenty years, and the shock of seeing her must have made Esperanza's heart stop. That's what I think happened to my big sister, Esperanza Morales. Rest in peace, Mana. And welcome home, Luz. Don't feel bad, *m'ija*, at least you killed your Mami Hope with happiness."

There was so much sobbing and sniffling in that room with the ghosts of Great Aunt Flaca and Double Great Grandma Maggie swirling over our heads and Great Aunt Lulu's words still echoing in our ears, all those *calaveras* jumping out of the closet, that for a moment the manager of the mortuary popped his head in the doorway to see what all the commotion was about. Then, as if on cue, the XYZ Club got up in unison, Ximena, Yazmín, Yesenia, Ysela and Ivón, followed by Zulema and Zoey, arranged themselves behind one of the lecterns and started to sing something about the turning of the seasons and a time for everything like crying, dying and being born.

"Turn, turn, turn," they sang in perfect harmony.

After the funerals, we all came back to Grandma Fátima and Grandpa Michael's house for hot chocolate and *menudo*. Everyone except the XYZ Club, who packed themselves into Uncle Patrick's van and went to Double Great Grandma Maggie's house where they were hosting their club's reunion.

All the kids, except Zoey, who was now officially a member of the XYZ Club, were spending the night at Grandma Fátima's. It wasn't till we were all eating *menudo* that folks realized Old Man Santiago wasn't around. He had refused to ride in the hearse with Great Aunt Betty, Great Aunt Lulu and Tía Luz, and nobody else remembered bringing him back from the cemetery in their car.

"Did he stay at the cemetery, the crazy old fart?" asked Uncle Joe.

"Crazy old stubborn-as-a-mule fart, you mean," groused Great Aunt Betty.

My dad and my uncles had to drive all the way out to the east side and back to Mount Carmel Cemetery where we had buried

Grandma Maggie and Old Flaca overlooking the Zaragosa Bridge. It was just me who waited up with grandma and grandpa for the phone to ring with the news that the old geezer had been found. They didn't come back until daybreak, all tired and discouraged. Uncle Joe paced up and down in the kitchen with the phone in his hand, trying to get the police to understand how scared everyone was that something had happened to old Santiago.

"He's an elderly Hispanic man, lady, memory-impaired, probably with dementia. What do you mean, I should calm down? Are you going to help us find him or not?"

It's freaky to see a grown man looking scared like that.

While my uncles and my dad chowed down on what was left of the *menudo* and *barbacoa*, Grandpa Michael and I took our microwaved cups of hot chocolate out to the back porch.

"Grandpa," I said, blowing into my cup, "can I ask you something? Who's Uncle Sam?"

"What do you want to know about Uncle Sam for?" Grandpa Michael frowned. "Poor man's been dead a long time."

"Just wondering."

"Was somebody talking about Uncle Sam?"

"Yeah, kinda. I came back from the funeral in the van with the XYZ Club, and Cousin Ivón was talking about Tía Luz, something about some picture she carried in her big rig that Uncle Sam had dedicated to the 'light of my Sundays.' I think this Uncle Sam was Cousin Ivón's dad, right Grandpa?"

"Where'd they get that picture?" He sounded suspicious.

"I don't know," I shrugged, taking a hot sip that burned all the way down my gullet.

"What else did they say, *m'ija*?" prodded Grandpa Michael.

Suddenly I remembered Cousin Ximena warning me not to repeat anything I heard in the van. It was a secret, she said, and the only reason they were gonna let me in on it was because I was old enough to keep my mouth shut. In this family, she said, if you don't know how to keep secrets, you're in deep shit.

"*¿M'ija?*" Grandpa prodded me again.

"I'm gonna be in deep shit with Aunt Ximena and the XYZ Club, Grandpa," I said, knowing I could talk that way to him without getting smacked.

"It'll be worse if you don't tell me," he said, glowering under his gray brows.

What was I gonna do? Lie? I had a feeling he knew exactly what they had said. "I'm not sure, but it sounded like there was some drama with Tía Luz and Aunt Lydia because of this Uncle Sam, which is why Tía Luz left and never came back." I took three quick sips of chocolate.

"Go on."

"And I guess Old Man Santiago sort of defended him and blamed Tía Luz, which is why he didn't want to ride in the hearse with them. Do you know what happened, Grandpa?"

"None of your business. You're too young to be passing on *chisme* like that."

Okay, really? I was old enough to keep a secret and too young to pass on *chisme*. Whatever.

Grandpa shook his head and whistled through the big gap in his front teeth. "Poor Sam, never could live that down," was all he said. And then, as an afterthought, he knuckled my head and said, "Don't you dare ask Aunt Lydia anything about it."

"I wasn't gonna say nothing to Aunt Lydia."

"You better not. She'll scold you for sure."

I was going to tell him that for my confirmation I wanted one of the XYZ Club to be my godmother, like a fairy godmother. But I kept the thought to myself and watched the sun rise and the thunderbird on the mountain glow bright red for a moment.

There were dumb things I wondered about sometimes, like how come I felt so close to these people who weren't my blood, or whether David and me were Mexican or Irish or Gypsy. That morning, I thought maybe David and me really weren't adopted, maybe whoever our mother and father were, somehow they'd been connected to this crazy family so full of secrets and skeletons and fairy godmothers.

"Grandpa, is it hard to tell what you're born with and what you learn through osmosis?"

"Osmosis?"

I yawned. "I don't know. Sometimes I think I was born to this family. Is that possible? Or am I just absorbing everything through osmosis?"

"You should ask your dad about that, honey," he said.

"Grandpa?" I yawned again. "When I grow up, can I change my name to something with an x, y or z so I can be in the XYZ club with Zoey?"

Grandpa tousled my hair. "You need to get yourself to bed, young lady, before your grandma skins your hide for staying up all night. Off to bed, now."

I trudged inside where my cousins were rolled up in blankets and sleeping bags all over the living room. I took the blanket off David and curled up on the couch. Just as I was falling asleep, the front door opened and in walked grandma and grandpa's neighbor, Judge Anacleto, with Old Man Santiago hobbling on his cane behind him. The old geezer was going on about how it wasn't his fault nobody thought to go knocking on the judge's door, all that *escándalo* everybody was making for nothing, couldn't a man go down the block to watch the soccer game with his *compadre* without getting the police department on his tail? He'd been gone all afternoon and nobody had even noticed he hadn't been at the funeral.

They left the door open and a long shaft of desert light sliced across the floor of the living room, landing on the different-colored hair of all my cousins: curly black, straight brown, wispy blonde, even red-headed David who liked wearing a ponytail like our dad. The grownups had all come together in the kitchen to hear the rest of Old Man Santiago's story, and I could smell fresh coffee brewing. I closed my eyes, wondering about my new name. There were too many Y's in the XYZ club already, so maybe I'd go with X or Z—Xena, like Aunt Ximena's favorite super-hero, or Zora, for Grandpa's alter ego, El Zorro.

Shortcut to the Moon

On good days, I think of Iowa City. Those are the days that I find coins in the street, someone gives me a smoke or treats me to their leftovers. When I've eaten and appeased the god of bile in my gut, or when the nicotine hits the bull's eye in my blood, I allow myself to remember that year in Iowa City. That's all it was for me: one year of college. But for lots of reasons, that little town is etched into my mind like it was a foreign country, or maybe, another planet.

When you're from El Paso, you get used to the rough grain of the wind. The leaves turn piss yellow or brittle brown in the fall, not every shade of red and gold and purple, and the winter wind doesn't frostbite your thighs or turn your tears to icicles. In Iowa City, you learn the meaning of seasons. At the Black Angel Cemetery, where I spent untold hours practicing Iowa-Writing-Workshop techniques that felt like they were making me change from being left-handed to right-handed, the colored leaves of oaks and maples stood out among the headstones like panes of stained glass. What I loved most about that year in Iowa, other than the cornfields and the blizzards and the daffodils blooming under the snow and the juicy double cheeseburgers at George's Bar, was getting blitzed on Cuervo and Colombian with my cousin Ivón in all-night heart-to-heart sessions that we called "shortcuts to the moon."

That's what I like to think about on good days, but I haven't had a good day in a long time. Until today, when that *gringa* tourist felt sorry for me, I guess, and handed me a five-dollar bill. I wasn't even asking for it. Just sitting there, huddled at the foot of the Cristo Rey statue that's perched at the top of the lookout over the little lumber town of Creel in the Copper Canyon. The days are longer than the nights, so it wasn't cold, but I was shivering. I guess the *gringa* could tell that I needed something to ease the pain, so without a word, she just walked over to me and handed me a bill. Abe Lincoln stared up at me, and I realized my eyes had crossed. I was like all shocked and forgot to thank her. Just opened my mouth and watched her walk away.

Took a while for it to sink in that this was not another fantasy of mine, and finally I dragged myself up from the nest of newspapers I'd made and went to the mission store to buy some essentials: a couple cans of tuna, a pack of Faros, a bar of soap and a roll of paper towels that I can use for drying, washing and wiping. I could barely fit it all into my grungy backpack. Who knows what happened to my suitcase, but I got three bikini *chones*, three baby T's and a pair of khaki shorts rolled up in the pack, along with my journal and my battered copy of *Siddartha*. The pack is heavy to lug around all day, but makes a nice pillow at night. The lady who runs the mission store just shakes her head every time I go in there, but she always throws in some *tamarindo* candy or a little pack of Chiclets and tells me to go with God. I want to say I'm trying, but she won't get it.

So today is a good day. A double good day, cuz I'm not passed out yet. After I've washed up at the public toilet in the train station and changed into a clean pair of *chones* and an almost clean T-shirt that says, "Life's a Witch and Then You Fly," I wander down to the plaza in town and allow myself to be around people. Sometimes, watching people breaks my heart. I remember my dad and my grandma and my stupid cousin Ricki. I never, ever allow myself to remember my mom, even though the smell of roasting *chiles* from a restaurant brings her front and center, whether I like it or not. It hurts so bad, I have to fuck somebody so's I can get the money for a bottle.

The train station is the best place to pick up men. The Germans and the Spaniards are the easiest. The Germans, to a man, have these burly pink bodies and perfect dicks. I haven't seen a crooked dick on a German yet. They have a strong smell, though, and their armpits are rank. Even their elbows smell. And their assholes are covered with thick blonde hair. The Spaniards don't smell as bad, though they've got more body odor than a Mexican any day, and they're funny as hell, but their dicks aren't as nice to look at. A lot of them aren't circumcised and they get this crazy tilt to their erections, which makes me laugh sometimes. Except, I don't laugh often. Only on good days.

These days, most of my clients have been from the States. I go for the young ones traveling in packs because all the beer they drink on the long, slow train ride from Chihuahua City makes them horny when they get to Creel. Hey stud, I call out, and the first one to turn around is my prey. They don't have a choice but to prove their studliness to their buddies. Me and Araceli, the local whore, have worked out a deal. I get the Americans, she gets everyone else. Works out fine with her. *Americanos* are cheap, she says. Besides, I got me some regulars that won't touch Araceli with a ten-foot condom.

And since today is a double good day and I'm cleaned up and I don't have to fuck nobody for money or food, and since even the families strolling in the plaza aren't putting a bug up my ass, I think I'll send another postcard to my dad. I bought three postcards when Ricki and I first got here, at the end of March, and sent one right away, a picture of polka-dot-painted Tarahumara men in headdresses and loincloths dancing their traditional Pascua Florida Easter dance. The other two I saved for later in the trip, all stamped and everything, a picture of the quaint little kiosk in Creel and another of a spectacular sunset over the copper formations of the canyon. But that was before Ricki went on that Holy Week excursion to the waterfall and didn't come back. Before I read in the paper that the decomposed body of a young man had been discovered by some hikers about two weeks after he disappeared. Nothing left to identify him but his teeth and tattoos. I didn't need to know the results of the dental plate match. Ricki had a juvie record in El Paso, so I knew they'd eventually find out who he was. It was the tattoos that told me everything. "Rita" on one arm, "Cunning" on the other. Not his mother or his girlfriend's name, as they surmised in the local rag, but her own name, or rather the name of the woman he was becoming. From Ricardo Cunningham to Rita Cunning.

"Rita, as in Hayworth," he would say, all husky-voiced and dreamy-eyed, naming off all the Ritas that he knew, in person or by reputation. "As in Moreno, as in González, Magdaleno and Mae Brown, as in Santa Rita. Don't you see, Mare? It's sexy and dark and down-to-earth at the same time. It can be the name of a *tía* or a saint, of a sister-in-law or a dyke." Though of course, he wasn't interested in the least in having sex with women. The Cunning part, short for Cunningham, he was especially pleased with until I pointed out it sounded a lot like cunnilingus to me. I have a way of bursting people's bubbles.

When I found out about the tattoos, I went to the police station in town and said I was Ricki's cousin and wanted to see the body, see the tattoos with my own eyes. Health hazard, they told me. Against the law to expose a body in that advanced stage of decomposition. They asked me his name and age and where he was from, and what we were doing in Creel. What else would we be doing in Creel but visiting the Copper Canyon, I said, brave as usual on tequila. I watched the cop clench down on the cigarette he was smoking, getting pissed off at the way I was talking to him, so I knew I was pushing it. Why did he go into the sierra? To bare his asshole to a Tarahumara, I wanted to say, but I just shrugged and mumbled something about a Holy Week excursion.

He looked at me all shifty-eyed and asked for my passport, said he was going to have to hang on to it for a few days. He wanted to know if I knew where Ricki's passport was. I lied, said he didn't have one, just a tourist visa. I gave him the name and address of his parents, Uncle Michael and Tía Fátima, and wrote them a stupid note saying I was sorry and didn't know what had happened to Ricki.

To prove I was really his cousin traveling with him on vacation, the cop wanted me to pay the fee to transport his remains to Chihuahua City and from there to El Paso. Five hundred dollars, he said. Are you out of your mind, I said, digging into my jeans and pulling up the rest of my cash: fifteen hundred thirty-one pesos in one pocket, a hundred-dollar-bill my dad had given me for emergencies in the other.

"That's all I've got," I said.

He scooped it all into his fat palm and gestured with his head for me to go.

Fact is, as I learned from the jail keeper a few days later, they'd had no way of lifting the body out of the canyon and had set it on fire, instead. They sent his parents a box of bones and dirt from the canyon. DHL Ground Delivery. I'm sure as hell it didn't cost them two hundred fifty bucks. That motherfucker took all the money I had left.

I toyed with the idea of putting in a collect call to my cousin Ximena, Ricki's older sister, and sort of the captain of all the cousins, fearless leader of the XYZ Club. If anyone could handle bad news, it was Ximena. I got as far as dialing Grandma Maggie's number, and then . . . I don't know . . . I snapped, I guess. Next thing I knew I was waking up in some seedy room crawling with cockroaches next to some naked Asian guy, empty bottle of Hornitos between us. I took a couple of twenties from his wallet and slipped out of there fast. Weird thing was I had all my clothes on, even my shoes, but when I went to the bathroom, I found my *chones* drying on the sink and my backpack stashed behind the toilet.

Next time, it was a white guy in Iowa Hawkeye boxer shorts I woke up next to. Talk about serendipity. Then the custodian of the jail, where the cop didn't pay me but at least gave me my passport back. Then a black guy, a safe-sex freak who wouldn't let me even jerk him off without a rubber, followed by a couple of Germans. I didn't care who it was or what he wanted, as long as he didn't try to stop me from drinking myself to death. And before I knew it, the sad little marching band playing the Mexican national anthem told me it was Cinco de Mayo, long past Easter, and I hadn't called anybody to let them know about Ricki. By then, I figured they already knew, so what was the use of calling. Somewhere in the small sane part of my brain, it occurred to me that maybe my dad would be worried about me and that I should call him to let him know I was okay, so to speak. But like I said, it was a small thought, easily overrun by a couple of shots of tequila.

If you really wanted to be generous, you could say that I stayed in Creel to figure out what happened to my cousin. And I did, for a while. Five days in a row, I went to that motel with the cute cabins we had stayed at when we first arrived and waited for the tour guide who'd sold the Basaseachic Falls Canyoneering Adventure to Ricki. He'd taken the two of us on a tour of the Tarahumara dwellings and the so-called Valley of the Monks that looked more like a forest of giant petrified penises. The guy kept disappearing into the woods to fuck his girlfriend. I didn't trust him, but he'd talked Ricki into the Basaseachic tour by saying it was a special tour for men only, led by a real Tarahumara guide, that took them to an area of the falls used only by the native men for some kind of spring ritual of renewal. Smelled real fishy to me, and I begged Ricki not to go, even threatened to get on the next bus back to Juárez if he did.

"Come on, Mary, you know me better than that. What's my favorite movie?"

"Wizard of Fucking Oz," I said, knowing what he was getting at.

"Exactly. 'Somewhere over the rainbow, dreams come true,'" he sang the whole stupid song as he packed his gear and his second-hand Polaroid camera into his Old Navy duffel bag. He didn't even care that I held on to his passport.

Horny little idiot. That tour guide must have seen the queer in him to tell him the excursion was for men only. Fact is, my cousin had this fantasy of getting fucked by a Tarahumara and figured this could be his one and only chance. When the tour guide finally showed up at the motel, swaggering under his cowboy hat and smelling of diesel, he acted like he had no idea who I was or what I was talking about. I told him I was going to report him to the police chief, but he laughed, said the police chief was his brother-in-law.

"I'll report you to the tourist bureau, *hijo de la chingada*," I shouted at him, but all he did was spit in my face and saunter away. So much for detective work.

I took to showing Ricki's passport picture to folks in the train station and the post office and the plaza, but every time I'd see a pretty guy in a ponytail, or a guy who walked with his elbows close to his body, like Ricki, I'd black out and wake up in some bed with some stranger. Most of the time I'd be fully dressed and they'd be naked, with cum splattered all over the sheets. I figured I'd worked them over pretty good with hand or mouth, and that was worth at least forty US dollars a pop. So I had a fee. A steady clientele. And a broom closet of my own with a tiny sink and a foldout cot at the rinky-dink Hotel Tarahumara.

Things turned to shit after they put me in jail, though. Crowded, stinking icebox of a jail behind the police station with an old drunk who kept farting "*pedos de muerte*," as the jailkeeper called them because they stunk of death. Stayed there for a week, I think, because I refused to blow the police chief, and that spoiled my reputation. I got kicked out of my room. I didn't look so hot, and I smelled even worse with the stench of *pedos de muerte* in my hair and clothes. No more easy clients at the train station. And Araceli gave me a major tongue-lashing and a good *desgreñada*, she was pulling-my-hair pissed when she found out about my regulars, said I'd been crossing the line into her territory and poaching on "her" men.

"*Pocha sinvergüenza*," she called me. "Go fuck the dogs in the plaza. This is my station from now on."

I had no money except the few pesos I could make in boxcars and the Cristo Rey lookout after dark, and no place to sleep but the great outdoors. Once, I gave a blowjob to one of the ticket takers behind the station and got a free ride to Divisadero. Figured I could ply my trade in dollars again up there where my reputation wasn't anything anybody cared about, where they didn't know I was the cousin of a young man found dead in Tarahumara country.

As far as customers were concerned, I had a pretty good stretch of luck for a few days doing the ticket takers while the train waited for the tourists to pose for pictures and buy some extra trinket or greasy quesadilla from one of the Divisadero stalls. I'd walk up to them after all the tourists had stepped down from the train, sidling up close enough to touch their belts, letting my hand wander down just far enough so they understood what I was offering for 200 pesos. I didn't always get 200, some of them actually tried to haggle over a hand job. I got them good, though, the cheapskates. Just as they were getting ready to squirt, I'd turn their dicks in the direction of their faces and give them a taste of their own medicine. They weren't too happy about that.

Things changed when someone reported a homeless drunk woman loitering in the lobby of the 5-star hotel that hangs off the ledge of the Copper Canyon. Before long, I was burnt up in Divisadero. So I got another free ride back to Creel, and I've been here ever since. My address now is Cristo Rey. Reminds me of home, except our Cristo Rey in El Paso is bigger and presides over desert and freeway. If I squint real hard at the limestone Christ statue, it transforms into my mom, arms outstretched, going, "Don't be afraid, Xochitl." She's the only one who ever called me by my first name, Xochitl, the one the Catholic nuns took away as soon as I started first grade, making me go by my middle name, María or Mary, the rest of my life.

I tuck in to a nest of newspapers each night, just me and the bottle or me and the delirium tremens. Sometimes I dream that I'm on the phone to my dad. "It's nobody's fault, *m'ijita*, your mamá was sick," I hear him saying, but his voice sounds like it's coming from a walkie-talkie underwater. Maybe it's me. Maybe I'm just swimming in tequila until I find my way back to the womb. It's funny what you can get used to. But I guess I'm getting tired of the party I've been on since Easter, tired of blacking out and sleeping on concrete. I've been trying to clean myself up, dry out enough so that I can bring myself to write that postcard to my dad. Maybe it's time to go home.

There's a kid sitting next to me on the bench now, watching me stare at Ricki's passport picture. A little snotty-nosed boy in a red jacket, about four or five years old. Looks like a Tarahumara kid, except they don't usually travel alone, not this young. I crane my neck over the plaza and spot a Tarahumara woman with a baby slung over her chest, sitting in front of the gazebo surrounded by palm-leaf baskets of all sizes. *Must be the boy's mom,* I think. For some reason, the kid is bugging me. Just sitting here staring at me, trying to figure out if I'm somebody he should beg from. My clothes are dirtier than his, but my face and hands are clean, and I've got a full pack of cigarettes and two empty tuna cans next to me on the bench. I could be sending some mixed signals to this kid. I sure as shit ain't gonna be sharing what's left of my five bucks with him.

I'm praying nothing happens between now and dinnertime so I can take that eighteen pesos I have left and buy me a big bowl of soup at Lupita's Restaurant. They're the only ones who won't kick me out, if I come in with money and can pay for my food. They've got the best *cocido de res* I ever tasted, other than my grandma's. A beef broth thick with carrots and *calabazas*, potatoes and cabbage, the meat practically dissolving in your mouth, bones rich with marrow and a big order of soft homemade corn tortillas. That's what I want more than anything. If nothing happens, I mean. I go back to staring at Ricki's picture. Little showoff with his slicked-back hair and bleachy smile.

Goddammit, Ricki! I pound my fist into the bench.

If this kid doesn't stop bugging me, staring at me with those crybaby eyes, waiting for me to fork over a peso or two, I'm going to take my money into that liquor store over there and get me a quart of Los Mochis Tequila.

Two Tarahumara girls, about eight and ten years old and wearing bright flowered skirts and paisley scarves, run up to the boy and one of them whispers in his ear, all three of them staring at me like I'm some circus freak.

"*Váyanse,*" I tell them, gesturing with my arm for them to get away from me. But the girls hold up a flat basket filled with magnets, little woodcarvings of girls in paisley skirts and bandanas, torsos wrapped in white cloth like *rebozos*, tucked inside a tiny palm leaf basket.

"*¿No quiere?*" says the older girl.

As long as I've been here, I've never seen a Tarahumara girl or woman begging. Only the little boys beg. Older boys and men don't usually come into town. Only the women deal with the tourists. More stoic than Apaches, they don't talk much. They'll tell you the price of whatever they're selling, and that's it. No "good morning" or "*buenas tardes*" or even "*gracias*" from them. And don't even think of haggling with a Tarahumara. They don't give a shit if you walk away. Money is just a daily means to an end for them, and they don't believe in possessions, either. Their measure of a good life is not "he who has the most toys wins." It's the one with the least toys that gets a ticket to Tarahumara heaven. You could say I've been trying to live by the Tarahumara code, you know, learning how to make do with as little as possible, for the last . . . what? . . . six weeks, give or take?

"*¿Cuánto?*" I say, picking up one of the magnets. The figure is carved of canyon *piñón,* and the face and legs are striated with brown and gray. I lift the skirt and see that it's wearing tiny paisley panties.

"*Diez pesos,*" the girls say in unison.

Maybe I could send this magnet to my dad, ask him to telegraph me some money for the fare back to civilization. I could still get a small cup of *cocido* with eight pesos. But there's this fucking hopeful look in the boy's eyes that does me in, makes me think of Ricki when we were kids playing *muñecas* in Grandma Maggie's backyard.

"One day I'm gonna be a mommy," he'd say, diapering his doll.

"Not me," I'd say. "I'm gonna be an astronaut so I can go to the moon."

Fucking memory turns the spit in my mouth to salt, makes me feel like I swallowed the salt-shaker. I need something to wash it down.

"*No, gracias,*" I choke out the words, returning the magnet to the girls.

Before I know it, I'm making a beeline for the liquor store. What can I say? The only place I want to be right now is on the moon. When I come back to the plaza with my paper-bagged bottle, the girls are still there, like they're warming the bench for me. I roll my eyes at them and start to walk in the opposite direction, toward the church.

"*¡Foto!*" one of them calls out.

"Leave me alone," I say, unscrewing the bottle. "I don't have a camera." I take a nice long burning swig of probably the cheapest tequila ever made. Feels like a live flame touching my gizzards.

The older girl comes up to me, points to Ricki's passport still in my hand, and says, "*Allá arriba.*"

What is this kid trying to tell me? I whirl around so suddenly it makes their eyes flutter. "You saw him?"

They don't understand me, so I ask again in Spanish.

The girls nod.

"*Allá arriba*," the older girl says again. "*Foto*."

I watch her reach into the pocket of her skirt and pull out a picture. She shows it to me, holding on tight to the corner. And there he is, the son of a bitch, posing shirtless in his own Polaroid moment with the two girls and the little boy. They're standing next to a washline strung on timber and hung with dozens of colored Tarahumara skirts drying in the sierra sun, the tattoos on his arms clear as day.

I grab the girl's arm. "Is he alive? *¿Está vivo?*"

Eyes round like pennies, the girl nods. "*Allá arriba*," she says for the third time.

I'm so startled I drop my bottle and it shatters on the flagstones of the plaza, all that good tequila soaking into the scuffed blue leather of my cowboy boots. I try to take the picture from her but the girl slips it back into her pocket.

"*Diez pesos*," she says, then wrenches her arm from my grasp, and she and the other girl and the boy scurry out of the plaza.

Fuck me running, I think, except I can't stand, much less run. My knees are giving out and I feel like I'm going to black out again. The bench. I have to reach the . . . But then everything spins out and I hit my head on the armrest as I fall.

When I come to, there's a familiar face, two of them, leaning over me. My eyes feel crossed and I have a hangover headache, even though I haven't had but one sip of my daily deadly dose today.

"I saw you falling? Are you okay?" she says, and her two faces dissolve back into one. It's her. The *gringa* who gave me the five-dollar bill earlier.

"He's alive," I tell her. "My cousin's alive. Those girls took a picture with him."

"How many fingers am I holding up?"

I try to focus on the fingers she's wiggling in front of my eyes, and for a moment, I think I'm going to vomit. The pain in my head feels like someone kicked me between the eyes.

"Here, drink some water."

"I'm okay," I say. "Stop fussing!"

She helps me sit up against the bench and holds a bottle of water to my mouth, but I turn my head. The thought of drinking anything makes me want to puke.

"My cousin. Police said he died in the canyon. All decomposed, they said," I tell her. I can't figure out how I could've gotten drunk on one sip of tequila. My words are slurred and I sound like I'm deranged. "Those girls took a picture."

"Just be still, okay. You may have given yourself a concussion. I think you need to go to a hospital. You need help."

I turn to face her and try to fix my gaze on something other than her blue eyes. "I need to call my family," I say slowly, staring at the spray of freckles on her nose. "See if they know . . . if they know about Ricki. Can you help me get to a phone? I'll do anything you want." I put my hand on her thigh to help her get my meaning. "Anything," I repeat.

"Brigit! Where've you been?" someone calls behind us. My head hurts too much to turn around, but soon enough, I have the misfortune of recognizing who it is. The shock sobers me a little.

"Jesus *pinche* Christ. X.M., is that you?"

"Now I know I lost my mind," I say. "You couldn't be for real."

It's my cousin Ivón Villa, partner in crime from my Iowa City days, standing there gaping at me with this horrified, pitiful look that makes me want to punch her.

"There but for the grace of the goddess go I," she says.

When did she get so holier-than-thou, I wonder.

"She's the one, Ivón," says the *gringa.* "The one I saw up on the lookout, the one I told you about. I didn't even recognize her. She's lost so much weight."

And that must be what's-her-name, the woman Ivón married in Iowa City.

"When you said you'd seen a drunk woman up there at the feet of Cristo Rey, sleeping in newspapers," Ivón says to her wife, "I thought, 'that's gotta be my cousin,' but I didn't want to believe it. Boy am I glad Uncle Joe's not here to see this."

"You know, sweetheart, maybe you should open a business for finding missing relatives," says the *gringa.*

"Right? That's what I get for being in the right place at the wrong time."

La Brigit helps me get to my feet and sit down on the bench. "Careful, now," she says to me, all maternal and shit. "Don't move too fast, or you'll lose your balance again."

Lose my balance? That's a good one.

"At least this one's not mauled by dogs," says Ivón. She's squatting down peering into my face now like she's extra near-sighted or something. "Unlike what happened to my little sister, this is all self-inflicted damage." She takes a seat beside me and puts her arm around my shoulders. "Huh, *prima*?"

"What in the holy hell are you doing in Creel, Pancho Pinche Puchi Villa?" I ask, using her childhood nickname and sounding like a total drunk. I know it doesn't seem that way but I am alert enough now to be aware of how embarrassing this looks. "Don't tell me my dad sent out the troops."

Ivón smacks my arm. "Girl, your dad is a mess. My mom said he'd had some sort of ulcer attack after your phone call, and he's been in the hospital ever since."

"My phone call?"

"You don't remember calling?"

I shrugged and shook my head.

"Your dad told my mom that you were ranting and raving about Ricki being murdered, something about his tattoos. Anyway, sick my ass. You were drunk, weren't you?"

"They know about Ricki, huh?"

"It's you everyone's been worried about, *pendeja*! Your dad was getting ready to come look for you himself. Good thing Brigit and I were still waiting for you in Mazatlán when Ma called. Remind me never to make any travel plans with you again. We had to take the ferry to Los Mochis and the slow-ass Copper Canyon train to Creel just to come and find you. It would've killed your dad to have seen you like this."

"So, what happened? Did his folks get Ricki's remains or not? The fucking police . . . "

"Ricki's remains? Girl, what the fuck are you talking about? Ricki went home weeks ago. Said he looked for you all over town when he returned from some side trip he took."

"You mean he's home?"

"The police told him you'd gotten on a train after having caused a disruption at the motel you guys were staying at. They made him pay a fine, too. He figured you'd gone back home, so he went back, too."

"The stupid shit's been home all this time?"

"Pigging out on Tía Fátima's pancakes the last I heard."

"His parents never got any notice of his death?" I'm beginning to put it together in my tequila-logged brain.

"Notice of his death? Girl, you must have been really tripping. All they got was a charge on their credit card that Ricki was using to pay for the damage you caused at the motel. Seems you set the room on fire, or something."

"Seriously?" I say and start to laugh. I can hear the freaky theme song of *The Twilight Zone* in my head. "A charge on their credit card?" For some reason that's the funniest thing I've ever heard and I can't stop laughing.

"I think she's hysterical," says Brigit.

The police had played the two of us and took us for whatever they could: $250 on my end, and who knows how much on Ricki's. There I'd been wandering around like the town lush, mourning my decomposed dead cousin in jerk-off sessions and blackouts, entertaining the locals with my theatrics. And there he was eating his mom's pancakes at home, no doubt showing off his Polaroid pictures of the Copper Canyon. I'm laughing so hard I can feel the piss soaking up my jeans. Not that it's the first time.

"You're a total nightmare," Ivón says to me.

"Don't be so mean, honey. You don't know what she's gone through."

"I been there, done that, Brigit," says Ivón. "Let's go, *loca!*" She yanks me to my feet.

"Look at that bruise on her forehead, Ivón. She should really see a doctor," says Brigit. "There's that little hospital by the train station, we could take her there."

"I'm not going to no hospital," I say, feeling the bump on my head.

"She'll be fine," Ivón says. She looks me right in the eye and tells it like it is: "Yo, listen up! We're taking you to our hotel so you can wash up, have a decent meal and get a good night's sleep. And tomorrow morning, we're getting on the first bus back to Juárez. We will not be taking the scenic route. This Copper Canyon train takes too long, and I've got to get back to Los Angeles before classes start."

"We'll run a nice hot shower for you," says Brigit, unzipping my backpack. "Do you have any clean clothes?" She looks inside and gags like there's a dead animal in there.

"I don't think so," Ivón sneers. "We're dumping all this stinky shit. You can wear some of my clothes."

Each of them puts an arm around my waist, and I feel like I'm five years old again, walking between my mom and my dad.

"What is it with this family?" Ivón is grumbling. "Do we all have, like, an alcoholic gene or something?"

"Remember Iowa City?" I ask Ivón, tears bubbling down my face, not so much because I want to remind her that she'd had her own pants-pissing days in college, but because I want her to say something nice about that year we shared in Iowa. I'm the one who talked her into going there, and she's the one who ended up staying. Got her Ph.D. and everything, the first doctor of the family. "Remember our shortcuts to the moon?"

"Shortcuts to hell is more like it."

We pass Lupita's Restaurant, and suddenly my mouth is salivating and the god of bile sends up a wave of nausea that makes me puke a bitter yellow liquid in the street.

"Get it all out," says Ivón, rubbing my back.

Brigit hands me the water bottle and I rinse out the tart taste, then chug what's left of the bottle. "Hey, do y'all want some good soup?" I say, drying my mouth with the back of my hand. "They got the best *cocido* in the known universe here at Lupita's."

"Not until you do one thing," says Ivón, getting in my face.

"What now?"

"Admit that you're killing yourself and that you need to stop drinking to save your life. Admit that you need to surrender yourself to your Higher Power. That you need to go to AA."

"Whatever!"

I can't believe what I'm hearing. Is this the same Ivón who could drink me under the proverbial table? We'd been getting loaded together since junior high. From the Smeltertown graveyard in El Paso to the Black Angel Cemetery in Iowa City, Ivón used to be my drinking buddy, my *Dark Shadows* blood sister in the Almighty Order of the Agave. And now, here she is doing the Twelve Step Shuffle on me?

"Fuck off!"

Ivón grabs me by the T-shirt. "Admit that you're an alcoholic, goddammit!"

"Don't be so rough on her, Ivón," says her wife. "She might have a concussion."

"Someone did this for me three years ago, Brigit, did you forget? Tough love."

Ivón knuckles my head and kisses me square on the mouth. There's tears in her eyes the size of Texas. "Admit it, *esa*!"

"*No chingues*," I say.

I glance up at the lookout and see my mom again in the outstretched arms of Cristo Rey. I can almost hear her going, *No tengas miedo, Xochitl*. Don't be afraid while I shoot myself up with insulin and trip out to talk to the Virgin. Trouble is, she died. My mom died on my watch. So what if I was only thirteen years old and just doing what I was told, counting 900 minutes before I woke her up from her self-induced insulin overdose with a cup of sweet tea? That's enough to terrify you the rest of your motherless life.

"Look, *cabrona*," I say, "the only thing I'm gonna admit to is that I'm happy to see you guys, okay? And if I weren't so messed up, I'd kick your high and mighty lesbian ass."

Ivón threatens me with her fist. I thrust my chin at her, like daring her to go ahead and hit her cousin when she's down and out. She punches my arm, just the same.

"Bitch," I say, and she hugs me hard enough to split a rib.

The True and Tragic Story of Liberata Wilgefortis, Who, Having Consecrated her Virginity to the Goddess Diana to Avoid Marriage, Grew a Beard and Was Crucified

2nd Century, AD

A Novella

Anonymous. "Hl Kümmernis süddeutsch." Süddeutsch. Neumister.com. April 16, 2018. Courtesy of Wikimedia.

“But Artemis swore the great oath of the gods:
By your head! Forever virgin shall I be
] untamed on solitary mountains
] Come, nod yes to this for my sake!
So she spoke. Then the father of blessed gods nodded yes.
Virgin deershooter wild one the gods
Call her as her name.”

—Sappho, fragment 44AA
(trans. Anne Carson, *If Not, Winter,* 2002)

The Bizarre Birth

Calsia Marcella, the wife of Lucius Severus, Governor of the imperial provinces of Lusitania and Gallaecia, stared in shock at what had issued from her loins after three days and nights of labor. Not another son to carry forth the governor's lineage, not the twins the midwife had predicted, but nine of them, nine girls, pale and skinny as whelps, with identical heads of red, matted hair. So still after having their limbs and backsides cleaned, they hardly seemed to breathe.

Calsia shuddered and looked away.

"They don't even cry," she said. "Are you sure they're alive?"

The Domina's voice had grown hoarse from hours of screaming and grunting to push the full brood out of her womb. The floor beneath the birthing chair was stained with blood, piss and excrement.

The midwife draped their mother's fleece-trimmed *palla* over the swollen umbilical stems of the sleeping babies, covering them up to their tiny noses. "Yes, thanks be to Magna Mater. The sweet lambs survived. All nine of them."

In the basin next to the bed, she had washed each of the babes as they left their mother's womb and placed them in a row at the foot of their mother's bed.

"It's so vulgar. To give birth to a litter, like a common bitch. What did you do to me, Basilia Quiteria?" Calsia asked, glowering at the midwife.

"This weren't my doing, Domina," said the midwife as she wiped the heads of each of the newborns with a cloth soaked in sage oil, to give them something sweet to smell instead of the offal of their birth. "You're the one that gave life to them and pushed them into the world. I but helped you bring them to light, with the help of Juno Lucina."

"You must have known," Calsia insisted. "You could have warned me that I was giving birth to an entire litter."

"I told you it was not one child you were carrying in that uncanny big belly of yours, Domina," said the midwife, gently wiping the dried waxy blood from the forehead of the last and littlest of the babes. "I could feel the two heads and the two sets of feet kicking on either side of the belly. Must've been number one and number two. They're the biggest. The others must've been nesting between and behind them. Poor souls. To be squeezed in like that for all those months. It's a miracle none of them died," she said as she dropped the bloodstained cloth into the pile of birthing linen next to the bed and rinsed her hands in the basin, leaving an oily film on the water.

"But how?" said Calsia, her pale lips trembling. "How could there be so many of them?"

"Perhaps your seed is stronger than your husband's, Domina. Nine times stronger."

"That's ludicrous. Don't ever say that again, Basilia, or my husband will be sure to murder me himself. Someone must have bewitched me. Made the *Strigla* get into me somehow."

Calsia swooned, and the midwife helped her lean back against the cushions of the bed. She took the other end of Calsia's heavy cloak and tucked it over her shivering body.

"I'll tell one of your ladies to bring you a *calda*, Domina," said the midwife.

"No!" Calsia grabbed the midwife's arm, digging her nails into the flesh. "They mustn't come in here. They mustn't see them. Nobody may see them."

"Try not to vex yourself, Domina. I will take the *calda* from them at the door. You need heat to stir your blood and close that wound. It was a hard birth. Hardest I've ever witnessed, and I've seen hundreds of births, Domina. You may not survive the night if you don't get some heat into you. The cold, wet humors must be quelled before they settle into your bones and chill your blood."

Calsia assented with her eyes and the slightest nod of the head. She was too tired to argue with the stubborn midwife.

Basilia took a pouch of herbs from her midwifery basket and went to the heavy oak door of Calsia's bedchamber. She slid the bolt back and pulled the door open a crack. Calsia's bevy of maids gathered anxiously in the hall.

"What happened in there?" someone said amid bodies swarming and pushing against the door.

The midwife pushed back. She was twice their age, but five times stronger after a lifetime of fortifying herself with her own strong *posca*.

"What was all that screaming? Sounded like she was being torn to pieces in there."

"You haven't killed our mistress, have you?"

"Did the child live? We heard no crying."

"Was it a boy or a girl? Should we send for the wet nurse?"

"Friends, please. Our Domina has come through it . . . "

"Praise Juno Lucina," the maids' voices echoed in the corridor.

" . . . but the birth weakened her," Basilia continued, "and she needs a good strong *calda* to regain her strength."

"Let us in there, you Druid hag. We need to attend to our Lady."

"Domina cannot see anyone right now. It was a brutal birth, I'm telling you, she needs her strength. Take this." The midwife handed the pouch of herbs to the closest lady. "Boil this in a cup of wine and water, add a cinnamon stick and a handful of cloves to it, and some honey if you have it. Bring it in a covered pot. She needs to drink it hot. Hurry."

"What witch's brew will you have us concoct, Basilia Quiteria?"

"It's the only thing that will save her, you imbeciles. Or do you want your Domina's death on your heads? The Governor will nail the lot of you to the nearest tree for failing to provide her with what she needed to keep her alive."

"But the child. What was it? What shall we tell the Governor?"

"Did the Governor return, then?"

"We sent a footman out with a message as soon as the labor started."

"No time to lose, then," said the midwife. "Our Domina must be restored before her husband arrives. Quickly, now, do as I say, and get her *calda* ready. Her life depends on it."

The midwife watched the maids retreat like a clutch of hens, the hems of their tunics dragging behind them, their candles flickering wide shadows down the dark stone corridor.

Once she was sure none had lingered behind to eavesdrop, Basilia shut the door and slid the heavy bolt back into place. Despite the sconces blazing on the walls and the candles flickering on the shrine that Domina had constructed to invoke the blessings of Juno Lucina, patroness of childbirth, the bedchamber felt colder now that the moonless midsummer night had fully settled into the stone walls of the villa. She expected her mistress to be asleep, but her pale eyes were wide open, reflecting the flames of the candles.

"The Governor's on his way back," Basilia said, placing the back of her hand over the cold foreheads of each of the babies. In the candlelight, they seemed almost normal, their little profiles peaceful, their little ears like perfect tiny shells, tiny nostrils drawing breath.

"It's been three days," said Calsia. "You'd think he'd be back by now."

"It's better this way, Domina. Gives you more time to recover. And me more time to figure out what to do."

"Why is it so cold?" asked Calsia, shuddering. "This is the coldest summer we have ever had."

Basilia added a large log to the fire and poked at it until the sparks caught on the dry bark, but the crackling flames did little to stop Calsia's trembling. Nor did they ease the anxiety in Basilia's belly. The Druid mage, who was training her to scry and other magical arts, always counseled her to keep silent about any doubts, as she would not want to influence the course of Fate. Although she was keeping her fears to herself, Basilia had a bad feeling about this birth.

"Lucius will have me killed for this. He'll think I was unfaithful to him. Nine times unfaithful. He could have me stoned to death, if he doesn't wring my neck himself."

"Poor things," said the midwife to the sleeping babies, stroking the downy hair of the oldest baby's forehead. "To lose their mother like that."

"I assure you, it's not they who will lose their mother," said Calsia, lifting herself up on an elbow. "But I who will lose them. You must get rid of them, Basilia. Expose them. Take them to the Minho River where it meets the sea, and drown them."

As if they had understood, the babies started to twitch and turn under the cloak, kicking it off little by little with their jerky arms and legs.

"But Domina, they're your children. Your sweet baby daughters." The midwife rubbed her hand in circles over the tops of the heads of the shivering babes.

"Don't be so simple-minded, woman. The Governor will blame me for cuckoldry. Or he'll see them as the devil's spawn. Either way it's the death of me. Now get rid of them. Get them out of my sight. This instant!"

With her red hair loose and matted and the grey irises of her eyes spreading into the pupils like ink, Calsia Marcella looked mad. The chalk-white flesh pulled taut over her cheekbones and the sharp bones in her chin gave her a demonic appearance, as if the *Strigla* witch had indeed taken possession of Calsia's body.

"Don't you want to keep at least one of them, Domina? The first one at least, she's the most perfect."

"What do you mean the most perfect? Are the others imperfect?"

"They are . . . how shall I say it? They are malformed."

"Malformed?" Calsia closed her eyes and moaned. "You mean they're cursed?"

"Did you not look at them, Domina?" The midwife held a candle aloft over the bed, casting a warm light over the babes. "Look here, Domina. You must look at them."

Basilia uncovered the babies and the frigid air made them spill their urine on the bed.

"Look what you've done, Basilia! Now I will have to burn this ticking and get a new one made."

As if the ticking were not already soiled from the birth, Basilia thought, but kept it to herself. "Come closer, Domina. This is your firstborn. She fed well, this one. She has strong limbs, strong lungs, a good-sized head, ten fingers and ten toes. You should hold her, Domina."

Gingerly, Calsia leaned in and quickly pulled away, grimacing as if the baby gave off a foul odor.

"She's not perfect. She looks like a monkey."

"It's just baby down, Domina. Some babies have more of it when they are born. She will shed it."

Calsia raised her hand at the midwife. "Enough. The Governor will never accept a baby girl with that pelt. What about the next one? She isn't furry at all."

"Seconda here is not covered in down, Domina," said Basilia, raising the child's hands, "but she does have six fingers on each hand. Touch them if you like, they won't fall off."

"Get that thing away from me, Basilia!"

"Terza, the third one, is a tiny thing . . . poor dear . . . she's so thin. You can almost see her bones through the skin. She must not have gotten any nutrition at all. She might get no bigger than a midget, if she lives. Might be short on brains, too."

"Quarta and Quinta are, see?" The midwife turned the babies' faces upward. "Harelips, both."

Calsia turned and lost the bile in her stomach on the floor.

Basilia waited for Calsia to compose herself. "From here it gets even stranger, Domina. Are you ready for it?" Basilia had swaddled the legs of the sixth baby. She unwrapped the swaddling. "Poor baby Sesta has a very bad case of clubfeet. She may never be able to walk. Otherwise, she's as hale as Number One."

Calsia's eyelids swelled with unshed tears. She shook her head. "Stop, Basilia. You must stop. And why have you dared to give them names? That does not fall to you. Only the *pater familias* can do that."

"They are not names, Domina, just numbers, to distinguish them, that is all. I meant no disrespect."

Calsia looked on her brood and wept bitterly.

"We are almost finished, Domina," Basilia said gently. "The next two, Settima and Ottava," Basilia said, "have these little flaps for arms, but no hands."

"By the Gods!" Calsia recoiled. "How could these things have grown inside me? They're more like tumors than children." She wept into her hands.

"Brace yourself for this last one, Domina." Basilia pried open the next baby's clenched legs. "Nona has a tiny male member growing over her female genitals. She was probably supposed to have been a boy, but could be the influence of so many sisters turned him around."

"I have never seen such a horrible mockery of a birth!" Calsia cried. "Don't show me anymore, Basilia. I order you to stop torturing me!"

The babies had all gone blue from the cold, nine pairs of legs kicking in all directions, their little faces wrinkling up, blue mouths gnashing as if they were about to let loose a loud wail.

"What have I done to deserve this fate?" Calsia started to wail at the carving of Juno Lucina on the birthing shrine. "Did I not offer enough sacrifices on your altar, Great Mother? Did I do something to incur this life sentence of dishonor and disgrace?"

At hearing Calsia's cry, the babies stilled, as if soothed by their mother's anguish. The midwife covered them again with the warm cloak.

"Domina, you must calm yourself," said the midwife, trying to get Calsia to lie down. "You will sour your milk if you don't calm down."

"Someone has cursed me, I tell you. Cursed the Governor. Those Christians! It must have been those Christians that Lucius had executed in the Circus. Why did I go to those games in my condition?"

"You come from a strong stock, Domina," Basilia said in a soothing voice. "A strong line of women, from what I can tell."

Calsia pushed away the midwife's hands, and sat up in the bed.

"Do as I say and remove these . . . these aberrations at once," snapped Calsia, anguish turning to fury. "I'm warning you, Basilia, if you don't get those creatures out of here, I'm going to smother them myself." Calsia's voice quivered with rage.

"And how do you intend for me to remove them without the notice of your meddling maids, who are all but ready to knock down the door? Would you have me drown them here in the basin like cats?"

"I care not how you do it, or where you do it, just get it done."

"And how will you explain it to the Governor? Even if you say the infant died, he would want to see the dead body. It is his noble offspring, after all, and must be attended as such, even in death."

"Did you tell my maids anything about the birth just now?"

"Only that you had a hard birth and needed a *calda* to restore your strength."

"So, they know nothing. The child could have died."

"Yes, but what will you tell the Governor when he asks to see the dead child?"

"He won't ask. Especially when I tell him it was a girl. I'll tell him it was a horribly deformed girl, a stillbirth, and that you took it away to protect us from malicious gossip."

"But the first one is perfect, Domina. Look at her. She's beautiful. She looks just like you."

"Very well!" said Calsia, getting up on her knees and reaching for the other end of her cloak. Basilia thought her mistress had come to her senses and was reaching out for the firstborn.

"I will do it myself!" said Calsia, pulling the cloak down hard over the babies' faces.

Basilia was not one to give up. "Domina, please! Don't hurt them." She tried pulling the *palla* out of Calsia's hands, but the Domina's grip was too strong. "You will offend Juno Lucina if you do this, Domina. No telling what ill fortune will befall your house if you smother your own children. Don't invoke Magna Mater's mighty wrath!"

The threat of displeasing the Queen of the Gods stilled Calsia's intention immediately. She dropped back against the cushions in defeat, her pale face haggard from the strain.

A plan occurred to Basilia. It was a bad plan but better than drowning the babies. She lowered her voice. "I will take the others, as you wish, Domina. I will pack them all into my basket and somehow find a way to get them out of the villa, but only if you agree to keep the eldest. At least you can say that all those hours of pain and labor yielded you one very hale little girl."

Calsia did not respond. She was staring at the flickering candles on the shrine, her eyes moving quickly from side to side. At last, she spoke. "Maybe I should keep the one that looks like a boy. Lucius would like that."

"And what will you do with him when his father inspects his genitals, as fathers like to do to their boys, and finds he has a eunuch for a son? What if this son can bear children? What kind of *monstrum* would that be for your good husband, Domina?"

The midwife lifted number one and offered her to Calsia.

"Please, Domina, I beg you. Keep your firstborn. The gossip will swell if you say you had another stillbirth, especially if people hear that it was deformed. Do you want evil tongues to play with the notion of a deformed birth?"

Calsia stared at the mewling, naked child kicking her hairy little legs in the midwife's arms. Despite the dark down growing all over her, this first one looked completely normal, with a fine patch of red hair, long curly lashes and a dimpled chin exactly like her brother's.

"She does rather look like Gaius Lucius," Calsia said, reaching a hand out to tap the babe's heart-shaped lips. A tiny smile crept into the baby's face. "I believe he was born with fuzz all over him, too, now that I think of it."

"And he looks perfectly normal now, Domina."

"His father considered it a good sign," said Calsia. "Said he would grow up to be more virile."

Basilia took the baby's tunic that had been draped in the arms of Juno Lucina on the altar and slipped it over the baby's head. Her little arms and legs got lost in the folds.

"Look at how beautiful she looks, Domina," urged the midwife. "She'll be a strong girl, and a fine lady. I'm sure of it. The Governor will have a daughter to lift up, and the young master a sister to play with and protect."

Gently, the midwife handed the eldest baby to Calsia. "Take her, Domina. The others don't exist. This one, she's your only daughter, your Wilgefortis."

"Wilgefortis?" Calsia asked, taking the child to her bosom.

The baby writhed, her head turning to and fro, her pink tongue searching for a mother's teat.

"It means *virgo fortis*, Domina, or strong girl, to pay homage to our virgin goddess Diana."

"That name sounds foreign, Basilia. Her father will never lift her up with a foreign-sounding name."

"Give her any name you please, Domina. She is the fortunate daughter of a magnificent mother, who has liberated her from the rest of this nightmare."

"Did you just entrap me into agreeing with you, Basilia Quiteria?" Calsia said, but her gray eyes were already softening as she gazed on her firstborn girl. "You have to shed all that hair," she said to the child, "and I will ask your father to name you Liberata. Wilgefortis shall be your secret name, known only to me and Juno Lucina . . . and you, of course, Basilia."

Calsia stroked the soft, fuzzy cheeks of her newborn. The babe sniffed and clawed at her mother's breast. A wet stain darkened Calsia's bodice, and she glanced helplessly at the midwife. Domina Calsia had never breastfed. That was the job of a wet nurse, but no wet nurse had been summoned yet. Calsia had no idea what to do.

Gently, Basilia helped her mistress remove her blood-stained tunic and release one heavy blue-veined breast. Calsia guided the swollen raspberry nipple into the babe's hungry mouth.

While Calsia rocked and fed the child, her face in a glamour, oblivious to everything save the squirming, suckling bundle in her arms, Basilia devised the rest of her, no doubt, foolish scheme. She would not drown the other eight babies and be burdened with their restless souls the remainder of her life. She would take them away from the villa, away from Bracara Augusta, if necessary, and have them adopted by different families. If they were meant to survive, they would. Their fate would be up to the gods, not to her.

Deep inside, she heard her mage's voice. *There you go, Basilia, doing exactly the opposite of what I taught you.* But how could she be expected to drown eight baby girls? Surely that could not be the bleak Fate of these innocent babes?

Basilia knew about the secret passageway behind the bedstead that lead to the Governor's chamber, and from there down to the cellars and out to the villa's burial grounds. Once outside the villa grounds, the eight strange sisters of Liberata Wilgefortis would be safe.

She lined her basket with another woolen blanket and laid the three bigger babies on the bottom—six-fingered Seconda, clubfooted Sesta and the hermaphrodite Nona—and the four lightest on top, the tiny Terza in between the harelipped Quarta and Quinta and the armless Settima and Ottava. With the two longer ends of the blanket, she tied a tight knot in the middle, leaving the shorter ends tented at the sides to make sure the babies could breathe. She wrapped the viscid afterbirth in her own woolen apron and placed that in the basket next to the babes, then knelt before the shrine and invoked her own trinity of sacred goddesses—Brigit, Isis and Minerva—for protection that the basket would hold and that none of the babes would smother to death in the time it took her to escape from the Governor's home. Spotting a pouch of silver denarii on Calsia's table, she scooped it quickly into the basket. It was probably her midwife's fee, so she wasn't stealing. And she would need currency to carry out her plan. Unfortunately, she would not be able to call for the birthing chair the following day, but that mattered little, as Basilia's days as a midwife had come to an end. She eased her left arm under the handle of the basket and lifted the heavy load on to her shoulder. She could carry it if she wrapped her arm around the basket and stiffened her back.

"I am ready, Domina. I will need to take one of these lanterns."

For a moment, Calsia fixed her gaze on the midwife, narrowing her eyes as if unsure who she was or what she was doing in the room.

"I'm taking them away, now," Basilia added.

Calsia blinked repeatedly and remembered. "Yes, hurry! Let no one see you!"

"No one shall ever see me again, Domina."

Basilia walked over to the door and slid open the bolt. "Your maids will return shortly with your *calda*," said Basilia. "We must hurry before they come back or the Governor arrives."

"Did you take the afterbirth and the soiled bedding?"

"I left some of the bedding, Domina, as you did give birth, after all, and you were in labor for three days. It would look odd if there were no signs of the delivery."

"Be sure to bury the afterbirth in the riverbank where you drown them."

"I shall take care of everything, Domina. Fare thee well. And may you have a long and healthy life, young Liberata Wilgefortis."

The Lodestone

Basilia had a difficult time maneuvering herself and her weighty basket behind the heavy tapestry, but at last, she was through, and the nightmare of Calsia Marcella's nonuplet birth was behind her. In the Governor's chamber, the hearth had been lighted and the bedcovers had been turned down in anticipation of His Lordship's return. But the room was empty, and Basilia managed to shove her squirming cargo through the narrow portal behind the tapestry in the Governor's anteroom that would take her to the secret tunnels leading to the burial grounds outside the walls of the villa. Once out of doors and away from the guards, she could escape to her little house in the woods.

She carried the lantern in her free hand, careful to keep the ends of the swaddling away from the flaming wick. The shadow she cast on the damp limestone walls of the passageway was that of a woman with a majestic belly. *Majestic belly*, she laughed at her own little joke. *Makes sense,* she thought, *for it to look like I be giving a second birth to these poor souls.* But she stopped laughing when she approached the narrow rickety bridge that arched over what could only be the sewers of the villa. For a moment, Basilia felt the awful stench drawing her down. One misstep to either side would plunge her and her cargo into the putrid water. Her knees started to quiver, her shoulder cramped up to her neck, the arm clamped around the girth of the basket started to loosen its hold. *A fitting end,* she thought, *to save the babes from drowning in the Minho River only to plunge them to their deaths in the cesspool at the very bowels of their family home!*

Quite a redeemer you are, Basilia Quiteria! She could almost hear her mage laughing at her. The absurdity made her cackle.

Still cackling, she stayed her course, keeping one foot firmly in front of the other, and got across to the safety of the other side. Instead of drowning the eight babies, she would take them to her cousin, Placidus the blacksmith, whose wife had been barren all their married life. Maybe Placidus and Demetria would want to raise these babies on their own, or maybe Placidus' brother-in-law, Eustace, who was a priest of the secret cult of the Christians, would want to show them some charity.

Tolerant as Hadrian's empire was of different religions, the same could not be said of Governor Lucius Severus. The provinces of Lusitania and Gallaecia were still governed by the laws of Nero. If the Governor even suspected that a midwife employed in his own house had Christian acquaintances, or that she, herself, was a practitioner of the old ways of the Druidae, he would have had her tied to a tree and burned alive, and she would never have been able to attend to Calsia's delivery of his noble spawn.

Now Basilia had to make good on the silent promise she had made to save the babies' lives. Outside the walls of the Governor's villa, she let the hefty basket slip to the ground. She couldn't carry it a step further. Her hands had become claws from gripping the handle so hard, the throb in her neck more excruciating, her thirst unbearable. The babies had been quiet through the tunnels, but now, in the cold midnight air, with the fog of the sea rolling in, they whimpered and started to thrash their little legs. Basilia squatted to urinate, the pain in her back gripping her buttocks. Sensing her impervious to their cries, the babies started to wail, and Basilia knew she could not risk calling attention to herself.

Walk through the woods, Basilia. *Remember your training as a creature of the woods*. In the early days of her training as a Druid, Ovidius had taught her how to focus her eyes in the darkness, to listen to silence and to smell fear in her surroundings. In this way, she learned to pay attention to the lodestone of her own inner compass.

"Hush!" she ordered the babies, "or do you want to lose your little heads before you're even a day old?"

The babies stilled. No doubt they were hungry, but Basilia had nothing to give them. She picked up the basket again and swung it over her other shoulder. Keeping one foot in front of the other, trusting that her feet knew where to go, she ended up standing outside the gate to her cottage in the wee dark hours of the morning.

Somehow, the cracks in the wattle and daub of her round house were aglow, smoke was curling out of the hole at the peak of the thatched roof, and she could hear voices coming from inside. *What is going on in there?* she wondered, dragging the basket into her overgrown kitchen garden. On the side of the house, she spotted two mules and two carts.

"Who goes there?" a man came out to the doorway and called out.

"This is my home, sir, what are you doing inside it?"

"Sila? It's your cousin, Placidus."

"Placidus? What are you doing here?"

It was not by pure chance that Placidus had come to visit Basilia. She suspected Ovidius had had something to do with why he was here. She lugged the basket with both hands, barely able to walk under the weight of all those babies. Placidus rushed down to the garden to help with the basket. Basilia collapsed to her knees. Placidus helped her up. Another man walked toward them. Eustace, the Christian.

"Steady, Basilia."

"What have you got here, Sila?" asked Placidus. He lifted the basket effortlessly and carried it inside with one hand.

"Can you walk, sister?" asked Eustace, still holding on to her arm while they walked slowly toward the doorstep.

She nodded. "I'm fine, sir. But I can assure you, I am not your sister. And I still don't understand what all of you are doing in my house."

"It was Ovidius, the healer," said Eustace. "He stopped by the temple and told us to get over here right away, that you were going to be needing our help."

"How did he know where I live? He has never been here."

"He told us to follow the lodestone," said Eustace. "Apparently, there is a lodestone under your hearth pit. We just pointed our compass toward it, and here we are."

"How does he even know who you are?"

"He called himself the Great Mage of the Order of Owls."

"The Order of Owls?" Basilia frowned. "He never said anything to me about any owls."

Eustace laughed. "Don't vex yourself, Basilia. Come, let me help you onto the doorstone."

She let herself be guided gently up over the threshold of her home.

Inside, Placidus had placed the basket on Basilia's long board table in the middle of the room but had not yet removed the cover.

"Let me do it," Basilia said, untying the knots of the fleece. "Might as well show everybody what Fortuna has bequeathed to us."

"You should not blaspheme in front of Eustace, Sila," said Placidus. "He is a Christian priest, he does not believe in the Roman gods."

Eustace waved away the comment. "God is one, and one is God," he said.

Basilia opened the fleece and all of them peered into the basket. Demetria and Aurelia both covered their mouths with their hands. Even Placidus stifled a cry.

"Wherever did you get all these babies, Basilia?" asked Demetria, her eyes agape. "They look like newborns."

"Aye, they came out of the Governor's wife, Lady Calsia. She was sickened by them, so she wanted me to take them away and expose them, drown them in the Minho River, but I will not."

"But why?" asked Placidus, raising Nona into his arms. "This little boy is stunning! Look at his red hair!"

"It is not a little boy, Placidus," said Basilia. "Look beneath."

Placidus frowned and raised the tiny penis with a finger.

"*Jesu Cristus!*" cried Aurelia.

"It's a girl?" asked Placidus.

"It's both," said Basilia. "It's a hermaphrodite."

"Aurelia, look at this one," said Demetria, lifting out Seconda. "Is this one the same . . . "

"No, look at her hands," said Basilia.

"Six fingers," said Demetria, gently stroking the sixth digit on each hand.

"Look at the feet of this other one!" exclaimed Aurelia.

"Clubfeet," said Basilia. "But she's a full girl. All of them but Nona are full girls."

"Why do you call her Nona, Basilia?" said Placidus.

"She's number nine," said Basilia. "Born last."

"If she's a hermaphrodite, she is part Hermes and part Aphrodite, and surely that deserves a better name. Would you mind Basilia, if we call her Herminia?"

"Placidus, you just corrected Basilia for naming a Roman god, and here you are naming two Greek ones," scolded Demetria.

"Are you lifting her up, then, Placidus?" asked Basilia. "If you are giving her a name, do you want to keep her, him, it?"

Placidus looked at Demetria, and Demetria shrugged then nodded, tears welling in her blue eyes.

"Yes!" said Placidus, taking the baby over to his wife. "Look, Demetria, God has given us a child, after all."

Aurelia peered into the basket. "There's more," she said, reaching her arms down, but Eustace stayed her grasp.

"Are they all . . . like that one?" asked Eustace.

"Tell us about these babes, Basilia," said Placidus. "Are you giving them out to whomever will take them?"

"I was hoping to, yes. I cannot bring myself to drown them."

"You would make a good Christian," said Eustace.

"I shall never give up on my goddesses, sir."

Aurelia reached into the basket again and took out one of the harelipped girls.

"There's two of these," said Aurelia, handing them both to Eustace, who handed them to Placidus.

"And two of these," added Aurelia, taking out the armless babes. "You poor things!"

Eustace recoiled. "What is that?" he almost shouted, waking Settima and Ottava, who started to wail.

At hearing their sister's cries, the others woke and joined in. Demetria rocked Nona and the harelipped girls. Aurelia soothed the others.

"We can take one, too," said Eustace. "Perhaps the six-fingered one."

"Seconda," said Basilia, a sudden fatigue overcoming her and making her dizzy.

"You're swaying, Sila," Placidus pointed out. "You look exhausted."

"Three days of labor and a very hard birth for the poor Domina. But at least she kept the firstborn. That one is perfect."

Basilia leaned against the table to steady herself.

"Not to mention a long walk from the Governor's villa carrying this basket," added Placidus. "Sit down, cousin," he said, dragging a wooden stool over to the table. "Give her some wine, Demetria."

"Here, Basilia," said Eustace, "let me cut you a piece of the bread we brought."

Basilia ate and drank like one coming out of a very long fast, explaining everything between bites and swallows. Despite the hunger and thirst, she could feel herself drifting off and had to pinch herself to stay awake.

The women wept, and they all agreed to help Basilia with her outlandish plan to safeguard the innocent babes. Eustace and his wife would raise not just Seconda, but also the tiniest one, Terza. Placidus and Demetria the hermaphrodite and Sesta the clubfoot. Eustace knew two families, he said, who lived in the neighboring towns who would, he was sure, take the harelipped or the armless pairs. Placidus and Eustace would take care of everything.

"Leave it to us, Basilia," Eustace reassured her. "The babes will land in good homes with good families like ours."

Basilia fell asleep at the board, and Placidus carried her frail body to the pallet on which she slept. Taking the eight babies with them, Placidus and Eustace loaded up their mule-drawn carts and set off for their respective homes in Bracara Augusta.

The next day, Basilia went with Eustace to deliver the remaining two sets of babes. A family of dwarves took Settima and Ottava. Quarta and Quinta were left in the care of an older couple from Eustace's parish. Each family was paid ten denarii for their trouble. They had said nothing about the other sisters to either of the families, only that the twins' mother had passed on at childbirth and that the innocents needed a safe and loving home.

The Mage

When Basilia returned home, she prepared herself for a visit from Ovidius. It was forbidden for Druidae to change the course of anybody's fate, especially those who could not make any choices for themselves. Basilia had done just that by saving the lives of the nine sisters. She did not expect to find Ovidius weeding her kitchen garden when she returned.

"Hello Basilia," he said in his sonorous voice.

"Master," she bowed low. "Have you been waiting long? I had no idea you were coming."

He stretched a thin, tremulous hand at her to help him get to his feet. "It's true. I do not come out very often since the passing of my mule, but I live closer to Bracara Augusta now, and the walk has done me good."

They walked inside and he gestured for her to take a seat at the board. He was full of pleasantries and seemed not the least bit angry or in a hurry, shuffling his long feet over to the hearth where he had already lighted a fire and started a cauldron of water to boil. His powers were such that all he had to do was imagine something and it would manifest.

"Thank you, master, for heating the water. How can I be of service?" From her herbarium, she took down an earthen jar filled with dried calendula blossoms to make tea, placed some of the dried stems and blossoms into clay cups, and waited for the water to boil.

"Are you practicing *goetia*, now, Basilia?" he asked.

"*Goetia*? Why do you ask me that, master?"

"Don't play the fool. We both know what you did with those eight babies."

He ladled some of the boiling water into each cup and let the infusion steep.

"I couldn't bear the thought of those poor innocent babes being put to death. That would have been so cruel. Why do you call that *goetia*?"

"It is a low breed of *magea*, my daughter. I do not teach *goetia*, only *theurgia*. If you cannot abide by the laws of *theurgia* . . . "

"Is there no reward for saving nine lives, then?"

"If you want a reward for your magic, Basilia, you have learned nothing and I refuse to continue as your mage."

"Of course not, master. I meant, is that not good magic? Should I not be praised instead of scolded?"

She handed him a cup of tea, but he did not respond. Magically, a round loaf of barley bread appeared on the table. A flask of olive oil. Some dried fish. She tore the bread and separated the fish, drizzled oil on everything and handed him a plate.

"This will one day be a bakery," he told her, biting into his bread with darkened gums.

She ate her own bread, savoring the rich briny taste of the mackerel, and sipped her tea, not knowing what else to say. He held his plate out for more food, and now, a wedge of cheese appeared. She sliced the cheese, another chunk of bread, more olive oil, and handed him another full plate.

"Thank you for the food, master," she said, wondering why making food appear could be considered high magic but not saving nine innocent lives.

Of course, saving lives is good magic, my daughter, he said, but his mouth was busy chewing up his food. She realized he was speaking to her through his thoughts.

When they are meant to be saved. The Fate of those nine girls has already been determined. You may have extended their lives, Basilia, but you did not save them. Alas, you may have even doomed them.

She wanted to answer him, but he shook his head, tapped his forehead and waited for her to speak to him using her own thoughts.

How could I have known that, master? she thought, amazed at this new skill. *It did not occur to me that there could be anything worse than their being drowned by my own hand.*

You must live a hermit's existence, he said. *You need more study, and more years of solitude to contemplate the errors of your ways. You are not yet ready to be initiated into the Druidae.*

She finished her tea. "How many years, master?" she asked with her voice.

"As many as it takes for the nine of them to find their singular path again."

And what will happen to my house, my practice? I have many women who rely on my midwifery skills, master. Am I to just abandon my whole life here?

Anybody can be a midwife. It is your skill with magea that will right things in the end. Until then, I will be watching you, Basilia Drusilla Quiteria! Do not try to fool me. You will know when it is time to come back home.

Where am I to go, master?

I'm taking you to my own cave to the north. It is several days away and gets very cold at night.

Should I wear something different, more ceremonial, perhaps? Or am I to stay in this clothing the whole time? Will there be food to eat?

Bring nothing but a blanket and the afterbirth you brought back from the birthing. This will keep you nourished for years. Are you ready?

He put down his empty cup and plate, picked up his blue crystal wand and blew on it until the wand glowed bright purple, then white.

Are we leaving right now, master? I have not even had time to wash up . . .

There's no time to lose, Basilia. You, too, have a destiny to fulfill, and it must begin now.

Suddenly, a fierce wind pushed them out the door and upwards into the night sky. She clung to his robe, looking down at the pointy thatched roof of the little Celtic house she had found in ruins so many decades ago and restored to a plain but comfortable dwelling. She was going to miss her old house. Whirling around them, in a vortex of night and wind and stars, she saw pages and pages of magical writings.

Master? she asked in her thoughts. *Are you with me?*

I will always be with you, Basilia Drusilla Quiteria. I will let you know when it is time to return to Bracara Augusta. If ever.

The Strange Child

I love my baby girl, but I curse the midwife, Basilia Quiteria, Calsia wrote in her scroll. *I curse her for deceiving me, for making me believe that this baby would be normal one day. It has been two years, and the baby has more hair than ever. I had to shave her little face and body when she was born so that her father would pick her up and name her as his daughter. He has not seen her since, but now he insists on arranging a marriage for her and wants to see how she is developing. If he sees her like this, there is no telling what he might do to her. Please help me, Juno Lucina.*

Lucius pounded on Calsia's door again. "Open up, Calsia!" he ordered. "I demand to see my daughter."

Calsia looked on the sleeping child in her crib and felt pity for her as well as a great love and a great revulsion, for the child had not shed the furry down she had been born with, and now she was entirely covered in a fine red hair. The only solution was to shave the baby's face and arms every third day, for that is how long it took for the hair to grow back.

"Leave her be, Lucius," she called out. "The girl is sleeping."

"How long do you mean to keep her away from me, Calsia?" Lucius Severus yelled from the other side of the door. "I have some viable suitors arriving tomorrow, and she will need to be present to make their acquaintance."

Calsia got up and approached the door. She would not open it now or ever, if she could help it. At all costs, she could not let Lucius see the girl in her natural state, else he was likely to drown her himself.

"Leave us be, Lucius," she hissed through the door. "She's but two years old, she doesn't need to be meeting any suitors right now. Are you so anxious to be rid of your own daughter?"

She pressed her ear to the door and held her breath until at last, she heard him stomp away.

I cannot continue to shave the child, Calsia wrote, *for the hair that was fine and downy is now growing back thicker and fuller. If this continues, she will have a man's beard by the time of her betrothal. Lucius means to tie her hand to a suitor much earlier, but I will not allow it.*

Calsia rolled up the scroll and slipped it into the mouth of the large earthenware vase where she hid her letters to her matron goddess.

Another knock on the door, much softer this time.

"Yes, Gaius, is that you?"

"Yes, Mama. I have the lyre you gave me. Can I play something for my little sister, Liberata?"

"That is very sweet of you, Gaius, but your sister is sleeping right now."

"I can wait until she wakes up. Meanwhile, I can play for you, Mama."

Her son's utter sweetness broke Calsia's heart. The same quality offended his father, for he wanted a boy who liked to hunt and go to the races, not one who preferred the company of a lyre. With no daughter to distract him, Lucius doted on his son, hiring the best teachers in the province to give him his reading and writing lessons, taking him weekly to see the gladiators in the Circus and teaching him how to hunt and kill wild beasts.

❧ ❧ ❧

"Why does Mother keep you locked up?" her brother asked through the door.

Wilgefortis was six years old, and she had not been allowed to set foot outside her room in that time. "Because of my face. She doesn't want Father to see me like this," said the girl.

"What's wrong with your face? Is it ugly? I heard the nurse say it was monstrous."

"It's furry, and Mama comes to shave it every morning."

The boy laughed. He thought she was joking. "No, really," he said, "what's wrong with you?"

"Nothing," said the girl. "I'm just me. This is how I am."

"Can I play you another song?"

"No, I'm tired, Gaius. Maybe tomorrow you can bring me something from the garden."

"What would you like? A fig, a pear, a flower . . . "

"Bring me something that you've never brought me. Bring me a toad."

"A toad? Aren't you afraid of them?"

"I have never even seen a toad, how am I supposed to be afraid of it?"

"How do you know you want a toad, if you've never seen one?"

"I heard the nurse say something about toads having magical powers. Maybe a toad will help me get out of this room."

"How will I be able to give you this toad if you can't open the door?"

"Don't worry about it. I have a secret to share."

"What secret? Can't you share it now?"

"No, not until you bring me my toad."

"They're very ugly, you know. Toads. And if they urinate on you, you'll get very sick and could even die."

"I know. That's what Nurse said."

"Are you trying to die?"

"Don't be silly. I just want to have a pet, that's all."

"Why don't you ask Mama for a bird?"

"I don't like birds. Are you going to bring me my toad, or not?"

"Yes! I'll bring you a toad every night if you want, but only if you tell me what your secret is right now."

"When you come see me tomorrow, don't come up the stairs. Go under the stairs on the second floor and you will find a secret door. Just push on the stone behind the statue, and the door will open. You can come up to my room through the secret passageway. Nobody will know where you are."

"Have you been going outside through this secret passage? Are those your footprints that we find every morning by the back door?"

❧ ❧ ❧

"Why don't you play your lyre for me anymore, Gaius?"

"I'm fourteen, now. Father doesn't want me to play the lyre any more, little sister."

"What news of my future husband?"

"I told you, Father is deciding between a Prefect and a Senator. The Senator has a higher rank and is requesting more of a dowry, but the Prefect is younger and will probably sire more sons."

"Have they mated you with anybody, Gaius?"

"Father wants me to join the legion. I want to go to Rome and study law. Mother just cries."

"I will cry, too, if you go to Rome *or* join the legion, Gaius. Please don't leave me here all alone."

"If I become a gladiator, I will still live in Bracara and can come visit you every day."

"Oh, Gaius! Tell me again what it's like? The Circus, the games and races. I so wish I could go with you and Father tomorrow."

"Father has taken ill. Mother will not let me go to the Circus without him. She says there are too many slavers around, looking for the next young gladiator to kidnap. Father won't even let me go with one of the guards. They tell me I'm a young man, now, but they continue to treat me like a child."

"Let's go, Gaius. You have your own horse. I would so love to see the games with you. Will you take me, Gaius? You don't need Mother and Father's permission anymore."

"I don't, do I? How is it that you are so much braver than I am, locked up as you've been your whole life, little sister?"

"I think it's all those toads you've brought me, big brother. I think it's their urine that makes me strong."

❧ ❧ ❧

Wilgefortis stared at the full moon outside her window and felt nothing but loneliness. She missed her brother, Gaius Lucius, more than even their mother, who had now also stopped visiting. Was it her fault Gaius was dead? Maybe Father had been right about not letting him go to the *Ludi Apollinares* by himself. Maybe if he had not taken so long trying to find the key to her room, he would have missed the lightning storm and nothing would have happened to him, save a scolding from Father for having disobeyed him.

"Maybe I should not have begged him to take me," she said to Freya and Nabia, the largest and oldest of her toads. "Is it my fault he's dead?"

Freya stared at her with one eye, Nabia with the other. Their heavy throats moved as they spoke, one echoing the other:

Gaius was a grown boy. He died because it was his time to die. But worry not, for he will visit you again, many times, and he will keep bringing you gifts from the other side. And he will continue to play his lyre for you, even when you hang on a cross.

She was too distraught to dwell on the riddles of the toads. She looked at all the things her brother had brought her over the years, other than the toads, the rocks and dried flowers and small wooden animals he had carved for her. She picked up a turtle and a lion and held them against her chest.

"Oh, Gaius! Who's going to make toys for me now?" she cried.

She remembered watching him gallop away from the villa in his magnificent black Galician pony. It was before first light, and from her window, she could see as far as the sea to the west, and as far as the High Road to the east. She saw the whole thing, the bolt of lightning that shot through the stormy sky, aimed for the huge cork oak tree that Mother said had stood at the gates of the villa for generations. The tree split in half and exploded into flames. The Galician pony her brother was riding suddenly reared on its hind legs, threw her brother into the flaming oak tree and fell on top of him.

Long days of mourning followed, with keeners hired to wail at the funeral rites while Wilgefortis, her mother and her father mourned in stoic silence. She was twelve years old and it was the first time since her birth that Wilgefortis had been let out in public, the first time since her birth that Father had seen her with his own eyes.

It wasn't until after her brother's sarcophagus was lowered into the family catacombs that her mother allowed herself to weep. And then, she wept for days, and days turned into weeks, and weeks into months, and still her mother mourned the death of her son. Her father ordered that his daughter join him for the *cena* every evening, so that he would not have to eat alone in the big atrium, now that his wife refused to leave her chambers.

But Liberata, as her father called her, was too despondent to eat. Gaius had been her only friend, her only confidante and through him she had come to know things about their father that perhaps a daughter should never know. That he had two other families in town. That he took slave boys into the bath house. That he gambled on how long it would take the gladiators to get disemboweled by wild beasts in the Circus. And now she was expected to sit beside this man she did not know, who glared at her under his black eyebrows most of the time and ate like a dog, chewing on bones and casting them over his shoulder, talking with his mouth so stuffed, pieces of food would fly out of his teeth. He did not notice that she only picked at her food, but never ate.

The girl was left alone with her grief, and the only one attentive to how much the girl's health was waning from her mourning fast was her brother's ghost.

When at last Calsia emerged from her long months of mourning, she was surprised to see Wilgefortis coming down the stairs for the evening meal.

"What do you think you're doing?" she hissed at her daughter. "Get back up to your *cubiculum* at once."

"But why, Mother? Father expects me to sit with him as I have done every night since we buried Gaius. You locked yourself away and he did not want to be alone."

"You have been sitting with him every night? What about the hair, who has been shaving it for you?"

"The hair is all gone, Mother, can you not tell?"

Calsia clapped her hands over her cheeks. "No more beard on your pretty face? Praise Juno!"

The girl nodded. "No more hairy face, Mother. It all fell out. Sadly, the hair on my head is falling out, too."

The girl reached up and pulled out a clump from her head. "The hair on my eyebrows is all gone. Even the private parts are free of hair."

"How did it happen?" asked Calsia, turning her daughter's chin from side to side to examine her skin carefully. "Did you eat something different?"

"I think the trick is not to eat much, Mother. I have had very little food in me all this time, just water and one biscuit a day with a bit of honey. The hair on my head is falling out, but the other hair on my face and body has not grown back."

"Praise be to Juno Lucina," uttered Calsia.

Because of her eating habits, Wilgefortis grew gaunt, her hair thinned out, dropping in handfuls when Calsia brushed what used to be her daughter's ruddy locks. Even the girl's teeth seemed overlarge in her mouth. Although he could not explain the reason for his daughter's sudden ugliness, her husband grew more and more repulsed by the girl's appearance, until finally, he could not stomach the idea of sharing a meal with her and had food sent up to her rooms instead. *To save you the trouble of coming downstairs*, he wrote in a note to his daughter, *it would be best if you dined in the comfort of your own quarters*. Calsia knew he couldn't bear to look at what the girl was becoming.

"What's wrong with the girl, Calsia? She's so skinny and ugly now. If she continues to look like that, there will be no suitor to take her off our hands. When is her blood going to flow so that we can marry her off?"

"In time, Lucius, in time."

Calsia dared not set foot in the topmost *cubiculum* on the third story. But in her bedchamber, she performed the rituals and sacrifices necessary to invoke the blessings of Juno, goddess of women, Mena, goddess of a woman's blood and Cybele, Magna Mater, to help bring on the girl's menses. No matter what she offered them, fruit, fragrant resins or pretty birds, nothing worked.

The Cave

Basilia had fallen asleep over her reading again, hunched over a stack of scrolls inside the Cave of the Mages, where she had already lived for more than a decade. At first, every time she heard horse's hooves clattering in front of the entrance, she would run to hide in the deepest corner of the cave, terrified that the Governor's secret spies were looking for her. She still had nightmares of being arrested for the treachery she had committed with Lady Calsia's eight babies.

Basilia kept herself alive on nuts and berries that she scavenged in the woods and bits of the afterbirth she had taken from Calsia's chamber that night, dried like jerky but still filled with the magical properties that had kept her vital all these years. She studied the Grimoires and Books of Shadows that Ovidius had written and collected during his own time of study in the Cave of Mages. She read all of the books written by Ovidius' ancestor, the fifteen-book *Metamorphhosis* more than once, the forty-book *Bibliotheca historica* of Diodurous Siculus, Pythagoras' texts on numbers and musical harmony, Heraclitus' mediations on opposites, the atomistic theory of Epicurus and Cicero's Latin translation of Plato's *Politeia*. To read the eighteen books of the *Hermetica* of Hermes Trismegistus, she had had to remember how to read Greek.

Every morning she cut cordwood with a rusty axe she had found in the cave, took a brisk walk in the woods, bathed in sunlight or rain, autumn leaves or snow, gathered nuts and berries. In the afternoons, she rested. At night, she read her scrolls, her eyes burning from the smoky tallow of the lantern.

She had no idea she would love the solitude so much. Here and there, she remembered her old life as a midwife, but the memory of the nine babies of Calsia Marcella made her profoundly sad, so she tried not to think about them.

And then one day she found a basket of food outside the cave, a round loaf of crusty bread and a hefty chunk of sharp cheese. There was nobody about, and at first, she was afraid to take it, fearing it was a trap. She hovered by the entrance to the cave, waiting in the shadows to catch a glimpse of whomever had left the basket. Her mouth kept watering profusely, until at last, she could stand the temptation no longer and grabbed the bread and the cheese out of the basket and hurried to the back of the cave to gobble it up in one sitting. She retched for two days, her body no longer accustomed to eating rich food.

Another day, she found a clay pot filled with *polta*, a huge bunch of green grapes and a jug of curdled goat milk. She savored the pork and chickpea porridge, but stretched it out across three sittings, saving the grapes and goats' milk for her evening meals. How odd to have forgotten what real food tasted like, how comforting it felt in her mouth and sliding down her gullet. She had stopped wondering who the provider of the food was, certain that it could only be the *mouras* of the forest. Why the fairy folk would be providing for her, when it was usually the other way around, for people to provide for the fairies, she could not say, nor did it matter.

The third time food appeared at the cave entrance, she found a string of salty sausages, a dozen fresh figs and a rusty mug of *posca*. She quaffed the drink in three deep swallows and belched loud before biting, first, into one of the sausages, followed by a few bites of fig, eating slowly, lying sideways and savoring each mouthful like a patrician, until late at night.

After that, a package appeared, wrapped in threadbare linen. Someone had left her a pair of worn soldier's sandals, the soles studded in iron. Inside the shoes, there was a handwritten note from her mage:

You have lived in solitude for twelve years, Basilia Quiteria, and I am pleased with the progress you have made in your studies. This is the last time I will contact you. Take heed. You are needed again in Bracara Augusta, but do not divulge your real name. This is your only chance to make things right. Ovidius.

I should have known, thought Basilia. *He always said he would never be too far to know what I was doing.*

It had to have been Ovidius making food appear, awakening the appetites she had taught herself to ignore. Now, there was no more food. Her belly complained, a strong gurgling that made her nauseous all day. The nuts and berries that had become her usual fare now felt like rocks between her loosened teeth, and there was but one sliver of leathery afterbirth left. The clear cold water that dripped steadily down the rocky wall of the cave now tasted of saltpeter. The time had come to leave her hermit existence. The hunger was killing her.

She slipped into the sandals, fitting tight against her swollen feet, the iron studs on the bottom making a loud clacking sound as she walked. She took nothing with her but the rusty mug and the denarii that had remained after she and Eustace had delivered the last of the twins to their adoptive families. She used the threadbare piece of linen to roll up the coins and tie the bundle to her waist.

Oh triple-faced Mother of the Moon, protect me! she entreated as she set off to whatever new life awaited her.

Return of the Midwife

Nobody recognized the midwife, Basilia Drusilla Quiteria, in the town of Bracara Augusta any more. They saw only an indigent old woman with grey hair matted into long, thick ropes, her shorn feet caked with years of grime and blood, her finger- and toenails like yellow claws. The stench emanating from her tattered clothes made anyone who crossed her path wince in revulsion. Even the drunks, who congregated in the town square to taunt and leer at any female who walked past, turned away from her. A few kind souls dropped a coin into her mug, recoiling quickly. Basilia wanted to laugh. She had never felt this kind of power, this ability to draw sympathy and disgust at the same time.

Even her cousin the blacksmith, who was unloading cords of chopped wood from his old cart in front of his shop, did not recognize her until she called him Placito, the pet name she had used to call him when they were children.

"Basilia Quiteria? Are you a specter risen from the dead, or is that really you?"

She put a gnarled finger to her lips. She did not want him to reveal her disguise. He could not bring himself to hug her, but allowed her to dip her rusty mug into the iron basin of water bubbling next to his forge. She gulped the boiling water with a voracious thirst, guzzling two more mugs before she squatted and let her urine flow on the dirt floor.

It was Placidus who told her that the eight sisters were back together, all of them living with Eustace and his wife in what used to be Basilia's house. Somehow, they had all found their way back to the lodestone in her hearth. The dwarves who had taken in the armless pair had been murdered, and the girls sold to a brothel, where they had been discovered by Aurelia herself, who would minister to the girls and women in that brothel. The harelipped pair had escaped their adoptive home and somehow found their way back to their sisters in Bracara Augusta. Even the two that Placidus and Demetria were raising cried bitterly each time they got together with their sisters and had to separate, begging Placidus to let them remain with Eustace and Aurelia.

"I need to see them," she said. "Can you take me to my house, cousin? Nothing looks the same anymore."

"Your house is gone, Sila. It has become an *insula*."

"I want to see the girls," said Basilia. "I care not about my old house."

"Only after you wash up, Basilia. You smell worse than a three-day old carcass."

She cackled and showed what was left of her yellow teeth. He went to the back of his shop and brought back a large half-barrel that he used for soaking his largest shields after their final forging, scooped hot water from the boiling basin into the barrel tub and hung a metal *strigil* off the lip of the tub.

"That's one of my own scrubbers," he indicated, "very popular with the bath houses."

Basilia was not paying attention to him. She had stripped off her crusty clothes and was already stepping into the hot water, naked and wrinkled, but gleeful as a little girl. He gathered up the stinking clothes and threw them into the flames of the forge.

The stifling stench of the burning cloth and the fish smell emanating from his cousin as she scrubbed happily at her rancid flesh made him gag.

"I'll go get you something clean to wear," he muttered, covering his nose and mouth. He bolted upstairs to his living quarters above the shop.

"What is that hideous smell?" his wife, Demetria, said, crinkling her nose.

"I've taken in a beggar woman," he said, "and she needs fresh clothes." Why had he lied to her? Demetria knew who Basilia was, and it would have been good for them to greet each other. But he realized he did not want his wife to see Basilia as she looked in her present condition. It would be undignified.

Used to her husband's excessive charity by now, Demetria shook her head and rolled her eyes. She stopped what she was doing, took a threadbare tunic and a thin cloak from a trunk and thrust everything at her husband.

"That's all I can spare," Demetria said.

"This will do."

"Where do you propose to put her up, Placidus, on the roof with your other strays?"

"She won't be staying here. I'm taking her to Eustace."

"Praise Jesus," said his wife. "But why?"

"Why not? He and Aurelia need help with all those girls."

❧ ❧ ❧

Placidus lifted Basilia into his cart, surprised at how light she was, and took her across town. Basilia felt lost. What had once been the outskirts of Bracara Augusta where her little house was located had become part of the town, now, and the trees had been cut down and rendered into shacks and blocks of houses with rented rooms.

How had Bracara Augusta become a bustling city in just twelve years? she wondered. Once her house had been a free-standing dwelling, a round house in the Celtic style, the woven branches of the round walls daubed with clay and dung, and a high, sloped roof thatched with rye. All that was left of her old home was the hearth pit, over which a great brick oven had been built. A three-story *insula* rose above and around it, so that now what would have been her house formed the lower floor of an apartment building, and where her hearth pit had once stood had now become a bakery. On the upper floors, lines of laundry hung across the narrow street that connected the two sides of the *insula*. The apartment building's din was deafening.

Basilia and Placidus stood in the road gazing on the eight red-headed girls who were helping Eustace in the *pistrinum*. Eustace was removing the baked loaves from the wide mouth of the great oven with a long wooden spatula, sweeping them into baskets that one pair of the girls carried to the counter to stack and sell. The tallest of them, long-boned and lanky as a boy, chopped wood and carried armloads of logs to the oven. The armless pair tended the fire under the oven by working two huge bellows with their feet. The hare-lipped pair kneaded the dough into damp loaves and handed them to Eustace to place inside the oven. The six-fingered one and the one that hobbled when she walked stood at the counter selling bread, while their sister, the midget, counted coins.

"Look at them, Basilia!" whispered Placidus. "Those are the lives you saved."

They were strong, strapping girls on the brink of young woman-hood, all with unruly red hair sticking out in all directions, and eyes like gray ice, exactly like their mother's. All of them wore white aprons over blue tunics, even Eustace.

"Are any of them promised in marriage?"

"They have all consecrated their virginity to Jesus Christ," said Placidus. "In the evenings, they minister to any Christian in town who has been maimed or mistreated for his beliefs. Even as young as they are, they are evangelists of the highest order."

Basilia and Placidus approached the front of the bakery, and Basilia noticed that each of the girls wore what looked like a neck-lace of small black beads, from which dangled a tiny fish carved in wood. Basilia felt the hair on her arms stand up, but she kept her mouth shut.

The girls recognized Placidus and dropped their chores to run out and greet him, each taking a turn to kiss him on the cheek and call him "uncle." Nobody knew who Basilia was. Even though her clothes were clean and her body washed, the long rolls of matted hair, her thickly calloused feet and blackened nails spoke to them of Basilia's beggarliness.

"Girls, this is the cousin that I grew up with, Basilia Drusilla Quiteria. She is a hermit recently come out of solitude, as you can tell by her appearance, and she seeks an audience with your father."

Eustace had been left to tend the oven by himself. From inside the bakery, he raised a hand to greet Placidus. Upstairs, on the second-floor gallery, Eustace's wife, Aurelia, leaned against the railing, eating an apple.

"Mama!" the smallest of the girls called out to Aurelia. "Can we give this lady with Uncle Placidus something to eat? She looks like she's starving."

The hobbled one went to the counter and took a loaf of bread.

"Here you go, Old Mother," said the girl.

"Thank you, Sesta," said Basilia.

The girl's eyes widened and she looked up at her mother. "The lady knows my name, Mama."

"Did they all keep the numerical names I gave them?" Basilia asked Placidus.

"It seems so, Sila. I had forgotten it was you who named them such."

It wasn't long before Eustace came outside, wiping flour from his hands on his apron. He clapped his arms around Placidus, then turned to look at Basilia with kind eyes.

"Welcome, Old Mother. Our home is your home."

"My home is no longer," said Basilia.

"Do you recognize her, Aurelia?" Placidus asked the woman in the gallery.

"How could I not?" said Aurelia. "Godspeed to you, Basilia. I thought you died long ago."

"We remember you now," the girls said in unison, and everyone laughed.

"I think not, girls," said Basilia. "The last time I saw you, you were but a day old."

"But we've all seen you in our dreams," said the shortest of the girls.

"Do you know who we are?" asked one of the harelips. Her cleft had healed more thoroughly than her sister's, but she was still disfigured by the scar.

"You two are Quarta and Quinta," said Basilia, "though I cannot tell who is who."

She looked at the tall one, "Nona, yes?" The girl shook her head, and said "My name is Herminia, Old Mother."

"Settima and Ottava," she named the armless pair. "And you, little thing, are Terza."

Terza jumped up and down.

She gazed on their hands. "Seconda, you can't hide from old Basilia," she said, making the six-fingered girl smile.

"And you're Sesta," she said, touching the girl's cheek, to keep from looking down again at the horse's hooves that the girl's feet had become, the feet twisted inward, ankles gnarled like tree roots.

"The years have been hard on you, Old Mother," said Eustace, leading her by the arm into the bakery. "You look famished and about to faint from thirst. Come upstairs and rest yourself."

In the heat of the shop, the aroma of baking bread overpowered her for a moment. Basilia swooned but Placidus steadied her from behind as they followed Eustace up the stairs to their living quarters on the second floor.

"We will be having supper soon," said Aurelia. "Won't you both sup with us? It's just fish head *polta*, but we have plenty of bread."

"My shop awaits," said Placidus. "I must get back before my wife burns everything down. But I will take a loaf if I may."

"Of course, brother!" Eustace patted Placidus on the back. "I will go down with you to close the bakery. You can take as much bread as you wish. And don't worry. We will look after our old friend, here, won't we, Aurelia?" He looked back at his wife, who was busy covering the birdcages that hung in the gallery.

"As if she were the girls' own grandmother," the wife called out.

The girls shrieked in glee.

Placidus put his arms around Basilia and hugged her tight. "You're home now, cousin," he whispered. "I was so worried I'd never see you again."

"Come, Basilia," said Aurelia, directing her to a bench by the front door. "Please take a seat so that we may wash your feet."

"Oh, no, that would be offensive," Basilia started to complain, but two of the girls helped Basilia to the bench. She took a seat and leaned back against the warm plaster of the whitewashed wall while four of the girls dragged a heavy basin of clean water from a separate room off the gallery. A third approached her with a rough sponge and a fourth with a bucket of greasy soap. Basilia's feet had not been scrubbed for twelve years. By the time the girls had finished scouring the caked mud and blood and excrement from the calloused bottoms of her feet, the water was black, the sponge was coming apart and the soap had dwindled to less than a quarter of the bucket. Her feet tingled from the scrubbing. The blackened nails looked even dirtier against her clean feet.

"We will get to those talons tomorrow," said Aurelia. "Girls, drag the basin to the *latrina*, and then wash up for supper," she ordered. Aurelia walked to the railing and called down to Eustace.

"Don't forget to bring up some loaves, Eustace. We'll need at least four."

❧ ❧ ❧

They sat Basilia at one end of the table and Eustace took the other. All held hands for Eustace's blessing of the food, and all but Basilia murmured "amen" after the prayer. Surrounded by eight pairs of bright grey eyes and mouths moving up and down, chewing food and talking so fast she could barely discern the mixed language they were speaking, Basilia slurped her fish-head soup and savored her crust of dark bread slathered with honey. After having lived so long in solitude, she found it difficult to follow their cacophony of conversations, but she was enjoying their company and being called Old Mother.

It was right to have saved their lives, Basilia thought, wiping a tear from the corner of her eye.

"I heard they're looking for a new nurse at the castle," Aurelia was saying.

"Another one so soon?" said Eustace.

"We have heard that the girl is troubled," said one of the harelipped girls.

"That she scares her nurses away," said the other.

"Why haven't we ever seen the Governor's daughter?" asked Terza. "Maybe she doesn't even exist." She had turned out a midget, as Basilia had predicted, but not at all short on brains, for she was the money person, and seemed to be quite clever and more talkative and bossy than any of her sisters.

"She exists. I've seen her in my dreams."

"You're always seeing her in your dreams, Seconda," said Settima and Ottava in unison. For an instant, Basilia saw them tied to a large wheel and being racked until their spines broke. Basilia shook her head. Why would such a vision come to her now?

"Is something the matter, Old Mother?" Eustace asked, concern in his blue eyes. "Are you cold? You're shivering all over."

"No, no, I'm fine," said Basilia. "I'm not used to so much sound all around me anymore."

"Shall we be quiet?"

"Please don't mind me, Eustace. I am very pleased to be here. I just need to adjust to being back in the world."

"Like I was saying," interjected one of the harelipped girls, "the Governor's daughter isn't allowed to leave the villa, not even to their own garden."

"They say her father keeps her locked away because she's terribly ugly," said the other.

"Where did you hear that, Sesta?" asked Aurelia.

"From the customers in the bakery. They tell us lots of stories."

"Such as what, Quinta?"

"They say her betrothed is a Roman Prefect, but that he's old and decrepit," said Nona-Herminia.

Eustace gave each of them a stern look.

"Girls, what have I told you about bringing home all this gossip? And in front of a guest, no less!"

"Leave them be, Eustace," said Aurelia. "It's better to know than not to know what our neighbors know."

"One lady told us that the Governor's daughter may be wrong in the head," said Terza, and again, Basilia's flesh went cold as she saw the girl's eyes getting plucked out with a strange instrument.

"Is she a dolt, then?" said Seconda.

"Bewitched, maybe," said Nona-Herminia. *Torn to pieces, torn to pieces, torn to pieces.* Basilia kept her eyes shut to the vision, but could not keep from seeing the snouts of the wild boar devouring the girl's flesh.

"Or just unhappy because she can't leave the house," said the practical Sesta.

"Poor child," said Aurelia.

Basilia understood, finally, why her mage and his *mouras* had lured her out of her cave and brought her to this table to hear this conversation. Her path must cross with Wilgefortis' once again.

After the meal, she thanked her hosts, got to her feet and stood stiffly. The girls enfolded her in their arms and called her grandmother. Aurelia wanted her to stay the night, stay as many nights as she wanted with them, but Basilia had to follow her own path.

Aurelia removed her own *palla* and wrapped it around Basilia's thin shoulders, raising it over her head to cover the matted locks.

"God bless," said Aurelia.

"Goddess bless," Basilia rejoined.

"Don't forget us!" the girls called out to her as she followed Eustace down the stairs.

"God bless you, Old Mother," said Eustace knowing full-well what she was going to do. "Perhaps you might be able to bring them together at last," he whispered into her ear. From a hook behind the door, he took a walking stick carved with fishes to help her on her long walk.

The New Nurse

With her new walking stick, Basilia picked her way through the muddy streets of the town to the High Road that led to the Governor's villa to the east. The road climbed a steep hill, winding up between groves of pine and alder trees. By the time she reached the ancient cork oak tree at the villa's gate, now charred and its wide trunk split in two, as though Jupiter's bolt itself had struck it, the sun had set. Twilight enveloped her as she approached the guards.

"My name is Sila Drusilla, I am to be the new nurse for the Young Lady Wilgefortis," she stated without ceremony.

At first, the guards laughed. "Go away, you dirty, old hag. There is no one by that name in this house."

"She is the only daughter of Lucius Severus and Calsia Marcella," Basilia insisted.

The guards looked at each other, raising their eyebrows.

"Take the message to the Domina that Lady Wilgefortis' new nurse has arrived."

They walked her down a long path that ended in the back door of the villa. The door was open, and Basilia could see into the kitchen, where women of all ages were busy with different tasks. The air smelled of rotting fish.

"Wait here," ordered one of the guards.

"Keep an eye on her," said the other guard to the cook's assistant, gutting fish by the door.

When the guards had gone, Basilia attempted a conversation. "Is it a feast day?"

"Young mistress is getting presented to her betrothed today," said the woman, shaking her head. "The poor thing."

"Why do you pity her?" asked Basilia.

"It's not her fault. She was born that way," was all she would say.

Basilia did not press her for more information. She watched the activity inside the kitchen until, at last, a tall woman in a brown tunic and gray *palla* led her upstairs to Lady Calsia's sitting room.

Nothing had changed. She saw the same tapestries hanging off the same walls, the same embalmed heads of boar and deer lining the hallway to the family's rooms. The Domina's sitting room felt cold, as usual, even though a good fire burned in the hearth. She heard a growling noise followed by two short yaps, and saw a small furry dog on Lady Calsia's lap. Were it not for the color of Calsia's eyes, Basilia would not have recognized her former mistress. She had aged so much even her rubicund hair had lost its luster and turned a pale reddish-gray.

"The guard says you called my daughter by an unusual name," Calsia said when the old woman was presented. "How did you come to know her secret name?"

"I don't remember. Perhaps someone in town was talking about it. Or maybe your husband told it to me when he agreed to hire me on as the new nurse."

Calsia turned around in her chair to get a better look at the old woman. "How old are you?" Calsia asked. "You sound quite ancient. Come closer, I can't see you clearly."

Silhouetted against the fire, Basilia's face was in shadow, so that even Calsia didn't recognize the midwife with whom she shared a terrible secret.

"How old are you?"

"I am well past my prime, Lady, but cannot give you an exact age."

"Don't try to fool me, old woman. My husband would only have contracted you if you were young and beautiful. He did not contract you, did he?"

"Alas, no, my lady. But all I require is room and board."

Calsia gave a little laugh, and Basilia noticed that she had a few teeth missing. "I warned him that if he brought one more young woman to nanny Wilge, I would be walking out with my family fortune."

"Has the girl, your daughter, had many nurses?"

"She's a sweet girl, my Wilge, but terribly willful at times, and impossible to reason with when she has her fits."

"What kind of fits?"

"Screaming and kicking and thrashing about. Spouting curse words like a soldier. The fits usually come after a nightmare. She has been having many of those lately. But that's not what really worries me."

"There's something worse?"

"She refuses to eat. It started the night we buried her brother. I didn't pay attention to it at first because I was buried in my own grief. But it's been two years, now, and she hasn't had more than tea and one biscuit a day. She's lost so much weight. I don't think she's developing properly. She doesn't even look like a girl. My husband can't bear to look at her, so he has her locked in her room until she comes to her senses and starts eating again."

"Is it just the loss of her brother that she laments, or is there something else, something in particular that she rages about? Does she perhaps not find her betrothed to her liking?"

"What do you know of her betrothed?" Calsia leaned forward to see her more clearly.

"Nothing at all. Just what I heard in the kitchen, that she is to be presented to him this evening."

"I'm afraid I haven't been a very good mother. Not to either of my children. I've been too . . . " Calsia paused and stroked the furry head of her little dog. " . . . Too distracted, I suppose. Although 'haunted' is probably a better word for it. Haunted by a memory I cannot shake."

"Haunted, how?" Basilia's belly tightened. She could only be referring to the memory of the multiple births.

"I can't speak of it," said Calsia. "But maybe you're right. Maybe she *is* angry about her betrothal. I daresay she thinks herself a vestal virgin. Her father cannot wait until she's someone else's property."

"Has the girl begun her monthly rule? Sometimes, girls begin too early and become too easily flooded with hot humors."

"I'm telling you, she's tall and skinny as a boy. She is to be presented to her betrothed this evening, and her father is anxious to get her married. But we are afraid the Prefect will refuse to marry her unless she is ready to breed. I don't understand why it's taking so long for her body to develop."

"She is only twelve. Some girls take longer. Perhaps she needs a richer diet? More olives and meat, cheese and bread, and plenty of wine."

Calsia turned her face from the fire and looked long at Basilia. "You sound hungry, old woman. How long has it been since you've eaten?"

"Forgive me, Domina."

"I am not your domina yet. What did you say your name was?"

"Drusilla, my Lady, but I am called Sila." It was Basilia Drusilla's old nickname, given to her by her father. She had not heard or used that name since her childhood in Galaecia. Basilia was her midwife's name.

"Do you know how to read and write, Sila?"

"It's been a long time since I held a quill, but yes, I am literate."

"What about music? Can you play an instrument? The Prefect sent my daughter a beautiful lute that he expects her to play for him on their wedding night, but the stubborn girl refuses to learn, says the strings hurt her fingers. Do you play the lute, by any chance, Sila, or the lyre, perhaps?"

"Alas, Domina, my education did not cover the finer arts. My mother taught me the alphabet and herb-lore, and that was the extent of it. I do know how to use a spindle, if that counts." Basilia left out that her mother, a wise woman herself, had taught her the alphabet in both Latin and Greek.

The Governor's wife did not respond. She scratched the little dog between the ears and turned her gaze on the now-dwindling fire. Basilia was expecting to be turned away. Why had she thought she could come and offer her services as a nurse to the Governor's child without having any of the social skills required of young ladies of her station?

"Have you any experience as a nurse, Sila? Do you know anything about children?"

"The truth is, Domina, I have never been a nurse, but I am not afraid of children."

"That's a good quality, I daresay. Especially with Wilgefortis. Her fits have terrified all the rest of her nurses. What makes you think you will be any different?"

"I have eight granddaughters, Domina."

"Well, that's a unique qualification. Very well. We shall give you a try. But look at yourself. You look awful. You look as if you've been living in a cave all your life."

"Not all my life, Domina, but circumstances made it necessary for me to live like a hermit the last twelve years. I once had a bustling business as a midwife." Basilia held her breath, afraid that she had said too much and that Calsia would discover who she really was.

"A midwife, you say?" Calsia turned to stare at her again, narrowing her eyes. "Hmmm, I knew a midwife once, poor woman. Drowned in the Minho River, I was told. In any case, you speak well, Sila. You know your letters, and at least you don't smell bad, unkempt as you look," said Calsia, turning back to gaze at the fire. "When can you start?"

"Immediately, Domina."

"I shouldn't wonder, if you've been living in a cave for over a decade. My instinct tells me I should hire you, even though you look a scare."

"You won't regret it, Domina. I am certain I am the only one for this position."

"You may be right about that, seeing how many previous nursemaids Wilge has managed to scare off. Very well, then. I shall ask the housekeeper to find you some decent clothing, and we shall have to cut off that dreadful mop of hair of yours. Only when you look like a civilized person and not a wild creature of the woods can I present you to my husband. He may not like what he sees, but he will agree to hire you if I insist that I want you for the post, and we'll pay you with room and board until our daughter's wedding day."

"I do have one condition, Domina."

Calsia turned to glare at her. "What! Setting conditions already?"

"All I ask is that I be allowed to come and go as I please," said Basilia. "I am a freewoman and have no wish to indenture my service to the Governor's household."

"I suppose that isn't too much to ask," said Calsia, "for someone who has managed to stay alive so long, however feral your existence may have been. However, I cannot promise that you will have any free time in which to come and go as you please. I'm afraid the position is night and day. If that is satisfactory, the post is yours."

Basilia tried to genuflect, but her knees creaked. Calsia rang a small bell in her hand. A pair of women slaves appeared.

"Take our new nurse here directly to the bath house, and see to it that she is scrubbed hard, that they cut off that wild hair, those claws on her feet and make her look human again. She will wear the long-sleeved tunic and *palla* of a nurse. And get her some decent sandals, too. Those things she's wearing are loud enough to wake the dead."

"What room shall I put her in, Domina?"

"I want her to be given my room on the third floor so she can be next to Liberata. But take care that the girl doesn't see her until my husband comes home and agrees to her employment. Oh, and see to it that she gets a spindle in her room so she can teach my daughter how to spin wool. I'm sure her future husband will appreciate her learning that skill."

❧ ❧ ❧

Sila was given a room larger than her old house, with an oak couch for a bed and a fireplace, a large window shuttered in dark wood, armchairs, an armoire and a writing desk. Sila was walking around the room in complete amazement, wrapped in a fleece with her hair dripping wet after the scalding bath she had gotten in the villa's bath house. Her hair, chopped to shoulder-level, hung in wet, wiry strands over the fleece. Her feet were bloody from the pumice stone, the toenails from the saw, but at last, her feet were clean. She was admiring the new sandals with long straps that she found on the bed beside her white clothing when she heard the scraping sound of stone against stone. A secret door opened to one side of the bed.

"May I come in?" said the girl. She wore a bright blue tunic and a short *palla* in gray wool, her red hair in buns above her ears. Sila expected to see a girl covered in hair, as she had looked at her birth, but instead, the girl's skin was pale and smooth.

"Liberata Wilgefortis, is that you?" Sila asked.

"Yes!" cried the girl, throwing herself at Sila. Sila clung to the fleece as though it would protect her from the sudden crush of the girl's arms.

"Nobody calls me that, except Mother," said the girl. "Are you my grandmother?"

"No, child, I am your new nurse, Sila."

"Oh, Sila, I'm so happy you've come back. I've missed you so much."

"But, child, what are you saying? You don't know me."

The girl stared at Sila with her disarmingly clear grey eyes. "I remember you, Sila. Really, I do. You appear to me in my dreams, and there are babies everywhere, crying so loud, and you are there, comforting all of them. I think I may be one of them."

"Oh, dear child," said Sila, pressing the girl's head against her fleecy bosom.

Basilia heard the scraping sound again as the secret door opened once more and a young boy stepped through with a fat toad in his hands.

"Gaius, look! My old nurse came back. Sila, this is my brother Gaius Lucius. He visits me sometimes."

"You look familiar," the boy said, bowing politely. "Aren't you the midwife that attended my mother at Wilge's birth?"

Basilia remembered that she had, indeed, seen the boy twelve years earlier, when as a two-year-old he had wanted to follow her into his mother's bed chamber while she gave birth.

"Yes, now I remember you," said Basilia. "But you would be a young man by now. How is it you are still a boy?"

The boy tilted his head sideways, narrowing his eyes at her, but he was distracted by the toad jumping from his hands and onto Basilia's bed.

"Now you've done it, Gaius," said Wilgefortis. "You better catch it before it stains Sila's bedclothes. Mother will think it was Sila who wet the bed."

The boy plopped belly down on the mattress and caught the creature in both hands before it jumped to the windowsill. Basilia realized she could still see the bed beneath the boy.

"This is Gaius' ghost," Wilgefortis explained. "Every time he visits, he brings me another toad. How many does this make, Gaius?"

"More than a hundred, I would guess after all these years," said the ghost boy. Basilia noted that although he looked like a real boy, there was a silver aura about him that made him shimmer in the candlelight, and it was the shimmering effect that made it possible to see through him.

"Take the toad to my room," said Wilgefortis. "Put it with the others."

Gaius ducked back through the secret door, but not before the toad caught Basilia's eye and winked.

Basilia kept her mouth shut. For the Druidae, a toad was a magical animal that represented female fertility. Either the toad was announcing the arrival of the girl's menses, or the toad itself was the menses, absorbing the girl's blood through the skin. She understood, now, why the girl's monthly flow had not started.

That evening, at the appointed hour for her presentation to the Roman Prefect, Wilgefortis developed a high fever, accompanied by tiny pockmarks all over her face. Sila announced to the Governor and his wife that the Lady Liberata had fallen ill, and could not come down to dine with them and their guest. Angrily, the Prefect swiped his cup and plate off the table and stormed out of the atrium.

"What ails my daughter this time?" asked the Governor.

"A fever, Your Excellency. Maybe the pox, too. There are red marks all over her face."

"The pox? And you stand here polluting us with her illness?" said Calsia.

"Who is this hag, anyway, Calsia?" asked Lucius Severus.

"I am the girl's new nurse," Basilia said, genuflecting as best she could, hurting her knees as she stood up.

"Rather old for a nurse, aren't you? And why do you look so familiar?"

"I thought you knew each other," said Calsia with a smug grin.

"With your permission," said Sila, unable to bend a knee again. "I must go back and tend to the girl's fever."

"She told me you had hired her, Lucius," Sila heard Calsia whisper urgently to the Governor as she left the room.

"I have seen her before, of that I am sure. But hire her, I did not. You know how much I despise old women."

Sila hurried off to the kitchens to find fennel and gentian for a healing tonic for Wilgefortis.

❧ ❧ ❧

Wilgefortis took to Sila like a newborn to a wet nurse. Under the old woman's tutelage and constant attention, the unruly girl became the obedient daughter that her parents expected. In short time, she learnt her sewing, her spinning, her singing—all that was required to be of service to her future husband, the Roman Prefect who waited less patiently now for the flower-head of his betrothed to blossom.

Four years passed quickly, and still, the girl's blood refused to flow. Calsia stopped in once a month to inquire if the girl's maidenhead had ripened yet, or the Governor would come in occasionally to pinch her cheeks and lift her in his arms to check on her weight. Both left the girl's rooms disappointed.

Wilgefortis had grown taller and larger about the shoulders, but smaller around the hips and waist. Her ribs protruded more than her breasts and the bones of her knees and elbows jutted in sharp angles. Her face had changed as well. The chin lengthened, the eye sockets darkened, the cheekbones grew even hollower. Rather than a radiant maiden at the first bloom of her life, Wilgefortis looked more like a crone or a skeleton. Calsia was so mortified, she stopped visiting her daughter and stopped calling for the nurse to give her weekly reports on the girl's health.

Calsia wrote dutiful letters to the girl's betrothed, keeping him apprised of his future bride's progress, extolling the girl's charms in the most florid language she could muster. *A prodigy on the distaff*, she wrote. *A paragon of domesticity. The sweetest and gentlest nature*. All were partially true, but Calsia omitted a few other truths from her letters—that her daughter kept toads for pets, that the girl was wasting away before her eyes and that Wilgefortis did not bleed and would likely never breed.

Calsia feared for her daughter's life, feared the girl was losing her mind from this self-imposed hunger, but she did not share her fears with the Governor, as he was already threatening to send the girl to a brothel if her womanhood tarried another year.

Dream of the Eight Sisters

"More dreams, you say?" asked Sila as she prepared the girl's bed for the night.

"I don't know why I keep seeing them, the same faces," the girl said, her eyes still resting on the full copper moon that seemed to be poised on the ledge of the roof outside her bedchamber.

"How many of them do you see?"

"I told you. I keep seeing the same eight girls, and the strange thing is, they all kind of look like me. But they're all different, somehow."

"What were they doing this time, these eight girls?" Sila placed a warming pan under the covers.

"They were traveling somewhere. I think they were riding on horses, two on each horse, because I remember seeing only four horses in the dream, each a different color: a white horse, a black horse, a sorrel horse and a beautiful golden horse with a long golden mane. But all eight of them were in the dream. I think they were taking a rest, and there were these craggy mountains on each side of the road, and a stream ran alongside the road, and there were these gold minnows in the stream, and one of them reached her hand down into the water and pulled out this big gold fish, only she had six fingers on her hand rather than five."

To hide her alarm, Sila bellowed the logs in the fireplace, wincing as a flame singed some hair from her arm.

"Is that all?"

"That's all I remember, but I think the dream continued for hours. Everything else is just a blur. Just those faces going around and around. What does it mean, Sila?" The girl turned to look at the old woman, her young trusting face full of concern.

It was what Basilia had always feared, that the older girl would develop clairvoyant powers that might connect her to her unknown sisters. All eight of them had, indeed, been traveling on four horses, or rather, being raised by four families, until they had all congregated upon Eustace and Aurelia, who still lived in fear that Governor Severus would learn there were eight girls in his province who looked exactly like his own daughter.

Wilgefortis tapped Basilia's shoulder. "Sila? Did you hear me? Why won't you tell me what that dream means? I think you know."

The girl had lined up her large family of toads along the windowsill to absorb the moonlight, stacking them four-deep.

"Nothing to be afraid of, child," Basilia said, and her voice sounded ancient and tired. "You're lonely, that's all. You need more than the companionship of an old woman. You need some friends your age."

"You know Father won't allow me to have any friends. Other than you, my only friends are Gaius' ghost and these toads. Father means to keep me locked up until the wedding. Am I his daughter or his prisoner? I hate him so much."

"Child, it's wrong to talk that way about one's father."

"It's just that I long to be outdoors, Sila. What harm could I come to if I just stepped out to the gardens for a walk? I would die for the chance to pick a fig from the tree, to gather flowers for my room. I would give anything to be on a horse and away from this place. To take a journey like those girls in my dream. Why can't I be one of them?"

If you only knew, thought Sila.

"Your wedding day is almost here. You must start eating again. And stop playing with those toads. They're keeping your blood from flowing."

"That's not possible, Sila. Stop being so superstitious. Besides, I told Mother I did not want to marry anyone. I have consecrated my virginity to Diana."

"Do you mean to starve yourself to death, then? Is that your plan? That would be offensive, especially to Diana."

"I want to go away from here, Sila. Can't you help me? Please? I'm sure you can help me. I fear a terrible fate will befall me if I stay and marry that horrible man that Father is so keen for me to wed. Gaius told me he's much older and uglier than Father. But even if he weren't, I would not want to marry him. Why must I marry anyone, Sila?"

"Will you promise to eat if I help you avoid this marriage?"

The girl's translucent eyes lit up. "Yes, of course, Sila! I'll do anything you want, truly I will."

"Learn to play the lute?"

"Fine!"

"Release all your toads and drink a potion I will concoct for you at every full moon to make your blood flow?"

"Anything you want, Sila! But it seems you want me to do the very things Mother wants, so that I can please this husband they've chosen for me."

"We must play along with your Mother and Father for a spell."

"Do you mean it, Sila? Are you really going to help me escape this terrible fate?"

"Thy will be done, child."

Although her wedding was planned to take place on her seventeenth birthday, the Governor was called away that year to an assembly of the Council of governors, prefects and consuls in Rome. The Roman Empire's eternal war with the Persians had devastated the Roman legion, and Emperor Hadrian required all his imperial governors to increase taxation and work at fortifying their own provinces, lest the Parthians or the Armenians break the *status quo ante* and invade Roman territory. For the next three years, Lucius Severus traveled the length and breadth of his provinces to recruit soldiers and collect more taxes for the armies of Lusitania and Gallaecia, while Quintus Flavius led the training of the new recruits. The two men did not return to Bracara Augusta until Wilgefortis' nineteenth year.

With her father gone, and nobody commanding her to eat, to bleed, to hurry up and get married, those three years were the happiest years of Wilgefortis' young life. Her appetite improved, a healthy flush came into her cheeks again and she stopped having nightmares. Her mother gave her a dog of her own (*to see if she stopped playing with reptiles*, Calsia told Sila), a sleek miniature greyhound that she named Boodica that followed her everywhere, slipping under the covers with her at night to keep her warm.

Once a week, Calsia indulged her daughter's desire to walk in the gardens, to feel the rain on her own skin, to cut flowers and fruit for her room. She could chase Boodica all over the house, bathe in the bath house with her nurse and dine with her mother in the atrium. It was then that she learned to play the lute, with the help of Gaius' ghost, which Calsia did not believe, though she made offerings to Apollo for his intercession.

Everything went back to miserable when Lucius returned, more determined than ever to wed his daughter to Quintus Flavius.

The Young Crone

"I am finished with this eternal off-putting of the wedding, Calsia. You and the girl are taxing my patience!" Governor Lucius Severus bellowed from his *lectus* across from his wife's. Each had their own side table on which the *cena* had been served: platters of roasted lamb and vegetables, a bowl of fresh figs, grapes, two kinds of bread, thick slices of cheese and a pitcher of mulled wine. He stabbed his knife into the leg of lamb on the serving platter and cut himself a thick chunk.

"She's nineteen and still no blood?" He stuffed the meat into his mouth, followed by a draught of wine. "What's the matter with her? Is she barren?"

Calsia had given up eating meat, as the smell of cooked flesh turned her stomach. Her side table held a platter of roasted vegetables, sliced eggs, olives, figs and a round loaf of barley bread. She served her plate and leaned back in her *lectus* to eat.

"It's the melancholia, Lucius," said Calsia, her throat in knots at the memory of her dead son. "She can't seem to shake the loss of her brother. She even thinks the boy's spirit comes to visit her."

"She's taxed my patience long enough!" boomed the Governor, his mouth full of meat again. "I swear by the testicles of Mars I'll have her locked up in a brothel if she dishonors her betrothal one more time. Quintus Flavius will tolerate no more excuses. He cares not whether the girl has fever or melancholia or the pox itself. He has waited eight years for this marriage, and he means to sue us if we don't comply."

"She made much progress while you were gone, Lucius. She can play the lute now, and she's put on some weight, and she is much happier now that she has her little dog to keep her company. But sometimes, she is overwhelmed by a terrible sadness, which I'm sure is the memory of losing Gaius. Please be gentle with her, Lucius."

This was Calsia's constant plea with her husband, and she used whatever excuse came to mind in explaining her daughter's delayed maturity. Calsia had consecrated the girl's maidenhead to Juno Lucina and could not explain why the goddess was taking so long to ripen her daughter's development.

"Has she started eating again, at least?" Lucius Severus asked, dipping a chunk of bread into some olive oil and stuffing it into his mouth. "I want her well rounded for the wedding."

"I told you, she put on some weight while you were gone," said Calsia, pushing away her food. She had lost her own appetite. Sila had brought the girl's diminishing appetite to Calsia's attention. Calsia took to watching her daughter closely and insisted that she eat just a few bites of her food and a few swallows of wine. But then Sila told her that the girl would bring it all up in the *latrina* after dinner. Calsia thought it best to withhold that information from her husband.

"A Roman man doesn't want a skinny wife," the Governor continued his usual harangue. "A skinny wife is a barren wife. We're fortunate to have such a man interested in her at all, a Roman Prefect. He could have his pick of women in the region, and he chose our Liberata."

"From the dimensions on her wedding dress, I can assure you, Lucius, that our girl is not skinny," said Calsia, trying to lighten the mood.

The date of the marriage ceremony was the fourth day of the month following the girl's twentieth birthday, nine months hither. Calsia knew the Governor would make good on his threat to send the girl to a brothel if for some reason her maidenhead failed to blossom by that time.

"Is the dress finished then?" he asked.

"Almost," said Calsia. "The *stola* is of pure white linen from Florentia, embroidered in gold thread. The *palla* is a rich blue Egyptian silk monogrammed with our coat of arms and trimmed in gold brocade and, of course, the veil, saffron-colored to match her hair. We await its delivery any day now."

"That must have taken a toll on her dowry," said Lucius Severus.

"I know it sounds extravagant, husband, but we can ill afford any talk of shortchanging our good Prefect, after all the years he's waited for his bride."

"I doubt a fine dress like that will make a difference to our man," said Severus, belching loudly. "He can do more with a dowry than a dress."

The Stranger

On the night of Lupercalia—a feast day that Calsia and Lucius Severus had stopped celebrating since the death of their son—a man clad only in a loincloth came to the front door of the villa and asked for shelter. How he had gotten past the sentries at the gate, he did not explain, but somehow, he had persuaded the housekeeper to ask the mistress of the house if he could speak to her, and he was escorted to the *impluvium* to wait. The housekeeper had even given him a cloak to cover himself before the lady of the house could see him.

Calsia joined him shortly, and they sat down at the small table facing the fountain. Two thieves had attacked him in the woods, he explained to Calsia, taking all his coin and clothing, his sandals, everything but his loincloth. He had nothing left, and begged for any kind of shelter she could provide him for the night. Calsia was troubled by the man, the wounds on his hands and feet, his long hair matted with blood, the deep scars of a whipping on his back. She gave him leave to take shelter in the stable at the front of the house, and ordered one of the house servants to take their guest food, wine and a warm blanket, as well as an old tunic and belt she borrowed from her husband's wardrobe.

Lucius had gone tax-collecting again for a new campaign to quell another vicious Jewish revolt in Judea and Libya, and it would be unlucky to turn away a mendicant on Lupercalia, the festival of love.

There was nothing wrong with Calsia paying a visit to her unusual guest, and make sure his needs were taken care of, but she could not fathom why she had offered to salve his wounds and wash the blood from his hair. Only Sila knew because it was Sila who carried the basin of water with which Lady Calsia cleaned the bloody gouges on the man's head, and it was Sila who ground the herbed paste with which Lady Calsia salved the punctures in the man's hands and feet. It was Sila who wrapped the bandages around the man's wounds.

"Bless you," the man said, stronger after taking the food and wine Calsia had sent him. "For your kindness, let me do a kindness in return."

Calsia frowned. She had not expected any reciprocity for her hospitality. She had surprised even herself with her desire to attend to this stranger's wounds. "You owe me nothing, sir. These are the customs of Lupercalia. It's time for you to rest now."

"Please, Domina," said the man, lightly touching Calsia's arm. "Anything at all. Whatever you need. Just ask and through my God's grace, I will reciprocate."

Suddenly stiffening her back, Calsia asked, "What god do you speak of, sir?"

"The god of all things," said the man, glancing upwards.

"Juno Lucina!" Lady Calsia exclaimed, kneading her fists into her shawl, "my husband will kill me if he hears I've offered refuge to a Jew or a Christian under our own roof."

"I am not a Jew, dear Lady. It was Jews who tortured me thus."

"What did you do," asked Calsia, "to deserve such punishment?"

"I was a healer, once, a follower of Hippocrates, but the Jews called it black magic, and had me flogged and crucified. Now you have healed me, and I would heal you and yours in return."

"Wilgefortis," Sila whispered to Lady Calsia. "Maybe he can help us with Wilgefortis."

"There is nothing wrong with Wilgefortis!" snapped Lady Calsia. "Enough of this ungodly prattle! What was I thinking? If my husband finds out you stayed here, he'll have my head taken off, and yours too, sir, for good measure. Sila, it's time for us to go!"

Calsia stood up suddenly and toppled the basin of bloody water into the hay strewn floor. "Sir, I shall expect you gone by first light. Sila, bring those things into the house!"

Lady Calsia picked up the hem of her *stola* and hurried out of the stable. Sila lagged, taking her time to gather up the food bowls, wine jug and empty water basin that were the evidence of someone having spent the night with the horses.

"My young charge, sir, she suffers greatly," Sila spoke quickly. "Her mother disbelieves it, as you saw, but the girl's body is wracked by an affliction I cannot cure. Perhaps a demon has taken control of her. I know not what to do. She doesn't eat or sleep, she has nightmares and fits, she wastes away day by day and looks more withered than I do, though she is but nineteen years of age. Her father has promised to incarcerate her in a brothel if she isn't married and with child in her twentieth year, but I fear it is the marriage that she most dreads and would starve herself to death before it happens."

"There will be no marriage, old mother," said the man, the dark pupils of his eyes shifting quickly from side to side, as though he were reading an invisible script. "I see the souls that haunt the girl, there are eight of them, but they mean her no harm. They are her sisters, and their souls beckon to her soul. Together will they be reborn and remembered for centuries, and a sacred spring will be named in their honor, but first they must be delivered unto their fate in the glory of their suffering."

"But, sir, how could you know about her sisters? Nobody knows about them but the Domina and me. Are you a Druid, sir?"

"Some have called me that, others a Christian, a prophet, a magician. I am what I am, and they crucified me for it. Just as they will crucify your young girl. People persecute anything that threatens them."

"No!" cried Sila. "I'll hear no talk of crucifixion."

"For her sake, understand that the girl is not long for this world. She will marry in her twentieth year, but it will not be a marriage of husband and wife. It will be a marriage of souls. Her soul was cleaved into nine pieces when she was born into this flesh, and now it is time for her to be reunited with her sisters. Her fate will be their fate. She is the lodestone that will draw them together, and they will all cleave to each other once more as one soul. Once you were a midwife to her birth. Now, your task is to release her into her glorious fate that she may be made whole again."

"Sila?" Lady Calsia's loud shrill cry echoed from the kitchens.

At first light the next morning, the stranger was gone. Sila told no one of his ominous prediction. She thought of sending word to Eustace that his daughters were in danger, but there was no one she could trust to deliver such a message, and she dared not leave Wilgefortis' side. The only trace of the stranger's visit was a red moss growing from the damp earthen floor of the stable in the place where the bloody water of the basin had spilled.

Sila knew what to do. She scraped the moss up with her fingernails, boiled it into a *calda* for Wilgefortis, sweetened it with honey and served it in an earthenware cup to hide the bloody color of the infusion. The girl drank the potion in small sips, and the next day, her blood started to flow.

The Blood

The blood brought changes to the girl's body that would have given Lady Calsia apoplexy, had she witnessed them with her own eyes. Two days after her first blood started, Sila noticed a shadow growing on the girl's face, as though the skin were darkening in patches over her cheeks and chin. The girl grew taciturn with her nurse and refused to let Sila bathe her, brush her hair or touch her in the slightest. She would ask Sila to sit as far away from her as possible and was not interested in anything but the view outside her window.

The blood brought much pain to Wilgefortis, pain that doubled her over and made her cry out to Sila to bring another warm stone to lay over her tortured womb. There were clots of dark blood on the menstrual linens that Sila soaked in boiling water and scrubbed for hours, to no avail, as the red stains remained on the stiff cloths. Sila concocted a special *calda* for the girl, of lion's tail and powdered poppy flower that she procured from the apothecary in town. The *calda* was the only thing that eased the pain and allowed the girl to slip into a few hours of restful slumber.

It was during one of these slumbers that Sila discovered what was causing the darkening patches on the girl's skin. Hair. The girl was growing hair on her face: the pores around the jaws and chin were all sprouting fine dark hair.

"Great Mother!" Sila said aloud, waking Wilgefortis.

The girl sat up quickly, covering half her face with the blankets. "Why are you standing so close to me, Sila?"

"Your face," said Sila, "it looks like you're growing hair on your face again." Sila removed the covers to expose the girl's limbs. "It's all over you now. You look as you did when you were born."

The girl pulled the blankets down and smiled wanly. "It came back. I'm so happy. Do you like it? Diana has answered my prayers. I'm going to be free, Sila! No man will marry me, now."

Not knowing what else to do, Sila dropped to her knees and wept for the tortured soul of that young girl she had helped bring into the world. How she regretted having once convinced her mother to keep her. *If I had just taken all nine of them,* she thought, *kept them all together, instead of singling this one out, she would never have suffered the way she suffers now. They should never have been separated. This suffering is all my fault.*

"Don't cry, Sila. I figured out a way to escape Father's terrible plan. But I still need your help."

"I meddled once with your fate, already," said Sila, sobbing. "I shall not do it again."

Wilgefortis narrowed her eyes, trying to discern her old nurse's meaning. But Sila said no more, though she saw the girl dangling from a Roman cross in a long blue cloak. She covered her face with both hands and begged her goddesses to put a stop to this agony.

But Ovidius' words came back to her, *You may have extended their lives, Basilia, but you did not save them. Alas, you may have even doomed them.*

The Summons

A fortnight before Wilgefortis' wedding, the Roman Prefect arrived on a litter carried by Egyptian slaves. Other slaves carried trunks of his clothing, his books, his hunting implements, even his bedding and linens. He had not changed his mind about the wedding, he explained to Lucius and Calsia, but after eight years of waiting for a wedding, he had decided to forego the wedding ritual itself, and would, instead, take the option of living in his betrothed's house for a year. If it was possible for the girl to attend to him and be with him that whole year, with no more than three nights' absence, then he would legally marry Wilgefortis and go through with the ceremony.

Calsia was incensed at the Prefect's presumptions. What did he mean he wanted Wilgefortis to "attend to him and be with him" for a full year? Did he think he could treat her house like a brothel?

"The man is out of his mind if he thinks Wilgefortis is going to sleep with him without a marriage ritual," Calsia warned her husband. "I will take the girl out of this house myself and consecrate her as a vestal virgin to keep that man from disrespecting her like that. He's disrespecting all of us, Lucius, but especially you, since you are the *pater potestas* of this household. Why does this man think he can come here and do whatever he wants with your daughter?"

"It's a viable option, Calsia, approved by the Roman Senate," said Lucius Severus. "Maybe if we had not kept him waiting all these years, he might not have a leg to stand on, but we have dragged out this wedding for years, and it's the least we can do to make up for it."

"But the man means to live here, Lucius, under your roof, eating your food and having his way with your daughter—without the sacred contract of a wedding ceremony. Do you realize how this will make you look, Governor?"

"It will be far worse to have our daughter rejected altogether, Calsia, and the man is this far . . . " Lucius held his thumb and index finger together to show how close they were to the Prefect turning his back on them. "He's this far from declaring the wedding plans null and void. There's nothing to be done about it but indulge his desires, Calsia. Disrespectful as they might seem."

Lucius ordered that the Prefect be given quarters on the ground floor of the villa, his rooms overlooking the fountain in the *impluvium*. Without waiting for a formal welcome by his host, Flavius Quintus demanded an audience with his betrothed. Since he had never laid eyes on her, he would look upon her now as a grown woman to make sure she was still desirable to him.

"This man is a barbarian," Calsia complained to her husband. "I don't take orders from barbarians. And I will not sit at a meal with one either, even if it is in my own home."

"The man has never seen the girl, Calsia," Lucius Severus said. "They should have married years ago, but we have been denying him that pleasure since the betrothal. A man has a right to ensure the quality of his bride, especially one who is no longer in her prime."

"Not in her prime? She's not yet twenty years old. The girl has years of childbearing ahead of her. What quality does he want to ensure, exactly? She's going to be his wife, not his cow! Is that what you think of your daughter?"

Lucius Severus ignored his wife's objections and ordered the cook to prepare a sumptuous feast, which would be served in the villa's seldom-used *triclinium*, or formal dining room. Musicians and a couple of tumbling dwarves were brought in for entertainment. When the feast was ready and laid out on the enormous table in the middle of the room, Lucius ordered the housekeeper to bring Wilgefortis down to sit at the *cena* with her parents and her betrothed.

Basilia panicked when she heard the Governor's summons. The hair grew thick on the girl's cheeks and chin, lush and red. The more

Basilia trimmed and shaved it, the hardier it grew, and so she had stopped taking the blade to it. The girl ate heartily now, and the flush had returned to her face and the glow of life to her eyes. Her breasts remained undeveloped, but her hips filled out, and her blood came regularly and without pain. From the back, she looked like a hale and ripe young woman with a narrow waist and long red hair. One would never know she sported a full beard.

"Tell the Governor that the Lady Wilgefortis is indisposed," Basilia said to the housekeeper. The housekeeper took the message to her Dominus, but soon returned with the same summons.

"The Prefect commands that his betrothed join him for the *cena*. Or else he shall have to send his soldiers to collect her."

"Let me go, Sila," Wilgefortis said to her nurse. "Let them see me. They are going to have to lay eyes on me soon enough. Perhaps if the Prefect sees me this evening he will change his mind about the wedding."

"Most definitely he will change his mind, child. It's what your father will do that worries me."

"Worry not, dear Sila. I go happily to meet my fate, don't you see? I am not afraid of anything any longer. This is my choice."

"I will go with you, then. You will not go alone into that bleak fate."

"I want to wear my wedding dress, and the ruby brooch that Mother gave me as a wedding gift."

Sila understood the wisdom of this, for the girl would not be wearing the dress to her wedding.

"Are you sure you don't want me to shave you, dearest? We could still try to . . . "

Wilgefortis shook her head and gazed with deep compassion upon her old nurse. "I am what I am, Sila. And I am happy for the first time in years that the truth about me will be known, and that I will never have to marry."

And so Basilia dressed her charge lovingly, buttoning up the pearl buttons at the back of her linen gown, draping the blue silk *palla* over her shoulders that shimmered in the light like quicksilver, and fastened it with the ruby brooch. The girl wanted her long red hair pulled back from her face and plaited into one thick braid down her back.

Basilia did not realize how much she had grown to love that child, precisely as she was, beard and all. She raised the girl's hand to her lips and kissed each one of her knuckles.

"Virgo Fortis," she said. "My strong virgin."

"Ever virgin," said Wilgefortis, kissing Basilia's hand.

Basilia asked the housekeeper to go on ahead and announce Lady Wilgefortis' entrance. She did not want the woman to lay eyes on Wilge's beard while they walked to the atrium.

The Bearded Bride

Basilia could hear the lute playing and people clapping and laughing as they approached the bottom of the stairs. Upon entering the atrium, a sudden silence fell over the room. Everyone, even the dwarves, had stopped what they were doing to gape at the bearded Wilgefortis.

Finally, Lucius Severus broke the stillness. "What is this travesty?" he shouted, his voice quivering with rage and echoing throughout the chamber. Even the dogs at his feet started to quiver at the pitch of their master's outrage.

Sitting across from him at the big table, the Roman Prefect turned his head and vomited on the tile floor. Calsia's face had grown ghostly pale.

"Good evening, Father," said Wilgefortis, genuflecting to her father. "Mother, it's good to see you again after all this time." Then she directed herself to the Prefect and curtsied, saying, "My Lord."

"Is this a jest?" said the Prefect, starting to laugh, a loud, mocking guffaw that filled the atrium.

"Nurse!" bellowed the Governor.

"I am here, sir," said Sila, stepping out from behind the housekeeper.

"Who is this creature? What witchcraft have you worked on my daughter?"

"I know nothing about witchcraft," said Sila. "I was as surprised as you, my Lord. I know not how to explain it. The hair came with the blood."

The Governor turned his angry gaze on his wife. "Did you know about this?"

"Me?" cried Lady Calsia. "Don't blame me, Lucius!"

"Surely you saw this . . . this aberration," insisted the Governor.

"I swear to you, husband, I had no idea. It's been a few . . . months . . . since I've even seen the girl. I've been so busy with the wedding preparations. I trusted she was being well cared for by her nurse. But the old woman never reported this . . . affliction . . . to me. I can assure you, our daughter did not look thus the last time I visited her."

"May I speak, Father?" said Wilgefortis, genuflecting again.

"Somebody better speak," said Lucius Severus.

"I shall speak," the Roman Prefect said, getting to his feet. Although he looked recovered from his nausea and his laughing fit, his eyes blazed with the same fury as the Governor's. "This is not only a travesty and an insult, Lucius Severus. It is a veritable conspiracy to humiliate me and doom my lineage. You have made me wait eight years for a bride, only to be affronted by this horrifying mockery of a woman. The marriage is cancelled, and you can begin counting your last days as Governor of these provinces, Lucius Severus."

"Quintus! Quintus Flavius!" pleaded Severus, now also on his feet. "Calsia and I knew nothing of this conspiracy. We speak the truth."

"Please, sir," Wilgefortis said to the Prefect. "Don't punish my father for what the goddess gave me in answer to my prayers."

"What goddess? What prayers, Wilge?" asked Calsia.

"I am so very sorry, sir, that you waited so long and traveled such a long distance for nothing. But I have consecrated my virginity to the goddess Diana, and it was she who saw fit to give me this countenance." Wilgefortis stroked the hair on her face as though it were a pet.

"By the gods," said the Prefect, stepping away from the table and skulking closer to Wilgefortis. His eyes bored into hers, his nostrils flaring in disgust.

"She's one of them!" sneered the Prefect. "My spies caught eight women in town last week, proselytizing for that Christian sect, all of them sisters with red hair and grey eyes. Some of them are downright freaks. Save for the beard and the fine clothes, this one looks just like those infidels." The Prefect turned his livid stare on Lady Calsia. "In fact, they all look just like you, Calsia Marcella."

Calsia gasped, her eyes bulging at Sila. Sila averted the Domina's gaze and looked at the girl.

"They're all witches or Christians," the Prefect continued, "probably both. Which is why we will make a spectacle of their execution in the Circus."

"Eight girls? They must be the eight I saw in my dream!" exclaimed Wilgefortis.

"What in Jupiter's name is going on?" demanded the Governor. "Calsia! What is this creature talking about? What eight sisters?"

Sila felt brave suddenly and spoke up, telling them the story of the nonuplet birth, revealing herself as the midwife who had attended Lady Calsia in her labor.

"Basilia?" gasped Lady Calsia. "You are Basilia Quiteria?"

"It is I, Domina." Sila curtsied with stiff knees.

"I told you to drown them," said Calsia.

"I knew it!" cried Wilgefortis. "I knew I kept seeing those eight girls in my dreams for a reason. Let me meet them. Please, let me meet my sisters."

"You want to meet your sisters?" said the Prefect, curling his lips in a false smile. "We can arrange that." He took a horn from one of his slaves and blew it, summoning the small company of soldiers and the centurion that always traveled with him.

"At your command, my Lord," said the centurion, pounding on his chest with a fist.

"Arrest that hairy thing trying to pass for a woman! We're taking her to the Circus with the other freaks."

The guards closed in on Wilgefortis. Sila stood in their way.

"Move aside, you old witch!" commanded the Prefect, backhanding the old nurse so hard she lost her balance.

"Take the old witch!" cried Calsia. "She is responsible for all of this. It was she that bewitched my belly when I was with child and caused me to give birth to a litter of deformed whelps. And now she has come back under a disguise with the intention of bewitching my Liberata as well. My daughter was normal until this hag showed up. Ever since she has been our nurse, my daughter has been afflicted with one curse after another. It's her fault! Crucify the old woman! She's the only witch here!"

"You heard the Domina," bellowed Lucius Severus at the guards. "Take them both."

"Not the girl!" cried Calsia, clinging to her husband's arm, "not your own daughter, Lucius. She is all we have."

"Let it be known that Governor Lucius Severus will suffer no witches or bearded women in his home, Calsia, or in his realm, Quintus."

The Prefect motioned to a slave, who brought him his purple-edged cloak and fixed it to the shoulders of his tunic. The veins in the Prefect's forehead bulged from under his reddened skin.

"Lucius Severus, I formally declare the end of my betrothal to your daughter, Liberata," pronounced the Prefect. "And, as reparation for each year I lost waiting for her to become a woman, I demand eight times her dowry."

The Governor paled at the amount of the Prefect's demands. It would leave him in ruins.

Wilgefortis removed the heavy ring the Prefect had given her, engraved with his image, and handed it to her father to return to Quintus Flavius. Lucius Severus had no choice but to pass the ring back to its owner, but he could not hold the Prefect's stare.

"I will be writing the Emperor about this," said Lucius, glaring at the ring.

"Yes, please do that, Lucius. And be sure to include the part about the bearded bride you were going to foist on me, polluting my family line for generations."

"She was not born this way, sir," said Calsia. "She has been a beautiful perfect girl all her life. The last time I saw her . . . "

Basilia gaped at Calsia's lies.

The Prefect cut her off. "Lady Calsia, if I were you, I would leave Bracara Augusta immediately, lest you be arrested as well for giving birth to nine Christian witches."

The Circus

Led by Quintus Flavius and Lucius Severus on horses, the processional from the Governor's villa to the amphitheater of the Circus drew hundreds of spectators, gawkers and hecklers into the streets. Within the hour, the rumors had started circulating. The two women in chains—one ancient and the other gaunt and bearded—were witches, no, prostitutes, no, rebels, Christian rebels against the true Roman faith.

Placidus heard the clamor from his shop and called out to Demetria, panic-stricken.

"They've arrested Basilia and the Governor's girl, Demetria. They're taking them to the Circus with the other girls."

"The Circus? Dear God, they mean to execute them. Placidus, do something!"

How had Basilia gotten herself arrested? He jumped into his horse-drawn cart and followed the throng, picking up the processional of the witches, as the gossips were calling it, from the town square, following the red-feathered helmets of the soldiers who were savagely yanking and shoving Basilia and the Governor's daughter by their shackles. Placidus winced every time someone cast a stone at the prisoners, spit at them or urinated on them.

He would not have lost sight of the company had he not been distracted by Eustace and Aurelia, whom he spotted kneeling before the Prefect's horse as he stood arrogantly at the entrance to the arena. They were pleading with the Prefect to release their innocent daughters, but Quintus Flavius dug his heels into the animal's withers, and the animal kicked them fast and hard, one hoof hitting Aurelia between the eyes, Eustace in the chest. Their bodies dropped. Placidus bolted his horse through the crowds, using the cart to scatter the throng and save his brother- and sister-in-law from a crushing death, but it was too late. Aurelia's eyes had already rolled up into her head, and blood poured from Eustace's mouth. The Prefect's horse had killed them, and their bodies were already being trampled by the restive multitude. Little beggar boys were quickly stealing their clothes and shoes.

"Stop desecrating the dead, you imbeciles!" he yelled, kicking off the young looters. He lifted Eustace, first, surprised at how heavy he was. Eustace had always seemed small to Placidus, almost delicate, but the tearing feeling in his groin as he hoisted the man's dead weight over his shoulder told him different. He barely managed to get Eustace's torso into the cart, legs dangling over the side. Aurelia was much lighter, but the tear in his groin kept him from lifting her completely and her body landed face-down in the cart.

A deep howl went through him. "Please, Lord, stop this madness!" he heard himself wail. "Why does our merciful God not show any mercy to the innocent and the faithful?"

His words were swallowed by the din. He struggled to calm the horse as he extricated the cart from the sea of bodies swirling at the entrance to the circus. And then, he saw them again, Basilia and the girl. It was the first time he saw the Governor's daughter and her long beard took him aback.

"By Jove, she really is bearded," he heard himself mumble.

Sila and the girl were shackled together by the neck and ankles, and they were struggling to lift the crossbeam for the crucifixion that the accused had to drag into the arena. The Governor and the Prefect were surrounded by a company of soldiers who looked as fierce as the praetorian guard.

A centurion approached the Prefect.

"What's taking so long?" the Prefect yelled.

"They can't carry the crossbeam, sir," a soldier called out. "And the old one can barely walk."

"Hitch the crossbeam to your horse, then. And take their chains off!" ordered the Prefect. "Have them enter the arena one by one. The girl, first. The hag is to be tied to the stake for witchcraft."

The crossbeam was hitched to the soldier's saddle with rope, and the centurion drew his sword and started swinging it in a circle to open a path for the prisoners to enter the Circus. By now, the crowd had become a pack of Maenads, possessed with bloodlust, their voices chanting, "Witch! Witch! Burn the witches!"

The soldiers released Wilgefortis and her nurse from their irons, and the crowd seemed to sway and heave. Hands grabbed Wilgefortis by the hair, pulled off her ruby brooch, tore at the brocaded border of her *palla,* smeared excrement on her linen wedding gown.

Somehow, in the scuffle that ensued, Placidus charged his horse and cart into the melee and managed to pluck Basilia from her captors. Pulling her up into the cart beside him.

Basilia scratched and bit at his hands, but Placidus held her by the waist in an iron grip.

"Let me go, Placidus! I didn't ask you to save me. I need to witness the slaughter of the nine sisters!"

"Why, Sila? Their fate is their fate. You can't change that."

She looked over her shoulder at the corpses of Eustace and Aurelia, and shook her head. "May you rest in peace, dear friends." She drew the sign of the pentagram over the bodies with her left hand.

"Take me back, Placidus. I must bear witness to their execution."

"But they will torture you, too, Basilia. They will burn you at the stake for witchcraft. Is that what you want? Is that how you hope to atone for your sins?"

"I could never atone for the sins I committed against Wilgefortis and her eight sisters. But I promised Wilge I would not let her die alone, and yet, here I am with you, and there she is, about to be crucified."

"If you want to bear witness, I will take you to the knoll just above the amphitheater," said Placidus. "As a child, I would watch the games from there. You will be able to see and hear everything, but I will not partake in your sacrifice, Sila, so do not ask me to take you back to the arena."

Sila wept silently but did not try to escape.

An Unearthly Croaking of Toads

Inside the Circus the master of ceremonies was announcing the punishment until death of nine Christian rebels, all secret daughters of Governor Lucius Severus and his wife, Calsia Marcella. Eight of them would lose their heads and the Governor's daughter would be nailed to a Roman cross until dead. Afterward their bodies would be fed to the wild beasts of the Circus.

Watching the nails being driven into her darling girl's wrists and through the high arches of her delicate feet, Basilia howled in sorrow. They were hidden in the grove of oak trees that grew wild on the knoll, but Placidus worried that the Governor's spies would hear her cries.

"Had I known they would come to an end like this," she wept, "I would have gladly helped Calsia drown the newborns the day they were born, all nine of them. I thought I was doing something good by not drowning them in the Minho River, as the Domina wanted. I thought your God would protect them."

Placidus put his arm around Basilia's shaking shoulders. "Our God seems to enjoy sacrifice as much as any other," he said. "One day it will be written that those brave young women died such brutal deaths for love of their Lord."

"I shall never understand a faith that allows its young women to be slaughtered for love of any lord," said Basilia. "But you know better, Placidus. You know that one of them gave her life for the goddess. When you tell the story to your followers, don't forget that Liberata Wilgefortis was meant to be free."

❧ ❧ ❧

Nailed to her cross, blood pouring down her arms and feet, Wilgefortis looked ecstatic. Her eyes gleamed with a joy that Basilia had never seen in her young charge. This was what the stranger had meant, she now realized, when he had said that together with her sisters, Wilgefortis would be reborn as one soul.

She is the lodestone that will bring them together, and together will they be reborn and remembered for centuries. A sacred spring will be named in their honor, but first they must be delivered unto their fate in the glory of their suffering.

That was the glow in Wilge's face, the glory of her suffering, as the one piece that had been cut off from the other eight was finally going to be made whole again.

Liberata Wilgefortis was the only one crucified that day, by order of her own father, her red beard and hair awry, a beatific glow in her gray eyes, a filament of a smile on her lips, even as her body started to sag on the crucifix, the weight of her shoulders closing her lungs, her heart bursting under her own weight. On each side of her, four sisters, half-naked and with their backs shredded from the whipping that was part of their punishment, each knelt to the henchman's sword. Their heads rolled to the foot of their sister's cross.

A bloodthirsty clamor arose from the spectators who were rabid for more gore.

"Bring out the beasts!" they demanded.

"The lions must be fed!"

Even through that din, Basilia heard the sweet, sad sound of strings playing. She glimpsed the shimmer first and then saw the ghost of young Gaius playing his lyre at his sister's feet.

"Where is the old witch that accompanied my daughter?" called the Governor from his dais. "I wanted her burnt at the stake."

"She escaped on us, Excellency!" the centurion explained.

"No, she dropped dead at the entrance," a soldier said. "Some plebian in a cart took off with the body."

"Who is playing that lyre?"

"What lyre, Excellency? We hear no music."

❧ ❧ ❧

On this wretched night, there was nothing else holding Basilia fast to the flesh. Her life's work was done. She had brought the nine sisters back together again. She was ready to return to Magna Mater.

A jolt of pain from the middle of her chest radiated through her body. She felt herself fall backward, her body slipping from the seat of the cart and down to the bracken of the woodsy ground of the knoll. And then she felt herself plunging headlong into a dark swirling stench that quickly consumed her.

❧ ❧ ❧

Placidus felt the tears sliding down his face. "I think I have lost my own faith tonight, Sila," he said to her lingering spirit. "I find no comfort in such sacrifice. I feel no closer to salvation because those innocent girls gave their lives for our faith. What I have witnessed here is not faith, just carnage. That a man could put his own flesh and blood to death like that and not be stricken dead by a divine thunderbolt seems supremely unjust. Demetria would say that we should never question God's will, but if that execution was God's will, then I want nothing to do with such a God."

He knew Basilia was gone. Her lifeless body had fallen from the cart and rolled down to a small bog at the bottom of the knoll. That was as good a place as any for his cousin's body to return to Magna Mater.

"Goodbye, Basilia Drusilla Quiteria," he said aloud. "May your soul always walk with the Great Mother. Rest in peace with your beloved Wilgefortis."

He turned his cart around and rode the horse down from the knoll and into town, carrying the trampled bodies of Eustace and Aurelia back to the only family they had left, his wife, Demetria.

The night air throbbed with an unearthly croaking of toads.

ACKNOWLEDGEMENTS

Many of these stories have been years in the making. Some form parts of novels that I started but never finished in numerous attempts at winning NaNoWriMo (National Novel-Writing Month); others are older pieces with interesting characters that I was hoping to come back to and flesh out one day. One was a legend that I revised based on the life of St. Wilgefortis, the bearded female patron saint of women who want to liberate themselves of abusive husbands, or who don't want to marry at all.

Upon reading all these pieces together, I realized that there is an energy, maybe even a theme, that connects them. They have a disjointed flow of their own, a coherent incoherence that makes for "a deconstructed novel." In the cooking world, a "deconstructed" dish includes all the main ingredients of a well-known recipe that are not combined by the cook, but by those who eat the meal, who then participate in creating their experience of the dish. Similarly, this book contains all the main elements of a novel, but I don't provide the missing link that connects these stories, and I leave it up to the reader to use their own constructive logic.

As always, I am so grateful to the Universe for heartening my life with the presence of my darling Alma Lopez. We have gone through so many challenges in this first nine-year cycle of our married life, and through each we have become stronger, our love more rooted and enduring. And now, we get to welcome the baby girl we've been waiting for, dreaming about and drawing to us since 2009. Bienvenida, Azul Fernanda, to your forever family.

Finally, I would like to express my deepest gratitude to Marina Tristán, Gabriela Baeza and Nicolás Kanellos—the powerhouse editors and publisher of Arte Público Press—for your patience, and especially for the encouragement that I needed to complete the manuscript. Nick, thank you, también, for the close readings, the marginalia, the old-school editing job you did that helped make this a better book.

Notes

An earlier version of "Lorca's Widow" was previously published in *Zzyzyva/The Last Word: West Coast Writers & Artists*, XXI, 1 (Spring 2005): 145-160.

The story about the petrified fetus referenced in "Lorca's Widow" is based on a newspaper article in *El Diario de Juárez* in 1984, about an 88-year-old woman in Ciudad Juárez (across the border from El Paso, Texas) who carried a petrified fetus in her womb for over sixty years. According to the story, a similar case appeared in the Netherlands in 1979, where a woman carried a petrified fetus for fifty years. I translated the article verbatim, which appears as "The Octogenarian with a Petrified Fetus Finds Herself in Good Health."

The story in "The Sacrament" was inspired by a 1925 Virgen de Guadalupe *retablo,* which I include in the text.

Earlier versions of "The Tattoo" and "Shortcut to the Moon" were previously published in Arte Público Press anthologies: *Hit List: The Best of Latino Mystery* (2009, pp. 29-42) and *You Don't Have a Clue: Latino Mystery Stories for Teens* (2011, pp. 59-74)—both books edited by Sarah Cortez.

My retelling of the legend of Saint Wilgefortis is based on the historical nine virgin martyrs of Portugal, Wilgefortis (also known as Liberata, or Librada) and her eight sisters (Marina, Quiteria, Genibera, Eufemia, Marciana, Germana, Basilia and Victoria) who were born in 119 AD and died in 139 at the age of twenty. They were said to have been early Christian activists whose mission was to liberate incarcerated Christians. Wilgefortis is known as the bearded female saint who was crucified by her own father when she refused to marry the pagan king to whom her father had promised her hand. She prayed for deliverance from the marriage and a beard sprouted on her face. As punishment, her father had her crucified.

The St. Wilgefortis cult flourished from the 14th-16th centuries, then extended to Spain and across the Mediterranean to England, the Netherlands, Germany, Austria, Belgium, France and Czechoslovakia, where she goes by many other names, such as Uncumber, Ontkommer, Kümmernis. The story of the nine sisters is linked to St. Ovidius, the third Bishop of Braga (Bracara Augusta under Rome), Portugal, who is said to have been martyred for his Christian faith in 135. According to Wikipedia, the Wilgefortis/Liberata/Librada cult was also popular in Argentina, Panama and New Mexico until Vatican II removed her from the calendar of Catholic saints. The official Catholic revision of her legend says that St. Wilgefortis is a "fake saint," and that the name derives from the Old German phrase for "Holy Face," the *Volto Santo of Lucca*, an ancient carving where Jesus is depicted on the crucifix, not in a loincloth but a long dress. Thus, naysayers of the Wilgefortis legend believe that the bearded woman on the cross was nothing but a misinterpretation of a fully robed Jesus. In many of the bearded saint's statues and visual representations, her crucified form is depicted with a young fiddler at her feet.

Online sources for the legend:

- https://saintsofmyheart.wordpress.com/2018/03/13/88788/
- https://almaleonor.wordpress.com/2015/02/08/wilgefortis-y-librada-las-santas-crucificadas/
- http://www.atlasobscura.com/places/statue-st-wilgefortis
- Ilse E. Friesen, *The Female Crucifix: Images of St. Wilgefortis Since the Middle Ages* (Wilfrid Laurier University Press, 2001).
- Rebecca Clamp, "St. Wilgefortis" (song) downloaded from Amazon.com on 9/11/2017.
- López Pilar, Alma Leonor. "Wilgeforths y Librada: Las Santas Crucificadas," *Helicon,* Wordpress, 18 Feb. 2015, URL.

- http://qspirit.net/saint-wilgefortis-bearded-woman/
- Cherry, Rittredge. "Saint Wilgefortis: Holy Bearded Woman Fascinates for Centures." *G Spirit,* 19 July 2017, URL.
- Ott, Michael. "Wilgefortis." *The Catholic Encyclopedia* Vol.15 NewYork: Robert Appleton Company, 1912, URL.
- http://www.newadvent.org/cathen/15622a.htm
- "Wilgefortis" *Wikipedia,* Wikimedia Foundation, 5 Jan. 2018, en wikipedia.org/wiki/Wilgefortis.
- https://almaleonor.wordpress.com/2018/03/01/visibles-en-anatomia-de-la-historia/

ALICIA GASPAR DE ALBA is the author of various works of poetry, fiction and nonfiction, among them a Lambda Award-winning novel, *Desert Blood: The Juárez Murders* (Arte Público Press, 2005); a collection of poems and essays, *La Llorona on the Longfellow Bridge: Poetry y otras movidas* (Arte Público Press, 2003); and two historical novels, *Sor Juana's Second Dream* (University of New Mexico Press, 1999) and *Calligraphy of the Witch* (Arte Público Press, 2012).

She is also the editor of *Making a Killing: Femicide, Free Trade, and La Frontera* (University of Texas Press, 2010) and *Our Lady of Controversy: Alma López's "Irreverent Apparition"* (University of Texas Press, 2011). Her *book, [Un]Framing the "Bad Woman:" Sor Juana, Malinche, Coyolxauhqui and Other Rebels With a Cause* (University of Texas Press, 2014), a collection of twenty years of academic essays, won the 2015 Book Award from the American Association of Hispanics in Higher Education.

A full professor of Chicana/o Studies, English and Gender Studies and Chair of the LGBTQ Studies Program at the University of California, Los Angeles, Gaspar de Alba is a native of the El Paso/ Juárez border.

Gaspar de Alba lives in Los Angeles with her wife, the artist Alma López, and their adopted daughter Azul.

Also by Alicia Gaspar de Alba

Sor Juana's Second Dream

Calligraphy of the Witch

Desert Blood: The Juárez Murders

Sangre en el desierto: Las muertas de Juárez

La Llorona on the Longfellow Bridge: poetry y otras movidas

The Mystery of Survival and Other Stories